D1007285

"Hold on to your seats! Handeland delivers a kick-butt heroine ready to take on the world of the paranormal. *Blue Moon* is an awesome launch to what promises to be a funny, sexy, and scary series."

—*Romantic Times*

"A fast-paced and thought-provoking story. Dynamic characters in *Blue Moon* will leave you with no doubt that you are reading something special . . . the beginning of an exciting new series."

—*Enchanted in Romance*

"This book has everything—excellent writing, fascinating characters, suspense, comical one-liners, and best of all, a super-good romance."

—*The Best Reviews*

"An incredible werewolf story with a twist . . . full of sass and with a delightful, sarcastic sense of humor."

—*Paranormal Romances*

"The action is fast-paced, the plot is gripping, the characters are realistic, and I absolutely positively cannot wait for the next book in this series."

—*Fallen Angel Reviews*

"A dry wit that shines . . . Everything about this book is wonderful: the sizzling sexiness, the three-dimensional characters, and the sense of danger."

—*Romance Junkies*

"Great intensity, danger, drama, captivation, and stellar writing."

—*The Road to Romance,* Reviewer's Choice Award

ALSO BY LORI HANDELAND

THE PHOENIX CHRONICLES

THE NIGHTCREATURE NOVELS

ANTHOLOGIES

Hunter's Moon

Lori Handeland

St. Martin's Paperbacks

HUNTER'S MOON

Copyright © 2005 by Lori Handeland.
Excerpt from *Dark Moon* copyright © 2005 by Lori Handeland.

All rights reserved.

For information address St. Martin's Press, 175 Fifth Avenue, New York, NY 10010.

ISBN: 0-312-99135-5
EAN: 80312-99135-7

Printed in the United States of America

St. Martin's Paperbacks edition / February 2005

St. Martin's Paperbacks are published by St. Martin's Press, 175 Fifth Avenue, New York, NY 10010.

10 9 8 7 6 5

For
Robert "Buck" Miller
I just call him Dad

I

They say the hunter's moon was once called the blood moon, and I know why. A full moon shining through a crisp autumn night turns blood from crimson to black.

I much prefer the shade of blood beneath the moon to its shade beneath the stark electric lights. But I digress.

I am a hunter. A *Jäger-Sucher* to those in the know—of which there are a select few. I hunt monsters, and in case you're thinking that's a euphemism for today's serial killers, it's not. When I say "monster" I mean hell unleashed, tooth and claw, supernatural magic on the loose. The kind of thing that will give you nightmares forever. Just like me.

My specialty is werewolves. I must have killed a thousand and I'm only twenty-four. Sadly, my job security has never been in jeopardy. A fact I learned all too well when my boss, Edward Mandenauer, called me early one October morning.

"Leigh, I need you here."

"Where is here?" I mumbled.

I am not a bright and shiny early person. This might come from living most of my life in the dark. Werewolves emerge at night, beneath the moon. They're funny that way.

"I am in Crow Valley, Wisconsin."

"Never heard of it.

"Which gives you much in common with the rest of the world."

I sat up, awake, alert, senses humming. That had sounded suspiciously like dry humor. Edward didn't *do* humor.

"Who is this?" I demanded.

"Leigh." His long-suffering sigh was as much a part of him as his heavy German accent. "What is the matter with you this morning?"

"It's morning. Isn't that enough?"

I did not greet each day with joy. My life was dedicated to one thing—ridding the earth of werewolves. Only then could I forget what had happened, perhaps forgive myself for living when everyone I'd ever loved had died.

"Liebchen," Mandenauer murmured. "What will I do with you?"

Edward had saved me on that long-ago day filled with blood and death and despair. He had taken me in, taught me things, then set me free to use them. I was his most dedicated agent, and only Edward and I knew why.

"I'm all right," I reassured him.

I wasn't and probably never would be. But I'd accepted that. I'd moved on. Kind of.

"Of course you are," he soothed.

Neither one of us was fooled by my lie or his acceptance of it. Which was how we both kept ourselves focused on what was important. Killing them all.

"The town is in the northern part of the state," he continued. "You will have to fly to Minneapolis, rent a car, go . . . east, I think."

"I am not coming to Shit Heel, Wisconsin, Edward."

"Crow Valley."

"Whatever. I'm not done here."

I'd been working in Canada at Mandenauer's request. A few months back hell had broken loose in a little burg called Miniwa. Something about a blue moon, a wolf god—I hadn't gotten the details. I didn't care. All I knew was that there were werewolves running north, plenty of them.

But as much as I might like to, I couldn't just blast every wolf I saw with silver. There were laws about such things, even in Canada.

The *Jäger-Suchers* were a secret branch of the government. We liked to envision ourselves as the Special Forces of monster hunting. Think *The X-Files* versus Grimm's Fairy Tales on steroids.

At any rate, we were supposed to work on the sly. A pile of dead wolves—threatened at the least, endangered yet in some places—would cause too many questions.

The *Jäger-Sucher* society had enough problems accounting for the disappearances of the people who had once been werewolves. Sad but true—it's easier to explain missing humans than dead animals, but such is the way of the modern world.

My job, should I choose to accept it—and I had, long ago—was to catch the werewolves in the act. Of changing. Then I was well within my rights to put a silver bullet in their brain.

Bureaucracy at its finest.

Catching them wasn't as hard to do as you might think. Most werewolves ran in packs, just like real wolves. When they went to the forest to change, they often had a lair where they left their clothes, purses, car keys. Going from bipedal to quadrupedal had certain disadvantages, namely, no pockets.

Once I found that lair . . . well, does the phrase "like shooting ducks in a pond" mean anything to you? It's one of my favorites.

"You will never be done there." Edward's voice pulled me from my thoughts. "Right now you are needed here."

"Why?"

"The usual reason."

"You've got werewolves. Shoot them yourself."

"I need you to train a new *Jäger-Sucher.*"

Since when? Edward had always done the training, and I . . .

"I work alone."

"It is time for that to change."

"No."

I was not a people person. Didn't want to be. I enjoyed being by myself. That way no one around me could get killed—again.

"I am not asking you, Leigh; I am telling you. Be here by tomorrow, or find another job."

He hung up.

Sitting on the edge of the bed in my underwear, I held the phone against my ear until the line started to buzz; then I replaced it in the cradle and stared into space awhile longer.

I couldn't believe this. I wasn't a teacher; I was a killer. What right did Edward have to order me around?

All the right in the world. He was my boss, my mentor, the closest thing to a friend that I allowed myself. Which meant he should know better than to ask me to do something I'd given up along with my life.

I *had* been a teacher, once upon a time.

I flinched as the memory of children's voices lifted in

song drifted through my head. Miss Leigh Tyler, kindergarten teacher, was as dead as the man I'd once planned to marry. And if she sometimes skipped through my dreams, well, what was I supposed to do, shoot her?

Though that might be my usual method for solving problems, it didn't work too well on the happy-go-lucky dream Leigh. More's the pity.

I dragged myself off the bed and into the shower, then packed my things and headed for the airport.

No one in Elk Snout—or wherever the hell it was I'd been hunting—would notice I was gone. As I did in every area I visited, I'd rented an isolated cabin, telling anyone who asked, and it was shocking how few people did, that I was with the Department of Natural Resources, studying a new strain of rabies in the wolf population.

This excuse conveniently explained my odd hours and my penchant for walking with a gun or three, as well as my cranky nature. The hunting and fishing police were not well liked by the common folk. Which got me left alone—my favorite thing to be.

I arrived at the airport, where I was informed only one plane a day flew to Minneapolis. Luckily, that single flight was scheduled late in the afternoon and there were plenty of seats.

I had ID from the *J-S* society, which established me as a warden and allowed me to ship my weapons—a standard-issue twelve-gauge Remington shotgun, my personal hunting rifle, and a Glock forty-caliber semiautomatic, also standard DNR issue. An hour after touching down, I hit the road to Crow Valley.

I didn't bother to call ahead and announce my arrival. Mandenauer had known all along that I would come. No matter what he asked of me, I would agree. Not because I respected him, though I did, more than anyone I'd ever known, but because he let me do what I had to do. Kill the animals, the monsters, the werewolves.

It was the only thing I had left to live for.

2

By the time I reached the little town in the north woods, the moon was rising. Not that I could see more than half.

But the orb was out there—waiting, breathing, growing. I knew it and so did the werewolves. Just because the sky wasn't glowing with a silver sheen didn't mean the monsters weren't changing and running and killing.

As I slowed my rental car, which I swear was the same four-cylinder piece of shit I'd turned in at the airport in Canada, a flicker of movement from an alleyway caught my attention. I coasted to a stop at the curb and got out.

The place had a deserted air that all small towns get after the supper hour. However, I wasn't sure if this was the usual "rolling up the sidewalks" tradition or the populace had started to stay indoors after dark because of the wolves.

Edward had to have a more serious motive than the common werewolf outbreak for bringing me here. Even if I was training a new guy, there had to be a reason to do it in Shit Heel. I mean Crow Valley.

The shuffle of a shoe against concrete drifted to me from the alleyway.

"Better safe than sorry," I murmured, and reached into the car for my sidearm.

The rifle or the shotgun would be better, but as much as I might like to, I couldn't waltz along Main Street carrying a firearm as long as my leg. I might have the necessary ID, but I wasn't in uniform. Someone would stop me; then there'd be questions, answers. I didn't have time. Nevertheless, if there was a wolf in that alley, he'd be close enough to pop with my Glock.

I crept to the opening and glanced down the aisle. The single streetlight threw the silhouette of a man against the wall for just an instant before he disappeared at the far side of the building.

I'd have let it go, except for the howl that rose toward the waiting night. The hair on the back of my neck prickled and I shook my head. Once upon a time the thick braid that had reached to my waist would have waggled and rubbed away the itch. But I'd hacked off my hair long ago and now sported a near military crew cut. Life was so much easier that way.

As I was slinking along the front of the structure in the general direction of the man I'd observed, a chorus of answering howls rose from the forest that surrounded the town.

I glanced around the corner just as a wolf padded toward the trees. I let out a sigh of relief. I wouldn't have to wait around. Only an amateur would shoot a werewolf midchange. Then you're left with a half-man, half-wolf, which is a little hard to explain. Believe me. I've tried.

Though I always burned the body, I never knew who'd wander across my path while the bonfire was blazing. Always better to wait until they were complete wolves to do the deed.

But dallying can be hazardous to the health. Lucky me,

I'd come across a fast changer—either an overachiever or a very old werewolf. This one wasn't as large as the usual male but definitely a wolf and not a dog. Even huge dogs have smaller heads than timber wolves, one of the differences between *Canis familiaris* and *Canis lupus*.

The wolf loped toward the woods as the howls faded into the night. I let him get as far as the trees before I followed. The wind was in my favor, blowing across my face as I scuttled across the street. Still, wolves had excellent hearing, werewolves even better, so I didn't want to get too close, too fast.

I didn't want to get too far behind, either. I took three steps at a half-run and entered the cooler, darker arena of the forest.

Immediately the lights from Crow Valley became muted; the air cooled. I'd been born in Kansas, land of very few trees, and to this day whenever I entered woodlands I got spooked.

The evergreens were gargantuan, as ancient as some of the things I hunted, and so thick it was hard to navigate through them. Which was probably why a majority of the wolves, as well as most of the werewolves, gravitated north.

My eyes adjusted to the gloom quickly, and I hurried after the bushy gray tail, my gun ready. I'd done this enough times to know better than to put my weapon away. I wasn't Wyatt Earp, and I didn't plan to draw down on a werewolf. They were quicker than spit and twice as nasty.

A sound to the left made me freeze and spin that way. I held my breath, listened, looked. Heard nothing but the wind and saw even less. I'd stopped in a small clearing— the shadowy sheen of the moon lightened the area just a bit.

I turned back, hurried forward, blinked. Where was that tail? Nothing lay ahead of me but trees.

"Son of a—"

A low growl was my only warning before something hit me in the back and drove my face into the dirt. My gun flew into the bushes. My heart was beating so fast I couldn't think.

Training kicked in as I grabbed the wolf by the scruff of the neck and flipped the animal over my shoulder before he could bite me. If there's one thing I'd hate more than being alive, it's being alive and furry.

He hit the ground, yelped, twisted, and bounded to his feet. I used the few seconds I had to spring to a crouch and yank the knife from my boot. There was a reason I wore them even in the heat of summer. Kind of hard to conceal a knife in a sneaker.

I'd yanked out tufts of gray fur when I flipped the wolf, and they fluttered in the breeze. The animal growled. Eyes pale blue and far too human narrowed. He was pissed and because of that didn't think before leaping.

The beast knocked me to the ground. As I fell, I shoved the weapon into the wolf's chest to the hilt, then twisted.

Flames burst from the wound. Silver did that to a werewolf, one of the reasons I preferred killing them from a distance.

The animal snarled in my face. I held on to the knife despite the heat, despite the blood, and as the thing died in my arms I watched his eyes shift from human to wolf. It was an oddity I'd never get over, that change at the end.

Legend says that werewolves return to their human form in death, but that isn't true. Not only do they remain wolves, but they also lose their last remnant of humanity as they go straight to hell—or at least I hope that's where they go.

When the fire was gone and the wolf stopped squirming, I shoved the body off me and yanked out my knife. Then I saw something disturbing.

The wolf I'd killed was female.

I scanned the area, searching for the male I'd expected. I was certain the shadow I'd observed in the alley had been a man's. I'd followed the wolf that had come out the other side. Hadn't I?

This one? Or had the male from town been following her as I had? If so, he would have attacked when she did. They couldn't help themselves.

Another mystery. Why wasn't I surprised?

I retrieved the gun, cleaned off my knife in the grass, then stuck it back in my boot. I wiped my bloody hands on my jeans—they were already stained, as was my shirt, but at least the dark material of both, combined with the less than bright sky, helped disguise *what* was staining them.

My palms tingled. A quick examination proved they were sore but not blistered, so I ignored them, following standard *J-S* procedure as I made a wolf bonfire to get rid of the evidence.

After sprinkling the body with a special accelerant—a new invention courtesy of the scientific division of the *J-S* society—I threw on a match. The flames shot past my head. Hot, strong, fiery red. Just what I needed to get my job done quickly.

Until recently, burning wolves took a long, long time. In order to remain secret and undetected, *Jäger-Suchers* needed to do their jobs and dispose of the evidence before anyone was the wiser. The new accelerant was a big help in that direction.

I thought to check in with Edward while I waited for the flames to abate. Unfortunately, I'd left my cell phone in the car. Oh well, if I woke him it would be payback for his waking me. And I liked payback—almost as much as I liked killing things.

"Isn't that illegal?"

The voice, coming from behind me without warning, had me pulling my gun as I spun around. The man stared at my Glock without blinking.

I frowned. Most people flinched when you stuck a gun in their face. And mine was in his face. He'd gotten so close I had nearly clocked him in the nose with the barrel.

How had he snuck up on me like that?

Narrowing my eyes, I gave him the once-over. This was fairly easy, since he wasn't wearing any shirt.

The veins in his arms stood out, as if he'd been lifting—reps for definition rather than weight for strength. His chest was smooth yet defined, with flat, brown nipples that only accentuated the pale perfection.

I'd never been much for beefcake. Hell, be honest, I'd never been much for men. Seeing your fiancé torn into bloody pieces in your dining room did that to a girl.

However, I found myself staring at this one, fascinated with the taut, ridged muscle at his abdomen. Even his shaggy brown hair was interesting, as were his oddly light brown eyes, which shone almost yellow in the wavering light of the moon. I figured in the daytime they'd be plain old hazel.

His cheekbones were sharp, his face craggy. As if he hadn't been eating well or sleeping any better. And despite the pale shade of his eyes, there was a darkness to them that went deeper than the surface. Still, he was handsome in a way that went beyond pretty and stopped just short of stunning.

He had managed to pull on some black pants, though the button hung open, and his shoes must be with his shirt. Which explained how he'd gotten so close without me hearing him.

Suspicious, I kept my Glock pointed at his left nostril. "Who are you?"

"Who are you?" he countered.

"I asked you first."

He raised a brow at my juvenile retort. He was awfully calm for a guy who had a gun staring him in the face. Maybe he didn't think I had silver bullets inside.

The thought made my hand tighten on the weapon. Was this the man I'd seen in the alley? The one I'd thought had become a wolf, then run into the woods.

"You mind?" He grabbed the barrel, shoving it out of his face, then twisting the gun from my hand in a single motion.

I tensed, expecting an attack. Instead, he handed it back to me butt first. I'd never seen anyone move that quickly. Anyone human, that is.

If he was a werewolf, he'd have shot me already or attacked along with his girlfriend. I relaxed, but only a little. He was still a stranger, and Lord knows what he was up to in the woods, in the dark, without his shoes.

"Who are you?" I repeated.

"Damien Fitzgerald."

Damien? Wasn't that the name of a demon? Or at least it had been in some 1970s horror movie I'd refused to see. I'd never been much for gore, even before such unpleasantries entered my life on a daily basis.

The name Fitzgerald explained the pale skin and dark hair, even the auburn streaks placed there by the sun. But the eyes were wrong. They should be blue as the Irish Sea.

Their hue bothered me almost as much as their soul-deep sadness, the flicker of guilt. I'd seen that expression a thousand times before.

In the mirror.

He folded his incredible arms across his smooth chest and stared down at me. He wasn't truly tall, maybe six feet if that, but I was five-four in my shoes.

I hated being short, petite, almost blond. But I'd learned that guns were a great equalizer. It didn't matter if I weighed a hundred pounds; I could still pull a trigger. A few years of judo hadn't hurt, either.

Back in my Miss Tyler days, I'd highlighted my hair, worn pink lipstick and high heels. I stifled my gagging reflex.

Look what that had gotten me. Scars both inside and out.

"What's with the dead wolf bonfire?" he asked.

I glanced at my handiwork. It was hard to tell what I'd been burning, but maybe he'd been hanging around longer than I realized. So I gave him the same song and dance I used with every civilian.

"I'm with the DNR."

He made a face, the usual reaction to the Department of Natural Resources, I'd discovered. But he didn't behave like most people did when I introduced myself— getting away as quickly as possible and never looking back. Instead he stared at me with a question in his eyes.

Finally I asked, "What?"

"Why are you burning a wolf? I thought they were endangered."

"Threatened."

His blank stare revealed he had no idea of the technicalities that surrounded the wolf population. Threatened meant wolves could be killed under certain circumstances by certain people. Namely me. As to the circumstances . . .

"There's an itsy-bitsy rabies problem in the wolves here," I lied.

One eyebrow shot up. "Really?"

He didn't believe me? That was new. I was a very, very good liar.

"Really."

My voice was firm. I didn't want any more questions. Especially questions I'd have a hard time answering. Like how did we know the difference between a rabid animal and one sick with something else?

In truth, we wouldn't without testing at the Madison Health Lab. Standard DNR procedure was to contact the local wildlife manager, then APHIS—the Animal and Plant Health Inspection Service, a federal agency that deals with nuisance animals.

Thankfully the common man didn't know government procedure, so my lies usually worked. It helped that the word *rabies* freaked everyone out. People wanted the virus obliterated, preferably yesterday, and if someone with a uniform or an ID was willing to do that, they didn't ask too many questions. They just got out of my way.

Too bad Damien wasn't like everyone else. He tilted his head, and his unkempt brown hair slid across his cheek. "Rabies? How come I haven't heard about it?"

I'd fed this lie a hundred times before, and it tripped off my tongue without any thought at all.

"The news isn't for public consumption. We'd have a panic."

"Ah." He nodded. "That's why you aren't wearing your uniform."

"Right. No sense upsetting people. I'm taking care of things. So you can go back to . . . wherever it is you came from." I frowned. "Where did you come from?"

"New York."

"Just now?"

His lips twisted in what should have been a smile but wasn't. "No, originally."

Which explained the slight accent—the Bronx maybe, I wasn't sure. A Kansas girl who'd spent the last few years in the forest chasing werewolves didn't have too many opportunities to check out the accents of hot Irish men from New York City.

"Have you lived here long?" I turned away, using a hefty stick to poke up the fire.

"You never told me your name," he countered. "Do you have some kind of ID?"

I continued to stir the fire, considering what I should say. It wouldn't hurt to give him my name. I had DNR ID in my back pocket. The resources of the *J-S* society were far-reaching, even downright amazing in some cases. But why was he so interested?

"What are you?" I countered. "A cop?"

"Actually, yes."

I let out a yelp and spun around. Damien Fitzgerald had disappeared as if he'd never been.

The woman who stepped into the clearing wore a sheriff's uniform. She was both tall and voluptuous, which annoyed me on sight, and she walked with a confidence that bespoke someone who could take care of herself, even without the gun. Her dark hair had been cut short to frame an attractive, though not exactly pretty, face.

Her gaze took in the wolf pyre, then lifted to mine. "You must be the *Jäger-Sucher.*"

3

I winced and glanced around the clearing. *"Shh,"* I snapped.

Her eyebrows lifted. "Who do you think's going to hear me? The raccoons?"

"There was a man—" I frowned. "Didn't you see him?"

"No. You were talking to yourself when I got here."

"I was not. There was a man." I waved my hand. "He was wearing pants."

"Always a good choice."

"But nothing else."

"Even better. The last time I met a naked man in the forest it was the start of something big."

"He wasn't naked. Completely."

The woman shrugged. "Too bad. Where'd he go?"

"I don't know."

"You're sure there was a man?"

Was I? Yes. Definitely. I hadn't lost my mind since . . . I'd found it the last time.

"He said his name was Damien Fitzgerald. Don't you know him?"

"Can't say that I do. But then Mandenauer and I just got here last week. From what you're telling me, he sounds like a prime candidate for the fanged and furry club."

Finally I heard what she'd said, what she'd been saying. She knew about the *Jäger-Suchers,* the werewolves, Edward. The guy I was supposed to train had just turned into a girl. "You're . . ."

"Jessie McQuade. And you must be Leigh, my trainer."

I scowled. We'd see about that. I could think of few things I'd like to do less than teach this spectacularly competent woman all my tricks.

"You *are* Leigh," she said.

I grunted.

She took that as a yes. "Mandenauer is waiting at my place. Follow me."

Without so much as a by-your-leave, she kicked apart the remnants of the fire and stomped on the cinders. Then she marched back in the direction I'd come.

My gaze scanned the clearing, but there was no sign of the half-naked man. I even hurried to the place I'd last seen him and crouched in the leaves to examine the ground for a footprint. But the earth was hard and he'd been wearing . . . hardly anything.

A wolf howled near enough to make me jump, far enough away so that I followed Jessie at a walk instead of a run. I wasn't going to let her, or them, know just how spooked I was.

Had there been a man named Damien? Probably.

Was he merely a man? Or had he been more? I might never know that for sure.

Jessie's place was an apartment located in a small complex adjacent to the sheriff's office. I parked beside the squad car and followed her up the flight of stairs to the second floor.

"Are you really a cop?" I asked. "Or is this just pretend?"

"I'm a cop."

She didn't elaborate and irritation flared again. Jessie got to do her chosen job while she saved the world. I got to pretend I was a warden and earn the scorn of every community.

But I couldn't exactly be a werewolf hunter and a kindergarten teacher. The very thought was ludicrous.

The door sprang open before she could touch it, and a tall, emaciated silhouette spread across the hall floor.

"Edward," I murmured.

Jessie cast me a quick, surprised glance, and I realized I'd said his name aloud in a delighted voice that didn't belong to me. I couldn't afford attachments, not even to him, so I straightened my shoulders, cleared my throat, and stuck out my hand. "Good to see you, sir."

"Jeez, why don't you click your heels and salute," Jessie muttered, pushing past him.

Edward Mandenauer was as unlikely a leader of an elite monster-hunting unit as could be imagined. Cadaverous thin, he owned every one of his eighty-plus years. But he could still pull the trigger, and he'd killed more monsters than anyone, even me. I admired him. More than I would ever say.

"Why did you not come directly to me, Leigh?" Edward stepped back so I could enter the apartment.

"I'm here."

"You took a detour."

"How did you know?" I scowled. "How did *she* find me?"

"Your car was abandoned in town. Jessie ran the license plate, then tracked you into the woods."

My interest was piqued. Tracking had never been my strong suit. I wasn't patient enough. Jessie had to be very good to have found me as quickly as she had in the thickness of a forest that must be as strange to her as it was to me.

"From the look of the bonfire," Jessie tattled, "she's already started blasting away."

"That's my job," I snapped.

"This is *my* town."

"Girls, girls," Mandenauer admonished.

"Don't call me a girl," Jessie and I said at the same time.

We glanced at each other, scowled, and turned away. Mandenauer sighed. "You need to work together. There is something odd happening in Crow Valley."

That got my attention. "Odder than werewolves?"

"To be sure. Did you make note of the name of this fair city?"

Crow Valley. I hadn't thought about it. Stupid me.

For reasons unknown to science, wolves allow crows to scavenge from their kills. Some naturalists believe that the birds fly ahead, locate suitable prey, then circle back and lead the wolves to it. In gratitude, or perhaps as payment for services rendered, the wolves don't chase the crows off the corpses.

Whether this is true or not is anyone's guess. But the fact remains, where there are a lot of one, there are a lot of the other. Wolves feel at home around crows. Werewolves appear to as well.

"The wolves in this area have always been abundant, but they increased in number recently."

"And you know this how?"

He just gave me one of his stares. Edward knew everything.

"When the sheriff in this town left—"

"Left or was eaten?"

"Not eaten. Not this time. The odd occurrences with the wolves disturbed him. He called the authorities with his tall tales, and I was notified. I convinced him to take a leave of absence, then gave Jessie his job."

You think there are a lot of conspiracies in the government? You don't even know about the ones Edward is involved with. Any odd report—unexplained events, wolves run amok, monstrosities wandering over hill and dale—the information is forwarded to Edward and he sends a *Jäger-Sucher* to determine what needs to be done, then do it.

"What about Jessie's other job?" I asked.

"We had accomplished all we could in Miniwa. The wolves ran from there. We waited, but they did not return."

"What's going on here?"

He glanced at Jessie. "Tell her what we know."

Jessie hesitated, but in the end she shrugged and flopped onto the couch, gesturing me into a chair nearby. The apartment was sparsely but adequately furnished, as if she'd only brought the essentials.

No pictures on the walls, no knickknacks on the tables, though Jessie hardly seemed the knickknack type. Instead, every spare surface was covered with books, papers, notebooks. She didn't seem the studious type, either, but then what did I know?

"Werewolves are being killed in Crow Valley," she began.

"Good for you."

You may wonder how we know the difference between a dead wolf and a dead werewolf. I'll let you in on a little secret. If you shoot them with silver, they explode. Live or dead, doesn't matter. I kind of like putting a bullet into the dead ones. Call me sick. Everyone else does.

"They were being killed *before* we got here," Jessie continued. "From what I can tell, it started a little over three weeks ago."

I sat up straighter in my chair. A little over three weeks ago would have been the last full moon. That couldn't be good.

I glanced at Edward. "You've got no one working in Crow Valley?"

"No."

"Rogue agent?"

"Doubtful."

"Why?"

"Because the werewolves are not being killed with silver."

"Then how can they be dead?"

"There is only one other way to kill a werewolf," Edward said.

"How come I never heard of it?"

"Because it rarely happens."

"And why is that?"

"The only other way to kill a werewolf, besides the silver, is for a werewolf to kill one of its own."

"They never kill their own kind. It's against the werewolf rules of conduct."

"Apparently we have come across one who can't read."

Humor again. What was *wrong* with the man?

"Wolves and werewolves may appear the same," Jessie said, "but they're not."

"No shit," I muttered. I was already sick of Miss Know-It-All-Come-Lately.

She ignored me. Point for her.

"Though it's rare, wolves *will* kill another wolf, but

werewolves won't. They'll fight, drive one another from their territory, but they won't kill. I'd say it was a remnant of their humanity shining through, but we all know that most humans aren't very humane."

How true.

"So what's going on?" I asked.

"That's what we're trying to find out."

"Why?"

She blinked. "I'm sorry."

"What difference does it make who kills them as long as they're dead?"

Jessie glanced at Edward and he took over.

"It does not matter who kills them. What matters is that there is a werewolf out there behaving unlike a werewolf. I do not like it."

"Because . . . ?"

"The last time one of them behaved oddly, we met the wolf god."

"You think someone's trying to raise another wolf god?"

He shook his head. "A wolf god can only be brought forth under the blue moon. That time is past."

"Then what?"

"I do not know. But I have a very bad feeling."

I'd been around Edward long enough to understand that when he had a very bad feeling, the shit was usually going to hit the fan real soon.

"What's the plan?" I asked.

"You teach Jessie all that she needs to know."

"Why?" I demanded. "You've always taught the new guys."

"I am not as young as I used to be."

"Yeah, join the club."

His lips twitched, almost as if he might laugh. Wonders never ceased these days.

"I have enlisted the help of an expert to search the pages of history. Perhaps we will find a mention of what they are up to this time before it is too late. Until then, I must go back to headquarters. Elise needs my help."

Elise was Dr. Hanover, head research scientist at the *Jäger-Sucher* Compound in Montana and Edward's right hand. There was something else between them, too, though I'd never quite figured out what that something was. He was old enough to be her grandfather.

"You're not going to leave me alone with *her*?" I demanded.

"There are at least four hundred people in this town. You will not be alone."

"You know what?" Jessie stood and put her hands on her hips. "I don't need her help. I did just *fine* in Miniwa without any training at all."

"Yeah, I heard about that," I sneered. "Thanks to you, the werewolf population has doubled in this area and there are fresh new recruits running all over Canada. I just spent the last three months thinning them out."

Jessie's fingers clenched into fists, and she took one step toward me before the apartment door opened.

I had only an instant to register that a man was running through the room; then he grabbed Jessie around the waist and lifted her off her feet.

I started forward, but Mandenauer's hand on my arm stopped me. Good thing, too, because the guy locked lips with Jessie and the two of them shared the deepest, hottest, wettest kiss I'd ever witnessed outside of a pornographic movie.

I knew I should look away, but I couldn't tear my eyes from the sight. In my line of work, I didn't get a chance to see much affection. I didn't get a chance to see anything but death, and that was the way I wanted it. So why was I watching Jessie and whoever with misty, longing eyes?

Because I'd caught my first sight of a half-naked male in several years. My libido was acting up. My skin felt prickly, my stomach wobbly. I couldn't get Damien Fitzgerald out of my head, and that just wasn't like me.

The man stared into Jessie's face and very gently touched her cheek with his knuckle. She smiled and covered his hand with hers. It was as if Edward and I, maybe the whole world, didn't exist.

True love. Hell.

"She's going to get us killed," I muttered.

4

Jessie and her boyfriend turned toward me. I gritted my teeth so my mouth wouldn't fall open. Not only was he Indian, but he also was quite possibly the most gorgeous man I'd ever seen. Even better than Damien, the possible figment of my imagination.

He towered over Jessie, his body lithe and strong. The way he held himself screamed some kind of martial arts training. His hair was short, and a golden feather swung from one ear. He was exotic—both wild and tame. I couldn't seem to stop staring.

"You must be Leigh. Welcome."

The man held out his hand, but Jessie yanked him back. "Just one minute there, Slick; the duchess is being a pain in my ass."

"Since that's awful easy to do, Jess, I'm not going to hold it against her."

I smiled. He had her number.

"I'm Will." He offered his hand again, and I managed to shake it before Jessie could stop us. "Will Cadotte."

"Leigh Tyler," I returned.

"And you think Jessie is going to get us killed why?"

Not only was he sharp, but his hearing wasn't bad, either.

"Attachments." I shrugged. "You can't have them if you're going to be a *Jäger-Sucher*." I glanced at Edward. "What's the matter with you? Didn't you check her out better than this? Or is he a new development?"

I couldn't say I blamed her. Cadotte was a damn fine development. But I wasn't going to get my neck torn out or my head blown off because Jessie couldn't keep her mind off his assets.

"He is one of us, too."

I stared at Edward for a long moment. "It's finally happened."

"What is that?"

"You've gone senile. I must say, you hide it well."

He narrowed his pale blue eyes. "Watch your mouth, young lady. I know what I am doing."

That remained to be seen.

I glanced at Cadotte. "No offense, but you don't seem like much of a hunter."

"Probably because I'm not."

"He is the expert I spoke of."

I looked Cadotte up and down. "I just bet he is."

Cadotte threw his arm out, stopping Jessie before she could spring across the room and kick my ass. Or at least try. We were going to go round and round before this was over. It was only a matter of time.

"You must forgive Leigh," Edward said. "She is devoted to the job."

"Don't apologize for me. I'm the one who has to train her. I can see she's gaga over him. If he's in danger, she'll be useless."

"On the contrary, Jessie was very useful, even when

Will was in grave danger. It is one of the reasons I chose her."

My eyes met Edward's. His were determined and I accepted the inevitable. Jessie was one of us now, and so was the boyfriend.

"What kind of an expert is he?"

"*He's* right here," Cadotte said. "I'm a professor of Native American history, with a specialty in totems."

"Which will do us any good why?"

His lips twitched. For some reason Cadotte found me more amusing than annoying, which only annoyed me more. Of course that was very easy to do. Jessie and I had more in common with each passing moment.

"I live to acquire obscure data."

"Will was invaluable during our escapade with the wolf god," Edward said.

"The wolf god is gone."

"But not forgotten," Jessie whispered.

A shadow flickered across her face. Will took her hand. I wondered what was up with that, and since I'd never been one to shut my mouth, I asked.

"You knew the wolf god well?"

"She was my best friend."

"Nice friend."

"At least I had one."

"Girls—" Mandenauer broke off as Jessie and I both snarled at him. "I mean, ladies, must you?"

"I think they must," Cadotte murmured. "It's a territorial thing."

"Why don't they just pee on the trees as we do?"

"It'd be quieter," Cadotte agreed.

I stared at Edward, then shifted my gaze to Jessie. "What did you do to him?"

Jessie frowned. "Nothing."

"He never made jokes before he met you."

"Then my work here is done." She brushed her palms together.

"Leigh, if we cannot laugh once in a while, what good is living?" Edward asked.

"I don't know; what good is it?"

Silence fell over the room. Edward glanced away. Jessie and Will stared at me with something akin to pity in their eyes. And they didn't even know me.

I threw up my hands. "Never mind. Where am I staying? Just don't say here, because you can forget it."

"As if," Jessie muttered.

"There was one room for rent in Crow Valley," Edward said.

"Only one? No cabin? No hotel?"

Jessie rolled her eyes. "You aren't in Kansas anymore, Duchess."

I winced. Kansas. Did she know? Or was that just a lucky guess?

Edward, ever sensitive to my pain, jumped in. "Crow Valley is not a resort area. No one comes to this town on vacation."

From what I'd seen so far, I understood why.

"Why *do* they come?"

"To retire."

"Here?"

"What's wrong with here?" Jessie demanded. "I've lived here—or near enough—for most of my life."

"My sympathies."

Her eyes narrowed. Yep, she definitely wanted to punch me. Which worked out well, because I wouldn't mind slugging her just for the hell of it.

Cadotte stepped in again. "Crow Valley was originally a mining town. That's why they call Wisconsin the Badger State."

"I thought it was because you had too many badgers."

In my opinion, one was too many. I'd met a few badgers in my travels, and they were mean little fucks.

"We do." Will's expression said he'd encountered a few himself and had about as high an opinion of them as I did. "But the nickname originated with the miners, who were called badgers because they dug in the ground."

"What kind of mines?"

"Lead mostly. Some zinc and copper."

"And there's a mine here?"

"Yes, but it closed a long time ago. The town remained. It's a beautiful area. Very peaceful."

"If you like snow eight months out of twelve, summer for one month, if you're lucky, and so many trees you can't see the sun half the time," I muttered.

"Some people do."

Cadotte was very good at smoothing the waters and imparting information without seeming to lecture, even though he was. He must have been an excellent professor. Just as I had once been an excellent teacher.

I put that thought right out of my head and focused on what he was saying.

"A lot of folks from the big cities who came north with their families for vacation have retired in Crow Valley. They don't want to live in a tourist trap."

"So this entire town is made up of old people."

Easy pickings for the werewolves.

"Not entirely. An older community needs a lot of services. Medical, restaurants, entertainment. I'd say Crow Valley is fifty-fifty between retirees and the regular Joes who wait on them."

"A very large transient population then." In my experience, waiters, bartenders, and other service people moved around a lot. I know I would. "Which makes it hard to tell if there's a new werewolf in town."

"I never said this was going to be easy," Edward murmured. "That is why I called you."

His praise warmed the cold spot in my chest that had been there since I'd met Jessie. She was too tall, too confident, too palsy with Edward, and too damned lucky to have Cadotte.

I needed to get over my jealousy. It wasn't as if I wanted her life. I knew better than to get close to anyone, and sooner or later Jessie would know better, too. I didn't want to be around when that happened. So I'd do my job and get out of Dodge.

"Point me toward my room, would you? Nighttime's a-wastin'."

Everyone exchanged glances.

"What?" I growled. I hated being treated like an outsider—even when I was.

"It's just . . ." Cadotte shrugged. "Since I'm not sure what's going on yet, it might be a good idea to refrain from killing them for a while."

"Sounds like a bad idea to me."

"What if killing them is what they want?"

"That makes no sense."

"Does anything make sense with werewolves?"

Good point. If I could believe in werewolves and assorted other creatures of the night, pretty much anything was possible. Even that killing them was what they wanted. Still, if I wasn't going to blast a few werewolves, what was I good for?

"You can train Jessie," Edward said, as if he'd heard my thoughts.

I scowled. She grinned.

"As soon as Will has some idea of what we're up against, the two of you can begin to hunt," Edward soothed.

There was no way I was hunting with Jessie or anyone else. There was no way I was sitting on my ass and letting werewolves wander free to do their dirty deeds and make more werewolves. But I didn't have to tell them that.

"Fine," I said. "We'll start tomorrow."

The way Edward beamed at me, I would have felt bad for deceiving him. If I were capable of such a feeling.

Everyone talked at once, offering to show me to my room—on the other side of town. But I wanted to be alone. How else was I going to sneak away?

"Just give me the address," I snapped.

"No problemo." Jessie snatched a paper from the end table, scribbled something on a corner, and tore it off.

Will flinched at the sound and sighed. "Jessie, could you check and see if that's a rare document or something important before you go tearing it into shreds?"

"Huh? Oh, sorry." She shrugged and handed me the corner anyway. Then dug into her pocket for the key.

I stifled a smile. As annoying as she was, there were times when I sympathized with her. How did she stand living with an egghead like Will Cadotte?

He pulled a pair of glasses from his pocket, settled them on his nose, then bent over the end table to read what was left of his precious paper. I got a good glimpse of his ass. Maybe this assignment wouldn't be so bad after all.

I'd never been much of an ass woman, even before I'd caught sight of Fitzgerald's chest and become bewitched by all that pale Irish skin and manly muscle. However, that didn't mean I couldn't admire beauty when it was displayed right in front of me.

I pulled my gaze from Will's jeans. My eyes collided with Jessie's. While most women would be mad to find another ogling their boyfriend's behind, she merely looked amused and shrugged as if to say, *What can you do?* For just an instant I liked her.

Then she opened her mouth.

"I'll be at your place at seven A.M."

"Like hell."

"Leigh is not a morning person," Edward explained.

"Well, I have to work at night, so morning is when we'll train."

"We'll train when I say we'll train. At noon."

I narrowed my eyes. She narrowed hers. We stared each other down. I was reminded of films I'd studied of real wolves. Dominance struggles. Alpha and beta animals. Well, I was the alpha around here, and she'd damn straight better get used to it.

We might have stared at each other all night, but Cadotte grabbed Jessie and kissed her again. Edward showed me to the door. The first round hadn't gone at all the way I'd planned.

He stepped into the hallway behind me. "I must leave."

"Already?"

My voice sounded wan and needy. Pathetic. What was the matter with me? Thankfully Edward didn't seem to notice my sudden regression to the wimpy girlie-girl I'd once been.

"Elise requested I come to the compound as soon as I could. There is an . . . issue which requires my attention. You do not need me here with both you and Jessie, as well as Will, on the job."

"When can you get back?"

"I am not sure. You'll be fine. Just show Jessie everything I showed you and anything new you have learned along the way."

He put his hand on my shoulder. His fingers felt like dry twigs. Would they snap under too much pressure? For the first time I could remember, I was worried about Edward. He was very, very old, and today he seemed even older.

"Keep me informed," he said. "On the lovely Internet. What an invention."

I smiled. Edward was fascinated with the Internet. His was both a charming and a convenient obsession.

We walked out together, climbed into separate cars. I watched his until the taillights disappeared over a far hill, then drove down the main street of Crow Valley, which had been quaintly labeled Main Street, until I found a road called Good.

"They are hysterical in this town," I muttered as the carriage of my rental car scraped along the rutted, gravel-strewn surface of Good Road.

I clattered along in the night for quite a while, even began to wonder if Jessie's idea of a joke was sending me off on a path that led nowhere.

The trees made a canopy over my car, shutting out any light, making the air seem to throb against the windshield in a cool, velvet haze. I could smell the forest—the evergreen scent of pine, the musty aroma of dying leaves, and the tang of summer gone away too soon.

I had almost decided to turn back when I heard it. The faint, exotic drift of music.

I kept driving. The sky glowed dimly, as if city lights pulsed in the distance. But I knew from the map I'd studied before leaving Minneapolis that there wasn't a town of any identifiable size within a hundred miles.

So what were those lights, and who was playing music?

I nearly ran into the answer. My car rolled up one side of an impressive bump, then slid down the other. I shot into a clearing and nearly slammed through the front wall of a tavern.

"What the—?"

Cars were parked all around the building at odd angles, as if the patrons had arrived drunk. Music spilled out the open windows—jazz—as out of place in this forest as I was.

There was no sign on the building, no neon lights announcing McGinty's or Cheers, just a bright yellow spotlight perched at every corner of the tavern, blaring into the trees as if to keep whatever lurked there at bay.

"One helluvan odd place for a bar."

But in the single day I'd been in Wisconsin, I'd noticed they did taverns up right. There had to be one on every corner of every town I'd driven through. Why should Crow Valley be any different? Although I didn't see a corner anywhere near here.

There also didn't appear to be anything resembling a room for rent. I was going to hold Jessie's head under a faucet when I got back to her place.

I glanced around for a space big enough to pull a U-turn and caught a glimmer of motion from the woods.

"Well, hell-o," I murmured as Damien Fitzgerald slid out of the trees and headed for the front door.

He'd found his shirt and his shoes since I saw him last. He appeared to have a penchant for black. What had he been doing between then and now? Only one way to find out.

I shut off the engine, climbed out of my car, and hurried across the grass toward the tavern without a name.

5

I stepped into a room so filled with smoke I could barely see. Since I hadn't had a cigarette in two years, my eyes burned and my throat clenched, even as I yearned.

I missed cigarettes. More than I could say.

The door slammed behind me, and everyone stared. I stared back, feeling as if I'd stepped into a backwoods edition of *Star Wars*. I even glanced at the stage to see if the jazz was coming from a bizarre collection of aliens playing instruments I'd never seen before. But the raised, open area was empty, the music wailing out of a jukebox instead.

People of every shape, size, color filled the room. That struck me as odd right away. Folks in the north woods were not known for socializing with the Indians, and this tavern must be way over their quota of African-Americans north of the great Green Bay divide.

There were women—young and old, fat and thin, black, white, and red. Men the same way. Even a midget—make that little person—was perched on a stool at the bar. I'd stepped into the twilight zone. But when?

Everyone still stared at me as if I'd invaded a sacred

place. This was a bar, wasn't it? My money was as good as the next guy's.

"Hi." I waved.

No one answered, but they did go back to their drinks and their smokes. I scanned the room for Damien, but he wasn't there.

I crossed to the bar, took a seat next to the little guy. He blew smoke in my face. So much for being welcome.

I didn't see a bartender. Not at first. Spinning my chair, I scanned the crowd again.

Damien had come in here. I'd seen him. He was not a figment of my imagination. But I was beginning to wonder what he *was,* since he seemed able to appear and disappear at will. I'd learned, over the past few years, that there were more things to fear in this world than werewolves. A lot more.

I turned back and let out a little shriek. The man I'd been searching for stood directly in front of me on the other side of the bar.

He may have found his shirt, but he seemed to have trouble with buttons. He'd only managed the bottom two, and an enticing V of pale, smooth flesh flashed against the black silk.

"What can I get you?"

I forced my eyes from his chest to his face. He lifted a brow. He knew I'd been looking. I only hoped I hadn't been drooling.

The thought made me straighten, scowl, snap, "Where were you?"

"Right here."

"No." I shook my head for emphasis—though I wasn't sure if the movement was for my benefit or his.

"I was rotating stock." He pointed behind the bar, toward the ground.

Relief rushed through me. I wasn't losing it. Not again. Or at least not yet.

"What can I get you?" he repeated.

"You're the bartender?"

"No, I'm independently wealthy. I come in here on Tuesday nights and wait on people for fun."

Since he said the words without a hint of humor or a trace of a smile, I almost wondered if he was serious. Until the midget snorted.

"Do you have white wine?" I asked.

I wasn't much of a drinker. I needed my wits about me all the time. I never knew when someone might turn into a werewolf and try to kill me.

This happened a lot more than you might think. It was usually the person you least expected it to be, too. I glanced at the tiny man sitting next to me.

He lifted his upper lip in what was either a bad Elvis imitation or a snarl; I wasn't sure which. Could he . . . ? *Nah.*

"The wine is more like vinegar." I returned my attention to Damien as he set a white soda in front of me. "You're better off with this, Miss . . . ?"

I never *had* told him my name. Oops.

"Leigh Tyler."

I reached for the glass, my hand heading down as his headed up. Our fingers brushed and a jolt of awareness shot across my skin, making the hair on my arms tingle and the back of my throat tighten.

Damien must have felt it, too, because he jerked back as quickly as I did and busied himself wiping a drop of condensation from the bar.

My throat wouldn't ease up. My skin wouldn't stop jumping. I had a feeling this was what it felt like to be hopped up on drugs or maybe coming off them.

I grabbed the glass and took a sip. The mellow, sweet

soda soothed both the dryness in my mouth and the tension in my body. I needed to get to work here, but it had been so long since I'd talked to a man, I wasn't sure if I remembered how.

I coughed gently, then rubbed my hands along my tingling arms, wondering if the sensation would ever fade. My gaze drifted over Damien's profile—the smooth wash of his hair across his cheek, the glint of light eyes in a pale face.

I sighed. Most likely I was going to feel like this every time I came near him. Damn.

"So, what's the name of this place?" I asked.

"Isn't one."

"A bar without a name?"

He shrugged. "Happens. They've tried to call it everything from Skunk Hill to Tavern in the Green. Nothing really fits. So the place is just . . ." he spread his hands, "here."

I nodded, took another sip of soda, and set the glass back on the bar trying to figure out how to broach the questions I needed to ask.

"How'd you find me?"

I opened my mouth, shut it again, stumped. He thought I'd tracked him down? Of all the nerve! But I suppose guys who looked like Damien Fitzgerald had women following them all the time.

I glanced at the midget. He slammed back a shot and a beer, then gave me that weird little snarl again.

"Stop that, Cowboy. She's going to think you're not housebroken yet."

Cowboy shrugged and jumped down from the stool. As he walked over to join an ancient Native American woman at a table in the corner I saw how he'd gotten his nickname. Tiny cowboy boots with three-inch heels graced his little feet.

"I didn't know they made them that small," I murmured.

"People come in all shapes and sizes."

I turned back to Damien. "I meant the boots."

"Oh." He shrugged. "They make those in all shapes and sizes, too."

"So I see."

Damien picked up a dish towel and started drying glasses. He kept gazing at me as if waiting for me to speak. I was happy to oblige.

"Why did you disappear earlier?"

He shrugged. "I don't like cops."

"I don't have much use for bartenders, either."

"Ouch." His lips twitched, but still he didn't smile. "Except I didn't mean you; I was talking about the sheriff."

I frowned. He was gone before Jessie had shown up. Or so she'd said.

"How'd you know she was coming?"

"Couldn't you hear her? She wasn't trying to be quiet."

I hadn't heard Jessie. Because I was distracted by his great chest or because he had supernatural hearing?

"Where'd you find your clothes and your shoes?"

"In my room. Where'd you find yours?"

"You have a room in the middle of the forest?"

He flicked his head toward the back of the building. His hair flew around his face, settling into a slightly more rumpled position than before. "There's a cabin out back. I preferred it to the room upstairs."

Room *upstairs*? Jessie hadn't been sending me on a wild-goose chase. She'd sent me to my room. Above a weird bar, in the dense woods. I was still going to hold her head under a faucet.

"What's wrong with the room upstairs?" I asked.

"What do you care?"

I let out a sigh and stifled the urge to curse. "Because it's mine."

"You're the one who rented the room?" He appeared as happy about it as I was.

"Yeah."

"What for?"

"I'll be staying awhile. From what I hear, that room is my only option."

"True. There isn't a Hilton for miles."

I could see why.

"So, Damien, what made you run into the big woods half-dressed?"

He cut me a quick glance at the sudden change in subject, then shrugged and picked up another glass to polish. I was reminded of his chest beneath the wavering moonlight, the smooth flow of his skin over rippling muscle. I took a third sip of soda.

"Have you ever seen a forest fire?"

Another lightning quick change in subject. I was getting dizzy.

"Not up close."

"You don't want to. They sweep across acres in minutes, killing everything in their path. Sounds like a train coming at you, and there's nowhere to go, nowhere to hide."

His eyes *were* hazel—very light—a combination of green, brown, and yellow. They made me wonder what else he'd seen. What else he'd done.

"I was getting ready for work and I smelled the flames, followed the scent until I found you."

"But you managed to put on some pants first?"

"Would you rather I hadn't?"

Yes.

The word whispered through my head, but thankfully it didn't come out of my mouth. From the expression on his face, he'd heard me anyway.

"You followed the scent of the fire through the forest?" I repeated.

"Got a problem with that?"

A big one. This guy's nose was too damned sharp for a human. Too bad I was going to have to kill him. But a were-wolf was a werewolf, and even gorgeous ones had to die.

"Can you show me my room?" I asked.

Jessie had given me the key and I hadn't needed help finding anything since I was ten, but he didn't need to know that. I wanted to get him outside. Even I balked at mertzing someone in front of a dozen other someones.

"Sure." He tossed the dish towel onto the counter. "Cowboy, I'll be right back."

The little man lifted a little hand and kept talking to the old woman.

As we left, I felt a dozen pairs of eyes on my back. Why were they so interested in me? Or maybe they were just interested in Damien. I know I was.

Hell. I was too interested. Even now, my hands were clammy; my heart beat too fast. I didn't want to kill him, and that was new. Usually I couldn't wait.

Of course I didn't often meet my prey. I never spared the time for a conversation.

We left through the back door. A set of stairs led up the outside of the building. His cabin was tucked into the trees, very small, damn near decrepit. I was glad I had the room instead.

Most people would be worrying about what they were going to do with the body, how they would explain where this man had disappeared to. I didn't have such troubles.

I'd burn the body, and the *J-S* society would take care

of the rest. Edward employed an entire division devoted to such explanations. Having the sheriff of the town on my side didn't hurt, either.

I did pause to consider if I was dancing too close to the line between human and psychopath. Sometimes I wondered. Usually late at night when I was all alone, rarely during hunting time with the silver moon shining bright in the sky and my memories alive in my head.

Damien opened the door. It hadn't been locked. Nothing new in town like this, I was sure. But considering the odd crew downstairs and the even odder ones loping through the woods, I'd be locking that from now on, thanks.

Reaching inside, he flipped the switch. I wished he hadn't. I couldn't bear the sight of blood beneath electric lights. Too many memories, too much pain, so damn red it hurt my eyes. I reached past him, planning to shut it off.

His fingers closed around my wrist and tightened. In an instant, the awareness was back, so powerful I couldn't make myself pull away. He could easily have killed me as I stood there wondering what his mouth would taste like, what his skin would feel like.

"What are you doing?"

His voice had lowered to a growl, rippling along my skin like a tactile sound wave. He was so close I could feel his heat, smell his skin, a tantalizing combination of air and water with a hint of pine. Or was that just the flavor of the wind?

Since he held my right hand in a tight grip, my left crept for the gun at the small of my back, not the most comfortable place to carry one but definitely the most secret.

I'd planned to use the knife, less noise, but I couldn't reach my boot. I was one step up from lame with my left hand. However, at this range I ought to be able to hit something vital without even trying.

I looked into his eyes. Did he know who I was? Why I'd come here? What I planned to do? I couldn't tell. It didn't matter. My fingers closed over the butt of my gun.

"You should let your hair grow."

I froze as an image slid unbidden through my mind. My twenty-two-year-old self, staring impassively into the bathroom mirror as I hacked off my braid with a butcher knife. I shivered despite the waves of heat coming from Damien like an open oven.

He released my wrist. I could have shot him then, even used my good hand. But he brushed his palm across the shorn stubble of my hair, then dragged his knuckles down my cheek.

I couldn't move, could barely think. His thigh brushed my hip, his breath kissed my temple, and I didn't leap back, didn't even think about slugging him.

I hadn't been touched in years, hadn't wanted to be. So why him? Why now?

I craved the brush of his skin against mine at the same time the pulse of adrenaline urged me to kill him. A small sane corner of my brain wondered if he was practicing mind control. Maybe that's what the werewolves were up to in Crow Valley.

His hand turned and I caught a flash of something I hadn't seen before, something that made my fingers fall away from the gun.

He was wearing a ring. A *silver* ring.

Any idiot knew a werewolf would never wear silver.

6

I stood beneath the flare of the electric lights, horrified at what I'd nearly done. There was a reason I wasn't supposed to kill them unless I saw them change, a reason I'd forgotten. Mistakes could be made, even by the most dedicated agent.

If I killed an innocent human being, that would make me no better than the animals I hunted. I hated them, but right now I hated myself.

"What's the matter?" Damien lowered his hand to my shoulder, gave it a reassuring squeeze. Why he was being so nice to me I had no idea. I certainly didn't deserve it— even without the gun in my pants.

"Nothing."

"You went white. Are you sick?"

Very.

"No. The light's just too bright. Hurts my eyes."

"I'll change the bulb for you."

He released me and stepped back so I could enter the room.

"Not much to it." He swept out an arm. "Bed, television, bath through there."

I nodded, taking in the tiny sink, refrigerator, and coffeepot that made up the kitchen. Good thing I didn't cook.

"I'll just get that low-watt bulb." He moved toward the door. "It's downstairs."

"Thanks. Damien?" He paused in the doorway. "I appreciate your help."

He smiled, though the expression didn't reach his eyes. Now that I thought of it, his smile was rare and always a little bit sad—as if he had memories he couldn't quite shake. Like me.

"No problem. The new kids in town have to stick together."

I stiffened. "You're new?"

"Just moved in about three few weeks ago."

When the dead wolves had started to appear. Coincidence? My eyes fell to the ring on his right hand. Probably.

"I thought you owned this place."

"I only work here."

"The owner?"

"Lives in Tucson."

"Lucky him."

He tilted his head and his hair swung free. My fingers itched to tuck it behind his ear. Why did I always have to tidy everything? The man, his hair, the world.

"You don't like Crow Valley?"

"I haven't been in town long enough to decide."

"It's not so bad. I've seen worse."

"You travel a lot?"

He shrugged. "Enough."

His eyes had gone dark and haunted again. I wanted to ask what *enough* was, but the way he held himself, as if he was waiting for a blow or warding off a memory, made me stop.

"I'll get that bulb," he said, and practically ran from the room.

I seemed to have that effect on men since I changed occupations. Once I'd been popular, pretty, the annoyingly pert cheerleader type. Hell, I'd *been* a cheerleader, in both high school and college. I'd dated the quarterback, planned on marrying him, too. Until he'd gotten his throat ripped out.

Then a whole lot of things had changed. I'd started killing for a living, and men avoided me like a lifetime commitment. Sometimes I wondered if what I did clung to me like a bad odor, or a permanent blot on my creamy white skin.

Mostly I didn't care. I didn't want sex any more than I wanted friendship. A relationship? Ha. I had better things to do.

So why was I thinking of how delectable Damien Fitzgerald had looked barefoot and bare chested beneath the silver light of the moon?

Because I'd lost what was left of my mind.

Maybe he wasn't a werewolf, but that didn't make him fair game. Any connection with me could get him killed—badly. It had happened before.

Despite his taut pecs and bulging biceps, he was out of his league in my world. He'd be meat to them, and I couldn't let that happen.

When I heard his steps on the stairs, I went out and took the bulb from his fingers. "Thanks. I'll take care of it."

The sharp dismissal in my voice caused a flicker of hurt to cross his face, before he squashed it and let the stoic mask drop. With a nod, he returned to the bar.

I had to force myself not to call him back, not to follow him and apologize. He'd been nothing but kind to me and

I'd blown him off. Even though it was for his own good, I still felt like a shit.

I changed the bulb, for appearances' sake, then glanced at my watch. *Midnight.* The bar beneath my feet was starting to rock. No one would notice me slipping away. No one would care.

But after what had happened tonight, I was nervous. Had I lost my touch? My edge? Maybe I *should* take some time off, as Will had suggested.

Even so, I felt naked without all my guns, so I hurried to my car, retrieved every one that I had, as well as my travel bag, then hustled up to my apartment. As I reached the landing, the distant, eerie cry of a wolf split the night. I slammed the door and locked it behind me.

Was I locking them out or myself in? I wasn't sure, and that worried me. I'd spent a little time on the other side of sane, and I didn't want to return. I stowed my rifle, my bag, then sat down and had a good long talk with myself.

I had almost screwed up. It happened. However, if I got sidetracked, if I got spooked, they would win and a whole lot of innocent people would lose.

I'd take tonight off. Get some sleep. Go back to work tomorrow with a clear head and a clearer plan.

That decided, I checked the locks, the windows, my ammo. I should have checked my dreams—at the door.

I didn't mean to fall asleep before the sun came up. I planned to do some Internet research, make a few calls, catch up on my paperwork. But the traveling, the stress, the steady beat of the music from the bar downstairs must have combined to lull me from my intentions. Once asleep, I went where I hadn't been in quite a while.

Nightmares were nothing new to me. I lived with them

even in the daytime. But I usually hunted the darkness away, slept in the light. I'd found that this kept the bloody trips down memory lane to a minimum.

In this dream, I was twenty-two again. Fresh out of school with a brand-new job teaching ABCs. I loved everything about kids—their innocence, their interest, their trusting cherubic faces. I loved them and I wanted some of my own.

Which was where Jimmy Renquist came in. We'd met as juniors at Northern Kansas University. I'd been leading the cheer "Go, fight, win. Yay," when Jimmy had been thrown out-of-bounds by a Neanderthal defensive lineman from Fresno. He'd landed on top of me.

"I'm sorry. I'm sorry," he kept repeating as he helped me up and brushed me off. "Are you all right? I didn't hurt you, did I?"

"Renquist, get your ass back in the game!" the coach shouted.

He'd shrugged, winked, and smiled at me. I was lost from that moment on.

Jimmy was sweet, strong, smart. He loved kids, too. He planned to become a phys ed teacher. He would have if he hadn't fallen in love with me.

Even in the dream my mind shied at the memory of what I'd done to bring the horror down upon us. In the way of nightmares, the scene shifted to Sunday dinner at my parents' house. Telling them the wedding date, showing Mom the ring, having her weep with joy and hug me tight.

My last sight of Jimmy—whole—had been of him smiling that smile I loved as he shook hands with my dad.

My little sister—Mom and Dad's midlife *oops*—was five years old. My seventeen-year-old brother was home, too. Everyone was grinning when the first wolf crashed through the picture window.

Jimmy shoved my dad aside, threw himself in front of me. The wolf, a huge white male, hit him in the chest and tore out his throat in a single, practiced motion.

The rest of us might have been OK if we'd run immediately—blockaded a door, found a gun, maybe some silver bullets.

Who am I kidding? We were goners from the moment the window shattered, if not before.

But it's hard to move when something like that happens in your dining room. Normal people don't react well to sudden death, and we were so normal it was pitiful.

We stood there watching as the great white wolf ate Jimmy. We stood there in shock as the room filled with others. Later I understood that the pack had behaved with true pack mentality. Cull the herd, survival of the fittest, only the good die young. My sister went next.

The nightmare continued as I watched my family die one by one. I was too shocked to wonder why I was left for last. Too horrified and sick to notice that the wolves didn't look exactly like wolves.

Then the white wolf, fur pink with blood, turned to me. The others parted, let him come. I stared into his eyes, and I knew who he was.

7

The screaming woke me up. I was on my feet, rifle in one hand, the other on the door, when I realized the sound had stopped.

I listened, straining my ears, trying to determine a direction, but all I heard was the wail of a sax from the bar downstairs.

My shirt was wet with sweat. My heart thudded in my throat. My skin was covered with gooseflesh. It still took me several moments to understand that I was the one who had been screaming.

"Shit."

I set the gun next to the door. My hand shook and I clenched it until my fingers ached. I went to the sink, shoved my head under the water, drank directly from the faucet, then ran the cool liquid over the pulsing veins in my wrists. Slowly my heartbeat returned to normal.

If Edward could see me now, I'd be in deep trouble.

Because of my history, I was required to visit a specially trained *J-S* psychiatrist four times a year. This merely meant I'd learned exactly what to say to be declared fit for duty.

I understand that killing the werewolves won't bring back my family.

No, I'm not searching for the white wolf on my own time.

"The dreams are gone," I whispered.

The empty room, which still rang with the echoes of my screams, mocked me.

I *hadn't* had a dream in a very long time. Sleeping in the daylight had taken care of the nightmares. But they were still there waiting for me to slip up. Just like the werewolves.

My head lifted. Droplets of water flew in every direction. I was dizzy. Breathless. Weak. I knew how to make that all go away.

Blood. Theirs. Now.

Only hours before, I'd decided not to hunt, but that had been before the dream. I no longer had a choice.

Scooping up my rifle, I headed out the door.

My watch said it was close to 4:00 A.M. I didn't have too much time before dawn. What I had would be enough. It would have to be.

As I reached the bottom of the steps I frowned. All the cars were still in the lot. The saxophone continued to wail. The lights remained on inside. Hadn't they ever heard of bar time around here?

The windows had been closed against the October night. I couldn't blame them. This far north, the first frost could arrive at any moment.

The glass was foggy. From age or a buildup of smoke, either way, I couldn't see anything inside but shadows. None of which moved. But then no one had been moving earlier, either, unless you counted the lifting of glasses to their mouths.

I dismissed the mystery of the bar patrons. I had better

things to worry about. I could ask Jessie about the rules of bar time. If I actually cared. Or complain to Damien, though I'd rather avoid him as much as possible. I didn't need any more complications in my life—and Damien Fitzgerald had complication written all over him.

I practically ran into the woods, crashed loudly through the brush. I wasn't trying to be covert. Drenched in nervous sweat how many times over, I must have smelled like a wild animal. My hair, despite the dousing in the sink, stood up in grainy, stiff hanks. I didn't mind.

I wanted them to hear me, smell me, come after me. I didn't have all night.

"Come on!" I shouted as I picked up my pace.

Edward had taught me to hunt from the trees as often as possible. Even when you found their lair, being up in a tree to take them out was preferable to being on the ground.

Wolves were quick; werewolves were slippery and sly. Wolf body, person brain, deadly combination. A tall tree was the safest place. Though these wolves were special, they couldn't fly—yet.

But sometimes an opportunity presented itself and there was no convenient tree stand nearby. If Edward ever found out just how many times I broke the rules in order to kill the monsters, he would revoke my hunting rights for more than a day. He'd lock me up in a white room. Again.

I picked up my pace, needing to get farther into the forest, farther from Damien and his incredible nose. I planned on having another bonfire before daylight.

I'd been in decent shape before I became a *Jäger-Sucher,* but once I signed on I learned how out of shape I was. Wolves would catch me if I ran. They can reach speeds of up to 40 miles per hour and cover 125 miles in a day, though 40 is average. Wolves can follow a herd at a run for 5 or 6 miles and *then* accelerate. Werewolves don't need supernatural abilities when just being wolves makes them superhuman. Which was why I always carried a gun.

"There's just one of me!" I shouted. "I'm out here all alone. Come and get it!"

The *J-S* rule book said we needed to be sure we were shooting a werewolf. One way to do this, the preferred way, was to watch the beast change. However, Edward had taught me a few other less certain but no less acceptable ways, to be sure.

Real wolves would run from a human. Only werewolves ran toward them.

Both wolves and werewolves culled the weakest from the herd. Only werewolves attacked the strong. Only animals with human intelligence did so with military precision.

The rasp of my breath, the stomp of my boots, the crackle of branches nearly drowned out the whisper of the wind through the trees, the buzz of any remaining mosquitoes, the rustle of night creatures in the underbrush. Because of that I didn't hear the silence. Not at first.

By the time I noticed how still everything had gotten—eerily so—it was too late. They were coming in fast from every direction.

"Standard attack formation," I muttered. "God, you're predictable."

My rifle had been modified from semi- to fully automatic by the geniuses of the *Jäger-Sucher* weapons division. The gun appeared normal, but it wasn't. One of the reasons I preferred it to the standard-issue DNR shotgun—a nice piece of hardware but not for supernatural baddies.

The automatic was completely illegal, of course, so arrest me. I didn't think the werewolves were going to call foul because I possessed the gun of a modern terrorist. When I got through with them they wouldn't be able to do anything but burn.

The first one burst from the foliage to my right. They were rarely able to wait. To stalk. To attack simultaneously. Someone always got eager, and then he was mine.

I waited until I saw the whites of their eyes. That they had whites was the reason I shot them. Look at a human's eyes, then look at a wolf's. You'll see what I mean.

I shot a gray wolf in the chest. Then the one next to that, and the one next to that. I put my back to those bodies and mowed the rest down in a sweeping semicircle of gunfire.

Werewolves are good at making a plan, what they can't seem to do is improvise.

The last wolf hit the ground and silence returned to the forest.

"Automatic weapon, sweep pattern. Screws 'em every time," I murmured.

My heart still pounded fast and loud, but my hands had stopped shaking. I no longer felt weak. I no longer heard the voices in my head or the screaming in my ears. Life was good.

I counted bodies. Eight. Not bad for a night's work. Damn good for an hour's.

I leaned down, planning to drag them into a pile—the easier to burn them, my dear—and a low, furious growl rumbled from behind me.

I spun around, bringing the gun up at the same time. I never set my gun down. *Never.* Stuff like this had happened to me before. What had not happened was the click that signified empty when I pulled the trigger.

The wolf, a russet monster with big brown eyes, grinned. He'd flanked me. Bastard.

"Smarter than your pals, hey?"

His lip lifted, turning the grin into a snarl. I shifted, bending my arms and pulling the gun back like a Louisville Slugger.

"Play ball."

He charged. I swung. The gun caught him in the head, but not hard enough. He hit me in the chest and followed me to the ground.

Edward had taught me a million things. The first, and by far the most useful at this moment, was how to grab a werewolf and keep him from eating your face.

I got one hand on the wolf's windpipe, the other around his muzzle, and held on. So far, so good. But how long could I hold him off?

Paws flailed, claws digging for purchase. I didn't worry about getting scratched. Lycanthropy is a virus of sorts. Like rabies, it's passed through the saliva. So a scratch wouldn't make me furry, but it *would* hurt. However, if those teeth so much as pricked my skin, I'd be eating my associates raw within a day.

I took a deep breath and tried to shove the werewolf away. I got nowhere. The animal was stronger than me. I was doomed.

A rustle, a snarl, then another furry body hurtled through the night. I tensed, expecting a second attack.

Instead, the newcomer hit the wolf straddling my chest broadside, and they tumbled end over end away from me in a flurry of teeth, claws, and tails.

I didn't waste any time scrambling to my feet, retrieving my gun, and loading it as the huge red wolf and the smaller brown one fought.

I'd never seen wolves fight, except on TV. Never seen werewolves fight at all. I was glad I'd missed it. The combination of animal body and human ruthlessness was horrific to behold.

They slashed and tore; blood dampened the ground; fur literally flew off them. I should have shot them both or at least run away. Instead, I could only stare, both repelled and fascinated by the savagery.

The russet wolf was bigger, broader, stronger. But the brown one was pissed. He snarled the entire time, as if teasing the larger wolf, egging him on to more daring feats. They were both covered in blood—their own and each other's—when the smaller wolf broke away, limping.

A real wolf would have let him go. The red werewolf charged. The other waited, waited, ducked as if giving in, then reached up and tore out the big bully's throat in one vicious yank. I had to admire his technique.

The injured animal took a few steps, as if to run away, hide, maybe heal, but it was too late. He crumpled, dead before he hit the ground. The brown wolf walked over to his prize, not a hitch in his step.

"Clever boy," I murmured.

He glanced up and cocked his head. Lifting my gun, I aimed right between his eyes. I couldn't see their color. The night was too dark, the moon too dim, the forest too thick. But they were human eyes. That much I could tell. That much was all I needed.

I thought of Jimmy, my sister, brother, parents. I remembered other people the werewolves had killed, other places they had decimated. The hatred that lived inside of me—every day, every night—flared, and my finger tightened.

The animal continued to stare at me. He didn't try to

run. I could swear he was begging me to do it. So I hesitated, thinking of what Cadotte had said.

What if killing them is what they want?

"Hell."

If the werewolves wanted it, I knew I didn't.

I lowered my gun. The wolf snarled. His hackles lifted. Something was very wrong here.

Werewolves craved human blood. They did not kill one another. So what was the matter with this one?

Could he be something other than a werewolf? I'd seen a lot as a *Jäger-Sucher*. Edward had seen even more. Every day, in amazing ways, new monsters came to life—one of the reasons Edward hunted less and stayed in the office more. The business he had started after World War Two kept growing and growing.

I stared at the brown wolf and considered my options. A monster was a monster, wasn't it? Just because I killed werewolves didn't mean I couldn't kill something else. Call it a freebie.

But I couldn't bring myself to shoot the wolf. I'm not sure why. The night's carnage didn't bother me. I'd seen a helluva lot worse, been the cause of it, too.

In all honesty, the bullets and the blood were exhilarating. Chalk up nine for the good guys. Except only eight of them were mine.

I hated to put an end to a perfect killing machine. Especially when he appeared to be on my side.

"Fine," I said. "Knock yourself out. Kill as many as you can."

The wolf did that canine head tilt again. Too bad his muzzle was red with blood. If I saw a dog like that, I'd be creeped out. As it was . . . I was creeped out.

Instead of waiting around until he ran off, then burning

the wolves like I should have, I took my gun and headed back to the tavern more quickly than I'd come.

It was against my nature to leave one of them alive, but as I told myself over and over as I waited for the sun to rise above the trees, I could always kill him later.

8

Someone was banging on the door and shouting my name. I glanced at my travel alarm.

Noon. I'd overslept.

I dragged myself out of bed, across the floor, glanced out the window, and flicked the lock. Jessie barreled inside.

"I woke you," she said.

"What was your first clue?"

"I don't know, your lovely naked ass?"

I glanced down. *Oops.* Must have stripped completely instead of leaving on my underwear as I usually did in a strange new place.

Since I didn't have a home of my own, all places were strange, and since I traveled with the wolves, most places were new. Naked sleeping didn't happen very often. About as often as I had sex. Let's see, that would be once in every millennium.

I wasn't frigid—much. I just had a little problem with intimacy, among other things. Maybe because the last time I'd had sex it had led to murder.

Another bright and cheery thought to greet the day. No wonder I hated mornings.

I headed for the coffeepot without stopping for clothes. I could care less who saw me naked. If they didn't like the view they could get the hell out of my way.

Considering my notions on sex and men, I suppose my ease with nudity was contradictory. However, if you didn't think of your body as a sexual object, what was the big deal with everyone seeing it?

"You plan on getting dressed anytime soon?" Jessie asked, staring pointedly out the window.

I smirked. At last I'd rattled her cage. "You shy?"

"I can see you're not."

Once I had been. Once I'd been a lot of things. I was none of them any longer.

I cursed as I opened and shut all the cabinets and the tiny refrigerator. "No coffee. Someone must die."

"When Mandenauer said you weren't a morning person, I figured you'd be OK after noon."

"You figured wrong."

"Why didn't you go shopping last night? Get supplies?"

I froze. Last night came back to me in a rush. I'd planned to sleep a few hours, then go back out and burn the evidence. Instead I'd slept for too long and left the dead wolves in the forest.

I was slipping.

I found my underwear tangled in the sheets, stuffed my legs into my discarded jeans, and picked up the same T-shirt I'd worn yesterday. I rarely bothered with a bra. Didn't need one. Never had.

"Ahem."

I glanced at Jessie.

"Maybe you want to put on some clean clothes?"

"What's wrong with th—" I looked down, and the words died on my tongue.

My pants sported streaks that could be rust paint but

we both knew weren't. My once-white T-shirt was full of soot, dirt, and more red streaks. I was lucky no one had seen me coming out of the woods last night. They might have thought I was burying a body.

"You don't listen very well, do you?"

I shrugged and yanked off the shirt, replacing it with one from my bag. I left the jeans alone. I'd change them after we got back. They were only going to get dirtier anyway.

"How many did you kill?"

"Nine," I lied, not wanting to mention the brown wolf, which I hadn't killed. I was supposed to be training Jessie, not teaching her bad habits.

Her eyes widened. "Nine? You're kidding."

"Unlike you, I'm not much of a yuckster." I stuffed my gun in my pants, adjusted the shirt over top of it, and headed for the door. "Come on."

"Where are we going?"

"To burn a few bodies."

"You didn't burn them?"

I winced. "Could you be a little louder? I don't think people in Toronto heard you."

"Mandenauer said we should always burn them immediately."

"Well, Mandenauer doesn't know every damn thing."

"Could have fooled me."

"I'm sure I can."

I opened the door and ran straight into the hard wall of Damien Fitzgerald's chest.

"Umph," I said, and would have fallen on my ass if he hadn't caught me by the forearms.

"Hey. Sorry. You all right?"

His hands were rough, hard, as if he'd done a lot of

manual labor recently—hacked up his fingers, worked calluses into his palms. You didn't get hands like that pouring drinks. You didn't get them from lifting weights, either.

Why I found his scarred hands so fascinating—hell, I'll admit it: I found them downright stimulating—I had no idea. It was all I could do not to lose myself in a fantasy of him running those hands over every inch of my naked skin.

He was dressed in black again. Loose cotton trousers, what appeared to be black Nikes—I didn't know they made those—and another long-sleeved black shirt. This one had a pattern embedded in the material, the only way I could tell it wasn't the same one he'd worn yesterday. Except he'd managed to button it. I kind of missed the smooth white flash of his skin against the silk.

"Who the hell are you, mister?"

His green-brown eyes flicked to Jessie. He let me go as if I had lice.

"Sheriff." He nodded.

"Do I know you?"

"This is Damien Fitzgerald," I said. "He bartends downstairs."

"Really?" she drawled. "And what else does he do?"

I remembered that I'd told her about him and that she'd thought he was a fanged and furry charter member. I turned just as she reached for her gun.

"No!" I said, too loudly. "I mean . . ."

I grabbed Damien's wrist. He started at the contact and tried to pull away, but I held on. "What a gorgeous ring. See his pretty silver ring, Jessie?"

She frowned, and her hand fell away from her service revolver. She crossed the room and peered at Damien's hand. "Hmm," she muttered.

Damien tugged again, and when I released him he shoved his fingers into his back pocket as if to keep us from looking at his jewelry any closer.

What did he have to hide? And why was I so suspicious of everyone?

Because I had good reason to be.

"I brought you some coffee." He plucked a to-go cup from the porch railing.

I managed to refrain from declaring my everlasting love. The steam rising from the Styrofoam container smelled almost as good as he did. I wondered what kind of soap he used—something that smelled both green and blue, a little bit of moss with a crust of ice on top.

"Didn't think I'd get shot for it, though." Damien's gaze returned to Jessie.

"Don't mind her. She's jumpy."

"I never would have guessed. Something going on in Crow Valley I should know about, Sheriff?"

"Nope." Jessie continued to watch him as if she expected Damien to shape-shift at any moment, regardless of the ring and the sun blazing down on his tousled head.

"Thanks for the coffee," I said.

"Anytime. There's usually a pot on downstairs. Help yourself."

"Let's go, Leigh."

Jessie was impatient. I couldn't blame her. I was getting a little nervous myself at the thought of all those dead wolves in the forest. They were miles from here, pretty deep in, but that didn't mean someone couldn't stumble across them. I didn't have time for the explanations that would require.

"Where are you guys going?"

"What's it to you?" Jessie demanded.

Man, I was a social savant compared to her.

"We've got work to do," I said as I brushed past him.

"Was there something else you wanted, Fitzgerald?" Jessie joined us on the landing.

"I—" He glanced at me. "I wanted to make sure you were getting along all right."

I got the impression he'd been about to say something else, though what I had no idea. But Jessie, with what I was coming to see as her usual bull in the china shop manner, hurried on.

"She's fine. Just very *late*. OK?"

She ran down the steps, then stood at the bottom, foot impatiently tapping.

I glanced at Damien and rolled my eyes. "Gotta go."

His lips twitched—almost a smile but not quite. "Be careful out there."

A warning or a joke? Why would I need to be careful in the woods, in the daytime, with the sheriff and our guns? Did Damien know something I didn't?

I was reaching for my rifle when he touched my elbow. I started. And I'd said Jessie was jumpy.

As I lifted my gaze to his, something passed between us, something that tugged low and deep. I liked the heat of his palm against my skin, the rasp of his rough fingers, the tickle of his breath across the stubble that was my hair.

I couldn't remember the last time I'd wanted to press my body against someone, slip my hands beneath his shirt, press my mouth to the pulse in his throat, and suckle.

I jerked back, rubbed at the place where my skin was still warm from his. Damien's smile was sad. "Bye," he murmured.

I joined Jessie and we headed for the woods. I could feel Damien watching us, and though I tried not to look back, I couldn't help myself.

He stood at the top of the steps in front of my door. I hadn't locked it. Not that it would do any good against him. He had a key. I made a quick mental tally of what I'd left inside.

Shotgun. Nothing unusual there, except for the silver shells. Since I possessed specially made *J-S* ammo, they appeared normal, just like my rifle.

My bag contained only clothes, a few uniforms, jeans, et cetera. I rarely wore the DNR uniform. It only raised more questions. Especially if I ran into a real DNR guy. Though Edward usually made sure any area where we were working undercover was cleared of such pesky troubles as the truth.

I carried ID in my pocket, which would only prove what I'd already lied about. My computer was the best government money could buy and unhackable, as far as I knew.

Nope, nothing incriminating in my room. That I worried about such things, that I suspected Damien of searching my space, only proved how far gone I was in my paranoia. Sadly, paranoia was what had kept me alive so far.

"There's something weird about him," Jessie said.

"There's something weird about you, but I'm too nice to mention it."

"Har-har. And you say you aren't a yuckster."

I almost smiled but caught myself. I was beginning to like bantering with her, and that wasn't a good idea. She was new, naive, untrained. She would probably be wolf bait by next month. It had happened a hundred times before.

I wondered if Edward had told Jessie the statistics on agent survival. About twenty to one, where twenty wasn't the amount who lived.

"What do you see in him anyway?" she asked.

"Who?"

"Fitzgerald. He's too stringy, too short, too pale. And what's with that ring?"

"What do you mean?"

"Silver filigree? Could he be more gay?"

"This from a woman whose boyfriend wears an earring."

"I like that earring. I was not a happy camper when one of the bad guys tore it out in Miniwa."

I winced. I'd stopped wearing earrings when I'd chopped off my hair for just that reason.

"When Will's ear healed, he got it repierced, and I haven't been sorry. That earring feels pretty good when it's trailing over my—"

"Too much information!" I shouted, and clapped my hands over my ears.

She laughed. "OK. Never mind. Fitzgerald isn't bad. For an Irishman."

"What have you got against Irishmen?"

"Nothing. Except my father was one." Her laughter faded.

Huh, Sheriff Laugh-a-Minute had an Achilles' heel and his name was McQuade. Well, none of my business. I certainly didn't want to hear all her troubles and hold her hand while she cried.

"I'll run him through the system," she said.

"Your father?"

She blinked, then glanced at me as if I'd said something interesting. Then she shook her head. "No. Fitzgerald."

"He didn't do anything."

"Doesn't mean he won't. Or that he hasn't."

"Isn't checking someone out just because you feel like it called harassment?"

"I call it fun."

"You would."

We continued to tramp through the woods for several more minutes before Jessie growled, "Where the hell were you when you shot these things? Arabia?"

"Almost there," I said.

But I'd been running last night, faster and farther than I thought, because it took us another half an hour to find the wolves.

Or what was left of them.

9

"What did you do?" Jessie whispered.

The clearing was awash with blood. There were body parts all over the place. The very air was still, not a twitter from the birds.

I had a hard time tearing my eyes from the sight. It reminded me of home.

I flinched and turned my back.

No, not home. There the blood had shone crimson beneath electric lights. The bodies had been human.

Here the blood had dried to brown beneath the morning sun. Nothing to be afraid of. No similarity at all. No reason to hyperventilate.

"Leigh?"

"I shot them. That's all."

"Then what happened?"

I forced myself to look at the clearing again. The sight bothered me less and less. I could admire the pure fury and amazing strength it must have taken to do such a thing. I'd often wished I could kill them more than once. Someone, or rather something, had.

I inched closer. My foot squished in the blood-drenched grass. I grimaced. It was going to be a little hard to make a bonfire out of this mess, but I'd manage.

I continued around the circle, observing, cataloging, for all the good it did me. I knew there'd been nine dead wolves. But now it didn't appear as if there was enough left to make one.

"What happened last night?"

Jessie continued to speak softly. I understood the need. The clearing was a haunted place. Something wasn't right. I could feel it, and she could, too.

Quickly I told her about the hunt, leaving out the reason I'd been driven to kill, leaving out my mocking shouts and kamikaze behavior. Some things were on a need-to-know basis, and she didn't need to know.

However, when I got to the part about the brown wolf, she interrupted me. "Are you sure he was a werewolf?"

"Of course. Why?"

"I just wondered how real wolves react to werewolves."

"They don't like them."

"Enough to do this?" She jerked a thumb at the mess.

I frowned. "No. Real wolves usually turn tail and run. They sense werewolves aren't like them; they're *other*. Wolves are a lot of things, but dumb isn't one of them."

"Do you think the brown werewolf did this?"

I considered the idea. That the werewolf had killed another was strange enough. I found it hard to believe he would go berserk and eat nine of his own kind, but anything was possible. This was, after all, a werewolf.

"He could have."

"Why didn't you kill him?" Jessie asked.

I'd been asking myself that since last night. I only had one excuse, and in the light of day, in the light of what we'd found in the clearing, it didn't sound very convincing, but I told her anyway.

"Your boyfriend said maybe they want us to kill them."

"You couldn't remember that before you played out your *Terminator* fantasy?"

I shrugged. "Oops."

Jessie snorted. I think she was starting to like me.

It took us the better part of the afternoon to erase the evidence of whatever had happened in the clearing. The *J-S* accelerant got the fire going despite the mushy nature of the ground. Jessie and I made sure no sparks ignited the surrounding dry grass or lush trees.

As we waited for the last of the embers to die, Jessie spoke. "He ate them."

Since she was stating the obvious, I didn't bother to answer.

"This is too weird for me," she continued, "and when werewolves start acting weird—"

"Werewolves are weird by definition."

"True. But they have their behavior patterns, same as real wolves. They might be human on one side of the moon, but on the other they're animals, and animals that behave unpredictably mean trouble."

She'd get no argument from me.

"We need to talk to Will."

"Maybe you do, but I think I can manage a few more hours without him."

"Funnier and funnier," she muttered as she headed back toward the bar.

There were already cars in the parking lot when we emerged from the forest. "A regular gold mine," I observed. "What's the attraction?"

"Can't say."

"And you thought this would be a good place for me to stay why?"

Jessie shrugged. "You hunt at night, so the noise won't bother you. It's quiet during the day, when you sleep, and so busy, no one's going to notice you coming and going. If they do, they'll be too drunk to care. Or at least drunk enough to easily convince they didn't see anything at all."

Though I hated to admit it, she'd chosen well.

As we got in her car, Cowboy got out of his, a huge Cadillac that appeared too big for his body. But then what wouldn't? He limped toward the door.

I hadn't noticed a limp last night. Maybe his boots were too tight.

"Who's that?" Jessie asked.

"Cowboy."

"So that's Cowboy." She watched him until he disappeared inside. "He's on my watch list."

I blinked. "Of werewolves?"

"Troublemakers. I have to at least pretend to perform the job I was hired for."

She started the car and performed a wide turn that brought us around the back of the tavern. My gaze was captured by Damien's cabin, then by a flicker of white in the trees behind it.

He emerged from the forest, fully clothed for a change, and leaned against the corner of the building.

Our eyes met. He lifted his hand. My chest tightened as my belly danced with an excitement I hadn't felt for far too many years. I was in big trouble if the mere sight of him got me all hot and bothered. I needed to be very, very careful about how I handled Damien Ftizgerald and my inexplicable lust for him.

Jessie hit the gas and took off down Good Road at a steady clip. My teeth clicked together, narrowly missing my tongue as she flew over an incline. I forced my mind away from Damien, not an easy task, and back to our stalled conversation.

"What did Cowboy do that got him on the Crow Valley troublemakers list?"

"He's a fighter. I'd say classic Napoléon complex, but that would be too obvious. He likes to get drunk and kick ass, but he's not particular about whose ass he kicks—man, woman, child, dog, he's an equal opportunity Napoléon."

Note to self: Stay away from Cowboy.

We reached Main Street and Jessie headed toward her apartment. I'd seen the town in the evening. I hadn't been impressed.

By day, Crow Valley wasn't so bad. Clean, charming even, with necessary businesses and frivolous shops co-existing side by side.

"Coffee," I said in a desperate voice as we zoomed past the coffee shop.

"You don't want their coffee. Prissy latte crap at three bucks a pop?"

I turned my head and sighed as the coffee shop receded.

"Baby," she sneered. "You haven't lived until you've tried Cadotte's coffee. If you're nice, I'll have him make you some."

"An earring wearer and a coffee maker, be still my heart."

Her eyes narrowed. "I said be nice."

"I don't think I know how."

"Learn." She stopped the squad car in front of the police station. "I just have to check in."

"Isn't that what this is for?" I tapped the car radio.

"When it works."

Now that she said that, I hadn't heard even a flicker of static from the radio during the entire drive, let alone any call for One Adam Twelve.

She disappeared into the station. Curious, I followed, stopping so suddenly just inside that the door hit me in the ass.

"I've stepped into *The Andy Griffith Show*," I blurted.

The sheriff's office resembled the one in Mayberry. Desk, jail cell, telephone, filing cabinets. I half-expected Otis to be sleeping on the military-issue cot.

Jessie looked up from her desk and scowled. "Be thankful. Hardly anything ever happens here."

"Except the odd werewolf attack."

"There is that."

"And Cowboy's Napoléon complex."

"That, too." She pushed the button on her message machine.

You have no new messages.

"See?" she said.

"No dispatcher? No deputy?"

"If anyone needs me, they call my cell phone or they leave a message. No need for a dispatcher."

For some reason, that comment made her sad.

"And Barney Fife?" I asked.

"Elwood Dahlrimmple."

"You're kidding."

"I wish." She rubbed her forehead. "He's been here since . . . the stone age maybe. His hands shake more than a leaf in a windstorm."

"And you let him carry a gun?"

"Not with any bullets in it."

She was serious, and suddenly pretending to be with the Department of Natural Resources didn't sound so bad.

"Can't you fire him?" I asked. "I mean, you *are* the boss."

"Now why would I want to fire Elwood? Everyone knows him; they love him. They try not to cause problems while he's on duty."

"And he's too out of it to question what you're up to."

"Bingo. I don't need help being the sheriff of a town of four hundred."

"If they were just people."

"Now you're catching on."

"Which is where I come in."

"Never said you weren't smart."

Actually, I thought she had, but I wasn't going to bring that up.

"Let's go to my place."

Jessie was already at the door.

"How do you know Will's there?"

"Where else would he be? He's got work to do."

She turned out to be right. Will was home, sitting at the kitchen table, surrounded by papers and books. More were strewn across the floor. His computer was up and running, printing pages even as he muttered and pecked at the keys.

His glasses were on top of his head; he squinted at the screen; a pencil rested behind each ear. What a geek.

I glanced at Jessie just in time to catch the dopey look of love cross her face.

I slammed the door. He jumped; she scowled.

"Honey, I'm home!" I called.

Will smiled, stood, and came toward us with his hand outstretched. "Leigh, nice to see you."

I wished I could say the same. I stared at the long vicious scratch on his forearm, then lifted my gaze to the overly large bandage on his neck.

My mind went back to last night—the werewolves battling, biting, bleeding.

The next thing I knew, my gun was pointed at his chest.

10

Will stared at the weapon and laughed. "Hey, Jess, friend of yours?"

What was it with the people in this town? Didn't anyone flinch at the sight of a gun anymore?

"What the hell are you doing?" Jessie snapped.

I ignored her. "Where were you last night?"

"Here."

"Anyone who can verify that but her?"

"What's wrong with *her*?" Jessie demanded.

"You love him. If he turned furry beneath the moon, you'd protect him."

"She's right." Will cocked a brow in Jessie's direction. "You would."

"But I don't have to. You're not a werewolf."

"Prove it," I demanded.

"He already has."

"How?"

"Take off your shirt."

"I don't think I will," I said.

Jessie sneered. "Not you. Him."

"I'm not into kinky."

"Shut up."

I wanted to say something smart, but Cadotte drew his T-shirt off. He knocked the glasses and the pencils to the floor. He had almost as good a chest as Damien. Almost.

There was a nasty just-healed wound in his upper arm. A bullet wound.

"Mandenauer shot him with silver."

That sounded like Edward. He might look like someone's granddad but wasn't. He could be the meanest, most ruthless son of a bitch I'd ever known, if he needed to be.

"Do you think our boss would let Will into the group if he wasn't certain he was safe?" Jessie asked.

She had a point.

I put up my weapon, taking my eyes off Jessie. Big mistake. She grabbed me by the shirt and slammed me against the wall.

"If you ever pull a gun on him again, you'd better kill me first." Another slam and my head thunked the plaster. I saw stars. "Got it?"

I got it. Any warm and fuzzy moments between us were just moments. She didn't like me any better than I liked her. But we had a job to do.

"Leave her be, Jess. I can't count the times you stuck a gun in my face."

"That was different."

"I know. You had the hots for me from the start." He smiled. "Did she ever tell you how she found me naked in the woods?"

I glanced at Jessie, remembering her comments the first time we'd met. "She did mention something."

"She thought I was a werewolf, too. But she couldn't keep her hands off me anyway."

I frowned. They'd slept together when she thought he was a werewolf? Ugh.

My disgust must have showed on my face, because Jessie rolled her eyes. "You've obviously never been in love."

I had been. But the werewolves had taken care of that. Since I didn't want to elaborate, she shrugged and didn't comment.

"Why did you think I was a werewolf?" Will asked.

Thankful for the distraction—which took my mind off the memories and my mistakes—I pointed at his arm, then flicked my finger toward his neck.

He clapped his palm over the bandage. "Oh, I forgot. I went to the grocery store." He peeled away the adhesive strip to reveal a hickey. "Kind of embarrassing at my age."

I glanced at Jessie. Her face was suspiciously red. I couldn't resist. "Miss high school much?"

"Not in this lifetime," she muttered.

Huh. High school was the most fun I ever had. Considering my present life, this was understandable. Sad, but understandable.

"What about the scratch on your arm?" I asked.

Will shrugged. "Jess needs to cut her fingernails."

Suddenly I was the one blushing.

I'd had sex. With Jimmy and . . . My mind skittered away from that mistake like a crab running for safety beneath a rock. There were some places I would not allow my memories to go, ever, and the only time I'd slept with anyone but Jimmy was one of those places.

Still, I'd never had sex that necessitated scratching and biting. I didn't get it. Didn't want to.

"What happened last night?" Will asked.

Jessie quickly filled him in.

Will's dark brown eyes narrowed. "Nine wolves were eaten?" He turned and sat back down at the table. "I saw that. I just saw that."

"Saw what?"

"Forget it." Jessie shook her head. "He's gone. He won't hear you until he comes back to a little place I like to call earth."

The two of us stood there, avoiding each other's gaze, watching Will mutter and shuffle papers. He tapped at the computer, squinted, patted his head, and blinked owlishly.

"Here." Jessie leaned down and picked up his glasses from the floor.

He took them without looking at or thanking her, set them on his nose, and kept muttering, shuffling, and tapping.

"Aha!" he cried, then tapped some more.

A half an hour later, he sighed, lifted his glasses back onto the top of his head, then turned to us.

"Weendigo," he said. "The Great Cannibal."

"Another manitou?" Jessie asked.

"Yeah."

"Someone better explain, in English, for us i-juts."

Jessie spread her hands. "All yours, Professor."

"Better have a seat." Will gestured to one of the kitchen chairs.

"Only if I get some of that coffee Jessie keeps taunting me with."

He laughed. "Sure. I have a fresh pot set to go. Can you pour the water through, Jess?"

"I guess. I've heard your spiel before. But don't go any further than Matchi-auwishuk."

She disappeared into the kitchen, and I returned my attention to Will. "Matchi-auwishuk?"

"The Evil Ones."

Well, this just kept getting better and better.

"You heard about the wolf god?" he asked.

"Some."

"It was raised in an Ojibwe ceremony. A totem with the markings of the Matchi-auwishuk was used in combination with . . . other things."

"What things?"

"Blood, death, fire."

"You people sure know how to throw a party."

"Always have."

"Where's this totem now?"

"Dr. Hanover has it. She thought she might be able to . . ." He trailed off, frowned. "I'm not sure what."

"You and me both." I wasn't sure what Elise was up to half the time, and that was just fine with me.

"At any rate, the Matchi-auwishuk and the Weendigo are the two evil manitous of the Ojibwe people."

"And a manitou is?"

"An all-encompassing spirit. Legend has it that Kitchi-Manitou, the great mystery, created everything. Manitous are guardians over humans, and everyone has manitoulike attributes."

"There's a little bit of God in us all?"

"Exactly."

"What about the evil manitous?"

"I like to think they aren't within us all, but sometimes I wonder."

After what I'd seen, what I'd done, I had to wonder, too.

"So the Evil Ones helped to raise the wolf god in Miniwa?"

"Yes."

"And the Weendigo?"

"Hold that thought!" Jessie shouted from the kitchen.

Seconds later she entered with three mugs. I could tell just from the smell of the steam that something wonderful was on the way.

"Sugar or cream?" she asked.

I shook my head, took a sip, swallowed, groaned.

Jessie winked. "Told you his coffee was almost as good as him."

"Can he cook, too?" I asked.

Will just smiled and sipped. I wished I were as at home in my own skin, as at ease with my differences, as he was. But I doubted I ever could be.

"Get on with it, Slick," Jessie ordered. "What are we up against this time?"

"I'm not sure." Will set his cup on the coffee table, far away from his precious papers. "Legend has it the first Weendigo was a fierce warrior who, after a particularly harrowing battle against mortal enemies, hacked off a piece of flesh from a fallen foe and ate it to show they were vanquished."

"That'll do it," I murmured.

"Except the warrior grew to like the taste of humans and, despite warnings from the elders, he began to prey on people for his food."

I remembered the brown werewolf. Had he eaten one—make that nine—of his own? The memory gave me food for thought. Ha-ha.

"After a time the great mystery ordained that any human behaving like a beast should appear as one, and the warrior became Weendigo. Cursed to haunt the forests and the wasteland of the north, forever hunting, forever starving, because no amount of flesh is ever enough."

Will rooted through the papers scattered across the kitchen table, pulled one free, and gave it to Jessie. Her eyebrows lifted. She handed the sheet to me.

Weendigo, read the caption. Lucky it did. Because I could swear the thing was a werewolf.

II

Well, maybe not *exactly* a werewolf. The drawing appeared both human and lupine and very, very thin. I suppose that was what happened when the great mystery cursed you to be forever hungry.

I handed the paper back to Will. "So what does this mean to us?"

"The legend is about a human-eating human that turns into a beast. We've got a werewolf-eating werewolf that turns into a human. Coincidence?"

"I don't think so," Jessie and I said at the same time.

Will glanced back and forth between us. "Me, neither."

"But what does it *mean*?" I repeated.

"I'll have to do more research." He grabbed a notepad, reached behind his ear for a pencil, then frowned when he encountered nothing but hair. Jessie scooped up one from the floor and handed it to him without comment.

They'd be cute, if I were into that sort of thing.

Will started thinking out loud and scribbling. "Last time they needed a werewolf army, formed between the two moons of a blue moon month."

I knew my lunar trivia. I couldn't be a werewolf hunter and not know it. Two full moons in one month caused a blue moon on the second course—both rare and magical according to many.

"The night of the blue moon," he continued. "Matchi-auwishuk totem, wolf clan, blood of the one who loves you."

"Charming," I said.

"Not so much," Jessie countered. "It was my blood they were after."

"And the wolf clan?"

Jessie jerked a thumb at Will. He didn't notice. He was still scribbling.

"One of these days you'll have to tell me all about that," I said.

"One of these days," she agreed in a voice that said very clearly, *When hell freezes over.* I couldn't say that I blamed her. I'd never told anyone, not even Edward, the entire truth about my own original werewolf encounter.

"This time we've got a werewolf-eating werewolf and . . ." Will frowned and stared into space. "What month is it, Jess?"

What *month* is it? Man, he'd drive me crazy. Pretty only goes so far.

"Early October," she answered.

"And the moon?"

"Full in eight days."

"So whatever is going on started around the harvest moon, and if they play according to their usual plan it'll finish up at the hunter's moon."

"The blood moon," I murmured.

He blinked, frowned, focused on my face. "Yes."

"I really hate the sound of that," Jessie said.

"You should."

My family had died on the night of the blood moon, the hunter's moon. I ought to be making a pilgrimage to their graves, bringing flowers, remembering them. Instead I had a bad feeling I'd be miles away, fighting werewolves. What else was new?

Will still stared at me. I stared blandly back. I wasn't going to tell him why I knew about the blood moon, didn't plan on ever telling anyone why the full moon in October was the worst kind, at least for me.

"Wait," I said as a thought occurred to me. "Wolves were being killed here, but no one said anything about them being eaten."

"That's true," Jessie murmured. "But that doesn't mean they weren't."

She went to the table and shuffled through the mess, pulling out a file folder. The room went silent as she read through the report. She shook her head. "There were chunks out of some of the bodies, but nothing like we saw the other night."

"How do we know the wolves were killed by other wolves?"

"Mandenauer checked the bite radius."

Trust Edward to think of everything.

"According to the legend, a Weendigo grows with every meal," Will continued. "The larger he gets, the more flesh needed to satisfy his hunger."

"So we're looking for a giant?" I asked.

"I doubt that. The growth is most likely theoretical; the hunger is real."

"The Weendigo began with a snack, but now he needs a buffet?"

"Basically, yes." Will turned his attention back to his notes. "I have to see if there are any ceremonies that take place beneath the hunter's moon."

"Ojibwe ceremonies?" Jessie asked, then crossed the room to lay a hand on his shoulder.

Will reached up and twined their fingers together. They were always touching each other—both casually and much more than that. Their outright affection made me yearn for something I'd long ago forgotten.

What I felt for Damien was very different. I wanted him for no other reason than that he was hot and I was horny. *Affection, love, forever* were not words I could ever use again.

"Any kind of ceremony," Will answered. "Though I'll start with the Ojibwe, since that was where we struck pay dirt last time. And the whole Weendigo thing points in that direction, as does their location—here, in the heart of Ojibwe country."

He turned toward the computer.

"What should I do?" I asked.

"Quit blasting them for one thing," Jessie snapped.

"Why?"

"Why do you think? I doubt our friend the Weendigo could have killed nine werewolves on his own. You helped him do . . . whatever it is he's doing."

Damn, she was right again. But I wasn't sure I could stop killing them, even if I should.

"I'll burn them immediately. My mistake."

Jessie gave an aggrieved sigh, as if she were dealing with a stubborn, wayward child. "Don't come whining to me if they take over the world."

"Don't worry. I won't."

Will ignored our squabbling and answered my question. "You two should be checking out any new people in town."

"How new?" I asked, thinking of Damien.

"Last few months."

"Couldn't this Weendigo have been here for years?"

Cadotte thought about that. "Could have been, I guess. I was thinking the werewolf came here for this reason, but maybe he or she is just *here*. The time is what's important, not the location."

"There's a blood moon every year," I pointed out.

Will flicked a glance first at me, then at Jessie. "Find out if anything similar has ever happened anywhere else at this time."

She nodded and dialed her cell phone. "Mandenauer?"

I leaned forward, trying to hear his voice. Foolish, but I missed him.

Once I'd refused to let Edward get close to me, fearing superstitiously for his life. But years had passed, he'd faced dangers I didn't even know about, and he was still kicking. So I'd allowed myself to care.

Jessie explained what Will had discovered. "Are there any other recorded instances of werewolf cannibals?" She listened. "OK, thanks."

"Well?" I asked.

"None. Werewolves have been killed, though rarely, but never eaten. Mandenauer's concerned. Strange behavior is always a bad thing."

"I'll question a few elders," Will said. "See what they know about Weendigos. Maybe I'll get an idea of where to start looking for . . . something."

"We'll check around," Jessie said.

"We?" I asked.

"Yes, *we*. Talk to customers in the bar. Make nice. Be friendly." She frowned. "Maybe I should do that."

Will laughed. "Right, Jess. You're not a people person."

Another thing we had in common.

"I can be a regular Miss Manners if I have to be," she protested.

Will and I snorted at the same time.

Jessie scowled. "Never mind. Find out who's new, who's not. Ask if there's been anything strange going on."

"Like?"

"Unexplained disappearances?"

"Haven't you checked the missing persons reports?" I asked.

"There aren't any."

I gaped. "But . . . that's impossible."

She shrugged. "Town's full of transients. No one's going to report them missing."

True. But still . . .

"I'll drive you back to the bar," Jessie said. "You can ask around there. I'll take the shops in town."

"How come I have to take the bar? I barely drink."

"Even better. Alcohol kills brain cells, and you don't have a lot left to lose."

My eyes narrowed. "Oh, yeah, you're going to win them over with your sparkling wit and genial nature. I can see that already."

She almost laughed but caught herself. "Let's get this over with."

A half an hour later I stood outside the bar as the taillights of Jessie's squad car disappeared down Good Road. There were a few vehicles in the lot, but not many.

I checked my watch. Nearing four o'clock. Not exactly a hopping time in any tavern. I decided to go upstairs, take the shower I'd missed that morning, check my E-mail, do some paperwork.

My best bet for hearing anything interesting would be when the bar patrons were inebriated. Besides, I wanted to work a crowded room, not a table full of customers. The more people I could talk to at one time, the better.

I stepped inside, and I knew someone had been there. Damien? Or another?

Nothing was out of place. Not really—though I could have sworn I'd left my computer on the kitchen table at an angle and not anally lined up with the corner. However, since I was anal, I might have done that and not even noticed. Nevertheless, I pulled my gun and checked the apartment thoroughly, but whoever had been inside without me was gone.

I stared at my laptop. Even if someone had opened it, turned the thing on, played around, he wouldn't have found anything. I knew how to protect my files. I'd know that even before I'd taken *J-S* computer training.

Regardless, I powered up the machine, did a quick run-through of my data. Everything was there, and I could find no evidence that someone had been tiptoeing through classified information.

I left the computer on. I had work to do. But right now I was starving. When was the last time I'd eaten?

Yesterday. Maybe.

The coffee sloshed around in my stomach like acid. I opened the tiny refrigerator more out of habit than hope. I'd looked in there this morning, and it had been as empty as my social calendar.

So how had it gotten full?

I blinked at the food—fruits, vegetables, milk, lunch meat, juice. I straightened and opened the cabinet above the sink.

"Praise God, coffee," I murmured.

As well as cereal, bread, and cookies. Someone *had* been in here. The grocery fairy.

"I love the grocery fairy." I ripped open the bag of cookies.

Damien had brought me food. Who else knew I was here? Who else cared?

The nature of my life had never bothered me. I had no home; I existed alone. No one would miss me if I didn't come back from the woods one night. Well, maybe Edward would, but he'd lost agents before. He'd get over it.

I'd lived through devastating loss. I didn't want anyone to feel the same heartbreak because of me. I wasn't going to quit doing what I was doing, so I was better off alone.

But after meeting Jessie and Will, watching them together, I missed Jimmy terribly. I'd loved him with all my foolish young heart. I still wasn't over him. Probably never would be. The life we'd planned to share was one I still dreamed of. When I wasn't having nightmares.

Beyond the lost dream, I'd enjoyed being with him, kissing him, touching him. I missed that closeness.

A sudden memory of Damien cupping my elbow on the porch returned, as did the tug of awareness. I hadn't had sex since Jimmy died. Obviously a bad choice considering my oversexed reactions of late, but the very thought of intimacy had nauseated me.

Until Damien Fitzgerald.

I stuffed my mouth with cookies, trying to satisfy one need with another. Didn't work, but at least I wasn't hungry anymore. For food.

To satisfy the nagging voice in my head, I ate an apple, drank a glass of milk. Though I could care less most days if I lived or died, to do my job I had to stay healthy. My body was a killing machine, and I kept it in the best condition I could manage. In addition to jogging, I did sit-ups, pull-ups, push-ups at every opportunity. Needed to work on that upper body strength.

Around 9:00 P.M., after a round of calisthenics, followed by the filing of some long-overdue paperwork, I checked my E-mail. Everything was work related.

I took a shower and changed my clothes, opting for tight jeans and a low-cut hot pink tank. I even gelled my hair and put on lipstick. If I wanted information, I might have to practice a few feminine wiles. If I remembered any.

Too bad I owned only boots and sneakers. Guys liked high heels, which was why I'd thrown all mine out the day after I was released from the psych ward.

I'd thought I was celebrating my liberation. I'd only been hiding from the truth. The doctors might have certified me sane, but I was still broken down deep where I'd never let anyone see.

"Not bad," I told the reflection in the mirror.

The hot pink Lycra tank top could probably use a necklace to spruce it up, but I'd thrown all my jewelry into the trash with my shoes.

I stuffed some money, some matches, into my pocket. I no longer owned a purse, either. My jeans were too tight to hide a gun. Damn.

I changed from sneakers to boots and concealed my knife. I wasn't going anywhere without a weapon ever again

"Show time!" I said.

Funny, I sounded as thrilled about it as I looked.

I stepped onto the porch. They were playing jazz again. I had no idea if the tune was old or new, not a clue as to the artist's name or the title of the song. I wondered if there was anything but jazz in that jukebox.

Last night I'd felt the music out of place, but now the

bluesy wail of the brass fit perfectly with the coolness of the night, the shade of the moon, the aura of expectation that hung over the forest.

Eight days, Will had said. I shivered beneath the muted silver glow.

I didn't think it was going to be enough.

12

I was headed toward the front of the bar when I caught a hint of cigarette smoke. Not too strange, especially around here, but the scent was hot, acrid—fresh. Some-one had stepped outside for a drag or two.

Why I decided to follow that smell I have no idea. Call it a hunch. I hear sometimes they're even right.

Retracing my steps, I strolled past the staircase that led up to my room, caught a billow of gray trailing from be-hind a shed halfway between the bar and the shack where Damien lived.

I followed my nose around the corner of the building. The spotlights didn't penetrate here, instead throwing their false sunshine over the roof and into the trees. Be-hind the shed, the air was cool, damp. Here darkness reigned, the only light a flicker of silver that filtered through the branches and the tiny glowing circle of red at the end of Damien's cigarette.

He leaned against the shed, head thrown back, lips pursed to take a long drag. As he exhaled, his eyes closed in bliss. I took a single step of retreat, meaning to sneak away before I disturbed him.

"Don't go," he whispered.

I hesitated. I shouldn't be alone with Damien in the dark. I wanted things from him I had no business wanting. But in the end I stayed. Because I couldn't make myself go.

"I didn't know you smoked."

I inched closer, sniffed the air, savored the aroma. Once I'd partaken of nearly every vice—alcohol, tobacco, drugs. Anything to take my mind off that night, anything to bring me closer to my loved ones, closer to death. Then Edward had showed me a way to make life worth living, and I'd had to give up all the things that made me less than aware.

But I missed some of them—cigarettes in particular. I understood why people couldn't quit. The habit both calmed and exhilarated, the rhythm soothing, the nicotine stimulating.

"There are a lot of things you don't know about me," Damien said.

"Wanna share some?"

He lifted his hand to his mouth. I caught a hint of his tongue flicking at the filter, before he closed his lips around the tip. A trickle of awareness passed over me, and I rubbed at the rising goose bumps on my forearms.

Damien drew on the cigarette. I breathed along with him—in, out—the effect just wasn't the same.

"No," he said.

It took me a moment to remember what in hell I'd asked. Oh, sharing his secrets. As if I'd expected him to say yes.

I was drawn to both him and the scent of the smoke. He wore black again. I was beginning to wonder if he owned anything else.

Smooth pale skin flashed between the open buttons of his shirt as he shifted in my direction and offered me a drag. I wanted to put my mouth where his had been with a desperation that frightened me. I took another step forward before I caught myself, shook my head. "Those things will kill you."

"I can only hope."

His words jerked my gaze from the cigarette to his face, which remained as unreadable as ever. "What's that supposed to mean?"

He shrugged and took another long pull, letting the smoke trail out his nose as he spoke. "In my line of work I'm more likely to get killed in a bar fight than by cancer."

"And you'd prefer cancer?"

"Ever been stabbed? I wouldn't recommend it."

His honesty left me speechless. Despite my violent profession, I was an upper-middle-class Kansas white girl at heart. Getting stabbed in a bar fight was beyond my realm of experience. Getting bitten by a werewolf was another story.

"You could try a different line of work," I suggested.

His lips curved, but he didn't bother to answer. I had the feeling he thought me naive, and I probably was. If he could get another job, he would. So what kept an attractive, reasonably intelligent man in a dead-end occupation?

If I didn't know better, I'd think he was a werewolf. Many of them were drifters who worked at odd jobs for cash. It was easier that way. No record of where you'd been when a bunch of people turned up dead.

There was also the added problem of living long past the time that they should. Something wasn't kosher when someone who looked twenty years old possessed the same Social Security number as a person born in 1925.

Whenever I hunted a new city, I checked out the occupations where being paid in cash was a common occurrence—bartending, waitressing, construction.

Of course there were those who found a way around this problem, faking their own deaths, manufacturing data, buying false identities, or hacking into government files. When you lived forever, you had a lot of time to practice useful skills.

Damien lit a second cigarette from the butt of the first and continued to smoke with barely a hitch in the process.

"Are you on break or something?" I asked.

"Something."

Well, that was enlightening.

"Do you—uh—work every night?"

"Pretty much."

"There's no other bartender?"

"There was, but she took off."

"When?"

"The night you showed up. That was why I was getting dressed so late for work. Sue didn't come in. No one's seen her since."

Uh-oh. I had a feeling I knew what had happened to Sue. Namely me. No one had reported her missing and probably ever would.

"She worked nights, too?"

A pertinent question. Werewolves had to hunt. It was their nature. They couldn't go indefinitely without a kill. Like the Weendigo, they craved human flesh.

In opposition to popular myth, werewolves didn't automatically change beneath the moon. They had a choice—except on the night of the full moon. Those nights were busy for me and mine.

"We switched off," Damien continued. "Neither one of us liked to work the same shift all the time."

Interesting. Most people preferred to stick to a schedule. I know I did.

"Now what'll you do?" I asked.

"Hire someone new. Maybe Cowboy. He's in here all the time anyway."

I saw an opportunity and I took it. "Cowboy's from here?"

Damien shot me a suspicious glance. "No one's from here. Except some of the Indians."

"No one?"

"Not that I know of. People who are born here can't wait to get out. People who visit can't wait to move in." He shook his head. "Go figure."

"Where's Cowboy from?"

"Cleveland?" He shrugged.

I waited for him to laugh. From his expression, I'd be waiting until the next millennium.

"You don't know?"

"I don't ask. One thing you learn in my profession: Listening is OK. Questions aren't."

Too bad questions were all I had.

"What do I owe you for the groceries?"

"Nothing."

"Come on. Let me pay you."

He shook his head. I could tell he wasn't going to accept money from me. Feeling awkward, beholden, I muttered, "It was very nice of you."

He made a derisive sound and flicked the end of his cigarette into the dirt. "I don't do nice."

Why did that sound both lewd and rude?

He ground the dying embers into dust with his black sneaker, then lifted his eyes to mine. My breath felt trapped in my chest. I wanted to run, and I wanted to stay. He both confused and fascinated me.

What was it about Damien that I found so attractive? He was nothing like Jimmy Renquist. Jimmy had been tall, broad, blond. A laughing, sunny boy who never got to be a man.

Damien was dark, slim, haunted. He rarely smiled; I couldn't imagine his laughter. The shadows in his eyes made him seem as old as some of the trees that surrounded this place.

I was drawn to those shadows, captivated by the darkness I sensed in him. It called to the darkness in me.

The air held a night chill, but I wasn't cold. Instead, my skin burned wherever his gaze touched.

"I didn't buy you groceries to be nice," he continued. "I wanted you to owe me."

"How much?" My voice was barely a whisper.

"I don't want money."

"What then?"

He moved toward me and I tensed, tempted again to flee. The shadows were gone from his eyes, chased away by the heat. He was no longer calm and cool but wired, his steps both hurried and determined.

I held my ground. I'd faced scarier things than him, and in truth, I hadn't been this aroused in a lifetime.

He stopped, so close I had to bend my neck to see his face. "I wanted you to owe me," he repeated. "I wanted you to give me this."

His mouth crushed mine in an openmouthed kiss. There was no giving involved. He took the kiss as he took my tongue and tasted.

I could have gotten away. Getting away was what I did. If I'd decided I didn't want this, Damien Fitzgerald would have been lying on the ground writhing in an instant. As it was, I was writhing, because I wanted so much more than a kiss.

The flavor of tobacco reminded me of a time when insanity had ruled me, as it ruled me now. My fingers slipped between the open buttons of his shirt and found their way across the silky expanse of his chest.

His muscles rippled, coming alive beneath my hands. I nipped his lip, then soothed the hurt with my tongue. Without warning he spun me around, pressed my back against the wall of the shed, and laid his body against the length of mine.

I was short—he wasn't tall; still his erection pulsed in a much higher location than I would have liked. With a groan, he lifted me, wrapping my legs around his waist, and suddenly everything fit together just fine.

He was hard, hot; the friction of our clothes only drove me faster toward the madness. It had been so long. I was on the verge of orgasm in seconds.

His palm cupped my neck, shifted my head. He gentled the kiss even as his fingers drifted lower, across my collarbone and the slight swell of my breasts.

He slipped my tank top from my shoulder. Cool night air bathed my skin. I shuddered as my breasts tingled in reaction, the nipples tightening, even before he touched me.

The contrast of hot and cold, rough and gentle, the firm thrust of his body against mine, made me come in a sudden mind-numbing wave that left me limp, breathless, and damp—everywhere.

He lifted his head. By an odd trick of moonlight his eyes glittered silver instead of gold. His mouth was wet, swollen. I reached up to touch his face and he flinched.

Slowly I lowered my hand, wondering what his life must have been like if the slightest gesture made him wary. Even though we'd just shared something I'd shared with only two others, I still couldn't ask him why.

A door opened and shut nearby. Voices, music, laughter. Someone was leaving the bar. Damien shifted, shielding me with his body, even though no one could see us at this angle, in this light.

A car door slammed. An engine. Seconds later they were gone.

Both of us were breathing heavily, harshly, the sound loud in the suddenly silent night. Damien slid my top onto my shoulder, and the movement brought me back to the earth.

"Put me down."

He hesitated and I tensed, prepared to make him. But he let go of my legs and my thighs slid along his until my feet hit the ground. Why that last touch seemed more intimate than all the others I couldn't say. But my face flared and my stomach rolled. What had I done?

Given in to the wildness I kept buried inside. A wildness that had gotten me nothing but trouble the only other time I'd set it free.

The flare of a match, a flame illuminated his face. I wanted to kiss him again, taste him, touch the hollows at his cheeks with my fingertips.

He glanced at me as he drew on another cigarette. The smoke trailed out of his mouth as he spoke. "I've been thinking of nothing but you all day. You're not my type, but maybe that's why you're so tempting."

I looked away. God, he reminded me of—

Suddenly Damien stood right next to me, and I hadn't even seen him move. "When I touch you do I leave a mark, a blotch, a smudge?"

His long, supple finger trailed down my arm. I lifted my eyes to his.

"I can't see anything," he whispered. "Except you."

For an instant I was dazzled by his words, captivated

by his smell, his heat and strength. Then I heard all of what he'd said, and it made me wonder . . .

"What did you do?"

Something flickered in his eyes, too fast for me to see if it was a lie or the truth.

"Nothing I won't do again," he said, and walked away.

The only thing left behind was the scent of smoke and the whisper of his touch. Despite the suspicion that he was much more than he seemed, both still tempted me—more than anything had ever tempted me before.

13

I was supposed to go into the bar and talk to the locals. I couldn't do it.

I couldn't sit on a stool and pretend I didn't want to take Damien up to my room and finish what we'd only just started.

What was wrong with me? I thought I'd been cured of my need to fuck the forbidden.

"Guess not," I muttered.

Of course, how could I be better when the very delusion that had sent me over the edge wasn't a delusion at all but the truth?

The only thing that made me feel sane was killing the things that had ruined my life. And Edward had shown me that, not a head doctor.

Maybe doing what I did best would help now. Maybe killing a few evil souls housed in wolf bodies could make me forget the taste of Damien's mouth and brush of his skin against mine. Maybe—but I doubted it.

I'd been around enough oddities to know that there was something not quite right about Damien. I needed to find out what that something was before I let him get any closer than he'd already gotten.

I glanced at the tavern, then headed for his cabin. The place was shrouded by trees, shaded from the moon. No one would see me creeping around back here, unless they knew where to look.

I tried the door. Locked. Well, that had never stopped me before.

I picked it in record time, even for me. Edward had taught me how, and I'd excelled at the lesson.

Once inside, I made sure the drapes were drawn before I turned on a lamp. The cabin was a replica of my apartment, only larger, with one room for everything but the bath.

The place was pin neat—the bed made, the kitchen pristine. Damien's clothes were still in his suitcase. Because he planned to leave in a hurry? Or because he was Felix Unger in a hot, studly body?

I opened his suitcase. I'd been right. He owned nothing but black. I guess that cut down on any clothing confusion.

There were no papers, no books, no notes—in the room or in the suitcase.

"Stranger and stranger," I muttered.

Only people who were trying to hide something had nothing.

Too bad I didn't think to lift his wallet.

Another trick I was very, very good at. If I ever lost my job as a *Jäger-Sucher* I could make a pretty good living as a thief.

I slid my hand under the chairs, the couch, the bed. All the usual places to hide interesting, incriminating evidence. The only thing I found was a .45 taped behind the toilet tank.

Odd, but not too odd. People who lived out of their

suitcases, their cars, often carried guns. Who knows what you might meet on the road? Living in the backwoods, working in taverns or worse, *having* a gun wasn't an issue. *Not* having one would be.

I left the revolver right where it was, shut off the light, put the curtains back where I'd found them. I glanced out the window and my heart slammed into my throat.

A white wolf stood between the cabin and the tavern.

I was running for the bathroom before I knew it. I fell to my knees, crawled a few inches, and yanked the gun from the back of the toilet. Tense, shaking, I waited for the sound of the window shattering. That it didn't only made me shake all the more.

I crept back into the front room, checking the gun as I went. One bullet. Damn. I'd have to make sure it counted.

Too bad I didn't carry silver bullets in my shoes. But even if I had time to get them from my bag, the bullets for my Glock wouldn't fit into a .45.

I'd just make do with what I had. A lead slug would slow him down, which would give me a chance to plunge my knife into his evil, murdering heart. I'd dreamed so often of having his blood on my hands; it was the only thing I lived for.

My breath rasped loudly in the dark, silent room. I inched to the window, looked out.

The yard was empty.

Dizziness passed over me in a sickening wave. I nearly fell to my knees.

"He was there," I assured myself. "He *was*."

I'd never seen the white wolf again after that night. Unless you counted my dreams.

I pinched myself. Yep, I was awake, in Damien's house, holding Damien's gun.

I opened the door just as a howl rose toward the half-moon. The howl was answered by another, then another. I followed the sound into the woods without a backward glance.

Ahead I saw the flash of a tail—white against the darker shade of the trees. Hatred welled within me, acrid at the back of my throat, a stinging tightness in my chest, a burning in my eyes.

I'd dreamed of killing him and now I had the chance.

It was foolish to run into a strange forest alone, with a gun I wasn't accustomed to—a gun that held one useless bullet. Even more foolish to think I would ever catch a wolf on foot. But I followed him anyway. I could do nothing else.

The .45 was heavy. My shoes slid in the mud. My shirt became wet with sweat, as did my hair, my face. I ran until I couldn't run anymore and then I ran farther. I'd lost sight of the white tail long ago. It didn't matter.

At last I stumbled, fell, lay with my hot cheek against the cool earth.

I don't know how long I stayed there, mind numb, heart racing. Eventually I got ahold of myself enough to admit I might have imagined the white wolf.

"Why would he be here?" I asked aloud. "Why now?"

Those were very good questions. Almost as good as the one I asked myself every day of my life.

"Am I losing it again?"

Hard to tell. Talking to myself wasn't helping. Besides, if I was losing my mind, I'd hardly be the first to know.

I flipped over. A huge black wolf crouched, ready to spring from the bushes near my feet. I couldn't see his eyes, couldn't discern any white. It was probably just a wolf, but when he lunged, I shot him anyway.

And was nearly blinded by the flash that blazed from the wound in his chest.

He howled, twisted, burned. I skittered back so he didn't fall on top of me. By the time I crawled over to him, he was dead, his eyes a wolf's, not human. Except he wasn't a wolf. Flames did not come out of a wolf.

I stared at the gun in my hand. Flames didn't erupt from a lead bullet, either.

Werewolf plus silver equals fire. Period.

The new question of the day: Why did Damien Fitzgerald have a gun with a silver bullet?

I couldn't wait to find out. Unfortunately, I had a wolf to burn. I'd learned my lesson. Couldn't just leave my kill lying around for any old Weendigo to eat.

I made a bonfire. Without accelerant, the process would take some time, so I stared into the flames and wondered what in hell was going on in Crow Valley.

Keeping my eyes on the trees, I strained my ears for a hint of sound. Not that there'd be any. The black wolf had snuck up on me without my hearing him. But where was the white wolf? Had he ever been here at all? And if so, was he *the* white wolf?

All the questions could drive a sane woman nuts. What did that say for me?

Later, when I stumbled back into the clearing that surrounded the bar, the place was hopping. I glanced down. No blood, a bit of dirt and soot. I'd take my chances that the patrons were too drunk and the bar too dark for anyone to notice.

Since it probably wasn't the best idea to walk inside with a weapon, I stowed the revolver behind a garbage bin. I'd fetch Damien, bring him out here, then question him until I knew who or what he was. There'd been enough pussyfooting around.

I yanked open the door and stomped inside. The same people who'd been there the first night stared back. Once again I found no sign of Damien. I strode to the bar and leaned over.

"What the hell do you want?" Cowboy snarled.

I jumped back so fast I nearly fell over a stool. Cowboy appeared on the other side, his chin just clearing the bar. He must be standing on a box.

"Where's Damien?" I managed.

"How should I know?"

"He isn't working?"

"Does it look like he's working to you, honey?"

Honey. Boy, I loved it when guys called me that.

"Where would he be if he wasn't here?"

"I'm not his social secretary. He asked me to work; then he took off."

Hell. He'd walked into the bar; then I'd broken into his house. Had he come back outside and seen me? If so, why hadn't he confronted me? Just another question of many.

"Thanks," I muttered, but Cowboy ignored me. I slipped outside and went to retrieve the gun.

It was gone.

I whipped around, eyes darting to the trees, the parking lot, Damien's cabin. Everything was still, silent, deserted. Nevertheless, I felt watched. Exposed. I could feel a huge bull's-eye on my forehead. My shoulders twitched. There was one on my back, too.

I sprinted for my car, jumped in, and tore out of the lot. As I bounced down Good Road far too fast, I remembered what Damien had said when I asked him what he'd done.

Nothing I won't do again.

I'd had no idea what he meant, but now I wondered.

Had he been killing werewolves with that gun?

14

The middle of the night in Crow Valley, Wisconsin, Jessie wasn't hard to find. My car and hers were the only ones trolling Main Street.

I stopped mine in the middle of the road, left it running, lights blazing. I felt safer that way.

She put the squad car in park, stepped out, leaned over the door. "What's your problem?"

"Got an hour?"

Her eyebrows shot up. "I got nothing but hours. They roll up the sidewalks around here at seven P.M. You wanna come to the station?"

"How about your place? I'd like to talk to Will, too."

Jessie shook her head. "He's sleeping."

"At night? What *is* the matter with him?"

She smiled at that. "He tried to get used to my schedule, but he just couldn't cut it."

"Maybe we should wake him up?"

"Maybe we shouldn't." Jessie's expression was set and mulish. I recognized it from the mirror. She wouldn't budge.

"Fine. Station it is."

I got in my car and followed her. Inside the Andy Griffith museum, she took a seat at her desk. "What's up?"

"Did you find out anything about Damien?"

Jessie frowned. "Why the rush?"

I hesitated. How much to say? How much to leave out? I decided to tell her everything that wasn't personal. Which turned out to be quite a bit.

"Do you think he's a rogue agent?" she asked.

Rogue agents had been *Jäger-Suchers* once. They'd gone off on their own, still hunting, still searching, but they no longer followed any rules but their own.

"Could be. All we have to do is ask Edward."

He knew every agent, past and present. I put the question on my mental to-do list.

"I talked to the owner of the tavern," Jessie said. "Fitzgerald is working for cash. The guy doesn't have his Social Security number, next of kin, address, or shoe size. The setup screams shape-shifter."

"Except for the silver ring and the silver bullet in his gun," I murmured.

"Which shoots that theory all to hell." She shrugged. "I ran the name Damien Fitzgerald, from New York. Without his Social Security number to narrow down the field . . . I got back a sheet of Damien Fitzgeralds as long as my forearm. None of them have records, which means no fingerprints or photos on file."

"Damn."

"Yeah."

Silence fell between us. I was thinking as fast as I could, but I wasn't getting anywhere.

"You didn't come speeding into town to talk about Damien," Jessie said. "Something else spooked you. Wanna tell me what?"

"Not really."

Jessie sighed and leaned back in her chair. "I know about your family."

My head came up so fast the room spun. My eyes narrowed.

"Relax. Mandenauer didn't say anything that wasn't in the police report." Her lips twitched. "Except for the part about the werewolves."

The police had decided that mad dogs killed my family. There were so many of them in Topeka.

"I can't imagine what it was like," she said gently.

"No, you can't."

"My best friend was a werewolf. She fooled me for years. Wanted to make me one of them. Then rule the world. I stopped her."

Our eyes met, and I saw how much what had happened in Miniwa had affected her. Having someone you trusted turn furry and try to kill you didn't happen every day. For an instant I wanted to reach out, but she just had to open her mouth again.

"You know something else, and I don't want to get killed because you're too much of sissy to tell me what it is."

I shook my head as if I'd been doused with a bucket of water, then wiggled my finger in my ear. "Sissy?"

"You heard me. What did you see out there tonight that scared you enough to make you run to me?"

Jessie might be the most annoying person on the planet, but she wasn't dumb, she wasn't slow, and she wasn't going to go away until I told her.

In truth, I *was* scared. Had I seen the white wolf or hadn't I? If I had, we were all in deep shit. If I hadn't, only I was. Either way, it couldn't hurt to ask a question.

"Have you ever heard the name Hector Menendez?"

"Should I have?"

"I don't know. You're the sheriff."

"You think he's here?"

I sighed. "Maybe."

"What does he look like?"

"Six-foot-two, a hundred and eighty pounds, black hair, goatee, blue eyes, Hispanic. Very . . . handsome," I managed.

Hector had been one of the most beautiful men I'd ever seen. Beauty was part of his allure. By the time I'd discovered what that beauty hid, it had been too late.

"I haven't seen him," Jessie said. "But that doesn't mean anything. People come and go. Did *you* see him?"

"I'm not sure."

"Maybe you'd better tell me who he is."

"Hector's the werewolf that killed my family," I said.

Her eyes widened. "And you saw him in Crow Valley?"

"I'm not sure," I repeated. "I thought I saw a wolf outside the bar. I followed him, but the one I shot was black, not white."

"You said Hector had black hair."

"He did."

"Then how could he be a white wolf?"

"His mother was blond and so was Hector."

He'd shown me a picture of her and him. Hector had been a true towhead as a child—the thick, wavy locks nearly white instead of blond. I'd thought it cute that he carried a picture of his mother and himself in his wallet. Later, when he'd told me the rest, the picture had disturbed me. Sadly, it hadn't disturbed me enough to make me stop seeing him. Although by then it was probably too late.

"His mother left the family when he was very young,

and he hated her. So he dyed his hair the shade of his father's. Hector is a tiny bit psychotic, I'm afraid."

"How can you be a tiny bit psychotic?"

"Fine." I threw up my hands. "He's a raving lunatic."

"Swell. A psychotic werewolf." She stood up, kicked the desk. "Just what we need."

Suddenly she whirled toward me. "Wait a second. We're searching for a cannibal. Now you tell me there's a lunatic in town. That seems like too much of a coincidence to me."

"But the brown werewolf ate the others."

"Did he? You told me you saw the brown wolf, he killed one; then later we found them eaten. It doesn't mean he's our man." She frowned. "I mean wolf."

"But if he isn't, that means we've got a brown wolf killing and a white wolf eating."

"Or two of them doing both."

"Hell," I muttered.

Silence fell.

"Jessie?"

She glanced at me and something in my face must have reached her, because she sat down and spread her hands. "What?"

"I'm not sure I saw Hector. I—" This was hard to say, especially to her. "I lost my mind when my family died. Saw a lot of things that weren't there for quite a while. Maybe I saw Hector." I took a deep breath, let it out slowly, wished like hell for a cigarette. "And maybe I didn't."

I expected her to make some biting comment, put me in my place, then tell me she'd call Edward and have him take me away. Instead she shrugged, pulled a pad of paper across the desk, and picked up a pencil. "That's Menendez? *M-e-n-e* . . . ?"

I stared at her. She made an impatient sound. "How the hell do you spell his name?"

"But—"

"But what? If that psycho is in my town, I want to know about it."

"But what if I was seeing things?"

"What if you weren't?"

"Doesn't it bother you to work with someone who was once certifiable?"

"No more than it bothers me to work with someone who's as big of a pain in my ass as you are."

We stared at each other for several more seconds, until she gave an annoyed growl. "Do you mind, nut job? I've only got so much time available to check out your delusions."

Wow, another warm and fuzzy bonding moment.

"*M-e-n-e-n-d-e-z,*" I spelled out.

"Gracias," she mocked.

Miss Politically Incorrect.

"I doubt you'll find much," I said. "Back when my family was killed . . . Well, by the time I was able to . . ."

Think without screaming? Talk without babbling? Breathe without crying?

"Articulate," I managed, "Hector was long gone. They checked him out."

"And?"

"He'd been pronounced dead in 1977 from a hunting accident. Kind of made it hard to put out an APB on him."

"What did the police do then?"

I rolled my eyes. "What do you think? When they arrived at the scene of the crime, I was in a corner talking to myself. Three months later I blame a dead man. They thought I was loony toons."

"In other words, they did nothing."

"What were they supposed to do, Jessie?"

"Let me ask a better question: What did Mandenauer do?"

Her words made me smile. "He saved me that night, then called the police and disappeared. I saw him next at the hospital." I lifted a brow. "The psychiatric hospital."

She shrugged and made a whirling motion with her finger. *Big deal; get on with it.*

"After weeks of being told I was crazy, he believed me. He got me out of there. I'm not sure how."

Having someone to talk to who didn't give me a pill every time I said "werewolf" had cleared my head better than a cold shower. Just being with Edward had made me feel sane again.

"He told me my family was at peace. He'd made sure they wouldn't rise."

"I hate it when that happens," Jessie muttered.

I glanced at her quickly. "You've seen one?"

"Not seen—no. But I had a few disappear out of the morgue. One went in there with her head blown off."

"Uh-oh, someone didn't use silver."

"Bingo."

I found it disturbing, to say the least, to have corpses with body parts blown off suddenly rejuvenate. But when you were dealing with werewolves such things happened all the time.

Being bitten will cause a change within twenty-four hours. Day, night, full moon, no moon, it doesn't matter. You're bitten, you change. After that, you can heal damn near anything—except silver.

Hector had murdered my family. He'd been after me. He'd been inches away from biting me, but Edward had gotten there first. Too late to save the people I loved, but not too late to save me. Even so, Hector had left his mark on me forever.

"After Mandenauer sprang you from the crazy ward," Jessie continued, "what did he do?"

"He taught me everything he knew."

"Blah, blah, blah. I meant, what did he do about Hector?"

Oh. "He used all the *J-S* resources to search for him, but we never found a trace."

"Which doesn't mean much."

"No."

Hector could be anywhere, using any name, doing anything he wanted. There was a certain freedom to being dead on paper.

"Do you know where he came from? How old he was? Who made him?"

The answers to any of those questions could help pinpoint where a werewolf might hide, who he might hang with. Sadly, I knew the answers to none of them in relation to Hector Menendez.

"I didn't know he was a werewolf until I saw him—"

I broke off as a vivid image flashed through my brain. My little sister, Jimmy, Mama. Hector's blue eyes shining from the face of a white wolf.

"Hey!" Jessie grabbed my hand, squeezed hard enough to make me wince. "I thought you were going to pass out there for a second."

I straightened and pulled away. I'd done enough fainting for one lifetime. "I'm fine," I snapped.

"Sure you are."

Being irritated with Jessie helped me focus on the here and now instead of my past. Which was probably why she was being so annoying. Or maybe she just came by it naturally. Like me.

"Hector told me he was from Texas. Corpus Christi. He sold drugs."

Her eyes widened. "Dealer?"

"Pharmaceutical rep."

Jessie turned a startled laugh into a cough. "And none of that was true?"

"None of it."

I'd met him in a restaurant where I'd gone for dinner with my parents. He'd been sitting in the bar alone, listening to music—Norah Jones, I think. Funny what you remember about one of the most important moments of your life.

He was tall and handsome; his dark skin and hair, combined with his light eyes and a well-trimmed goatee, gave him an exotic appearance. To little Miss Kansas and her white-bread, perfect life, Hector had been danger and desire all rolled into one.

I'd gone out with him a few times—secretly, of course. I'd been young, foolish, captivated, for a little while. Hector was quick to take insult—both real and imagined. He had a short temper and very little tolerance for anyone who was different from himself. An odd trait in a man named Menendez.

"You haven't heard from him since?"

I hesitated. "He called me at the hospital."

"How did he manage that?"

"I don't know. I may have imagined the calls."

As I'd imagined so many things.

"What did he say?"

I didn't want to remember all that Hector had told me—his plans, our future, his obsession.

"Nothing important."

She eyed me for a long moment, then let it go. "Why would he be here? Why now?"

I'd had the same thoughts. That Jessie had them, too, helped. I relaxed just a little. "I don't know," I admitted.

"I'll keep my eyes open. A guy like that shouldn't be hard to spot in a town like this."

She was right. And if I saw him first I wasn't going to wait around to see the whites of his eyes. I doubted Jessie would, either. The very thought made me feel stronger, more in control, safer.

"There's one more thing." I paused, then forced myself to blurt, "He has a tattoo."

Jessie lifted a brow. "Not a good thing to leave out, Leigh. A tattoo of what?"

"Pentagram."

She frowned. "Isn't that supposed to be protection against a werewolf?"

Surprise, surprise. Jessie didn't know everything.

"Not exactly. A pentagram is a five-pointed star. Some believe it's evil; others believe it's good."

"What do you think?"

Since the only time I'd ever seen one was as a tattoo on Hector's chest, I kind of thought the pentagram was Satan's tool.

"Supposedly, depending upon how the star is positioned, it can summon the powers of light or the powers of darkness."

"I guess we know which one Hector was after."

"Yeah."

"So where was this tattoo?"

I tapped a finger between my breasts.

Jessie's mouth fell open. I glanced away. I didn't need to explain how I'd seen Hector's chest. I'm sure she could figure it out.

"I doubt I'll get a good look at a stranger's breastbone," she remarked.

I doubted she would, either, but I'd told her all I knew.

Now we had to figure out if he was slinking around town. Knowing Hector, we wouldn't see him until it was too late.

"I ran an Internet search on cannibals."

"Excuse me?" Jessie's rapid change of subject left me blinking. "On what?"

"You heard me." She shoved some papers across the desk. "Will said the original Weendigo was a man who ate human flesh."

"That's just a legend."

"So are werewolves."

She had a point. I picked up the papers and started to read.

Albert Fish—1935
Stanley Dean Baker—1970
Omaima Nelson—1993
Nathaniel Bar-Jonah—1996

And, of course, Jeffrey Dahmer, the man who made Milwaukee famous.

The accounts were gruesome, nauseating, thorough. I read them anyway. When I was done, I shoved the papers back across the desk, unwilling to hold on to them any longer. My fingers felt slimy already.

"What exactly are we trying to find?" I asked.

"Hell if I know. Something out of the ordinary."

"In there?"

Everything I'd read had been far from ordinary.

"I noticed one thing," Jessie continued. "Before World War Two, there were very few serial killers."

"Maybe it was just harder to catch them then."

"Could be."

"You don't think so."

"Do you remember what happened in World War Two, Leigh?"

"Wanna be more specific?"

"What happened that involves us?"

Oh, that.

During the war Edward had been a spy. He'd discovered that Josef Mengele had been doing more than experimenting on the Jews at Auschwitz. He'd also had a secret lab deep in the Black Forest.

There he'd manufactured monsters. Hitler had demanded a werewolf army, among other things. Edward's mission had been to eliminate everything Mengele had made. By the time Mandenauer reached the lab, the Allies had hit the beaches and Russia was closing in. Mengele panicked and released all his creations into the world. They had been multiplying, mutating, spreading, ever since.

Edward, being Edward, was still following the orders he had never completely carried out.

"You think the increase in serial killers has something to do with the Nazis?" I asked.

"You got a better idea?"

I thought about it. We didn't know to this day everything Mengele had been manufacturing in his lab. Sure, there had been monsters before he started making them. History was full of 'em. But after—there'd been a whole lot more.

"What's your theory?" I asked.

"Maybe some of these cannibals were werewolves, too. Maybe they can't control themselves even when they're human."

"Maybe."

Or they could just be nuts.

"What does that mean to us?" I asked. "Here and now."

"Maybe this Weendigo started out as a human."

"They all started out as human."

"Let me finish. Instead of being bitten, he was cursed by his lust for flesh. He became a beast, like the legend. But even in beast form he can't stop being a cannibal."

She was making a weird sort of sense.

"I still don't see how we're going to figure out who it is that we're searching for."

"What if there's a suspect in a cannibalistic serial killer case who suddenly disappeared?"

"Yeah?"

"And what if a lot of dead, half-eaten wolves had turned up in the same place?"

She could be on to something, except—

"Edward said there'd been no incidences of cannibalistic werewolves but this one."

Jessie cursed. There went her theory.

But something tickled at the back of my mind. "Wait."

I held up my hand, tilted my head, thought hard, and suddenly there it was. "What if he's been soothing his need for cannibalism in human form and he just started satisfying that particular peculiarity in wolf form?"

Jessie stared at me as if I'd just said something very interesting. "I guess it couldn't hurt to get information on open serial killer cases."

"Right. But we don't want the FBI showing up here. They never can manage to blend in."

"Who has a contact at Quantico?"

"Mandenauer," she said, at the same time I said, "Edward."

Jessie picked up the phone.

15

Before she could dial, the door crashed open. Jessie and I pointed our weapons toward the sound.

Will stopped dead. "I have to go."

Jessie waved her .44 toward the sign that read: REST-ROOM. "Go."

He shook his head. His earring waggled, catching the light and throwing speckles of gold across his jaw. "I found something."

In the act of putting away our guns, Jessie and I tensed.

"What?" she asked.

"I'm not sure."

"There's a lot of that going around," I muttered.

"Huh?" Cadotte's eyes were unfocused behind his glasses. He stared at me as if he couldn't remember who I was. Then understanding dawned. "Oh, hi, Leigh. What are you doing here?"

"Never mind her, Slick. What did you find?"

"I did an Internet search on Weendigo, and I came up with the Legend of the Power Eater."

Jessie and I exchanged glances. "What's that?" she asked.

"I've never heard of it. But there's a book—"

Jessie groaned. "Not another book. Haven't we been through this?"

Confused, I looked back and forth between them. Jessie explained. "Will had a book on raising the wolf god. Sadly, a page was missing. A very important page."

"I ordered another one," he said.

"Which the werewolves conveniently intercepted."

"That's why this time I'm going *to* the book."

"Pardon me?"

"There's a copy in Madison. I'm leaving now."

"Now?" Jessie sounded forlorn. I stifled a smirk.

"I should be able to see it first thing in the morning. If there's anything useful I'll bring the book back or make a copy." His gaze softened. "I'll be home by tomorrow afternoon, Jess."

"Fine. Whatever. I've got plenty to do here."

"Uh-huh."

Cadotte wasn't buying it. He crossed the room and scooped her into his arms. Jessie was a big girl, but he was an even bigger man. He held her as if she were a child. Her usually stern face went all dopey with love. I turned away. But I could still hear every word.

"I'll be back before you even miss me."

"Too late."

Smoochy sounds followed. I tapped my foot, stared at the ceiling, considered leaving the room.

"Take this."

I spun around. Jessie was holding out her service revolver. Will stared at it with obvious distaste. "I don't like guns."

"I don't like dead boyfriends. I'm silly that way."

"I don't want a gun."

"Last time, Will, they needed you for the ceremony."

"You, too."

"But I can take care of myself."

"And I can't?"

She sighed. "For me? Please?"

He took the gun, holding it between two fingers, as if the thing might go off at any moment. Jessie glanced at me and together we rolled our eyes.

"He's going to shoot off his toe," I commented.

"Oh well, he's got nine more. Just don't shoot off something I'll need later. Especially something you've got only one of."

I blushed. I might be a big, bad werewolf hunter, but bawdy sexual innuendos flustered me.

"I think I embarrassed the duchess."

"Leave her be, Jess."

They were both staring at me. Jessie's gaze was contemplative. She saw more than I wanted her to. Will's was sympathetic. I didn't like his any better.

"I'll leave you two alone to say good-bye." I practically ran outside.

The half-moon slid toward the horizon. Soon the sun would come up and I could sleep. Here I was a werewolf hunter living like a vampire. That might even be funny, if I did much laughing anymore.

I took a minute to observe the clear navy blue sky. Living in Topeka for most of my life, I hadn't known how brightly stars could shine away from the glare of city lights.

A flash at the corner of my vision drew my gaze, and I watched a star flare, then drop. City dwellers rarely caught a glimpse of a falling star. Every time I saw one, I was amazed and humbled. There was so much out there we didn't understand.

"I wish I . . ." My words trailed off into the chill of the autumn night. What did I wish?

That I could catch the Weendigo—kill a killer at any cost?

Or that I could have back the life I'd lost?

Did I want death or to start anew?

I had no idea anymore, and that scared me. Until I'd come to Crow Valley I'd only wanted to kill them, not caring if I died, too.

But suddenly there were people I liked all around me, not friends exactly but no longer strangers, either.

There was sexual attraction, something I hadn't experienced in years. Lust had made me want to live. At least until I tasted it again.

That wasn't good.

The not caring had made me damn near invincible. I took chances no one else dared to. The monsters sensed I'd die before I let them live, which gave me an edge.

Suddenly the edge was lost. What if in the middle of a death battle I started remembering Damien and his kiss? Longing for it, for him? I'd sneered at Jessie because of her attachment to Will. Was I any better?

I couldn't afford to be distracted. So what was I going to do about it?

I had a pretty good idea.

The door opened and Jessie, then Will, stepped out. Her uniform was untucked, her shirt buttoned wrong. His pants were unzipped; his glasses had fingerprints all over them. Talk about a quickie.

I wanted one.

"Take care of her, OK?" Will asked.

Jessie snorted. "Right."

Will ignored her, focusing instead on me. "Please?"

"Of course."

Then he was gone.

Jessie made an impatient sound. "Let's get one thing

straight, Duchess. I can take care of myself. I don't need you or anyone else to help me."

"Me, either. But we can humor Edward. And the boyfriend."

She scowled at my term for Will and I almost laughed. It was so easy to yank her chain.

"Come on. *You* can call Mandenauer this time."

I'd forgotten that we'd been about to call him when Will showed up. I went into the station and sat at Jessie's desk.

"Make yourself right at home," she said.

"Thanks." I picked up her phone.

Edward answered his direct line on the second ring. *"Jawohl? Was ist es?"*

I frowned. It wasn't like him to speak in German. He'd been in this country for longer than I'd been alive. I'd only heard him revert to his native tongue when he was very, very tired, sick, or hurt—which had happened maybe twice since I'd known him.

"Are you all right?" I asked.

"Leigh? Yes. Of course. I was sleeping."

Something he rarely did. But when he slept, he'd always awoken completely alert and ready to deal with anything at a moment's notice. Military training did that to a guy, or so he said. His behavior concerned me.

"Is Elise there?"

"No," he said shortly.

"Why not?"

Elise watched over Edward like a mother hen. Drove him nuts, but she wouldn't stop.

"Because I am in my room and she is . . . I don't know where. Now what do you want at . . . four A.M.?"

Quickly I filled him in on what he didn't know.

"Can you contact someone in the Violent Criminal Apprehension Program?"

"Certainly. You will have your data by midday."

Edward the efficient.

"There's one more thing."

I glanced at Jessie. She made a whirling motion with her hand. Get on with it.

"Have you ever had an agent named Damien Fitzgerald?"

Edward thought for an instant. "No. The name is not familiar. Why?"

I filled him in on a little bit more.

"He could have changed his name," Edward murmured. "I will send you photos of the rogue agents I am aware of."

"Thanks."

"So why did Elise need you back there pronto?" I asked.

Silence settled over the line. I wondered if he'd hung up.

"Edward?"

"I am here."

"Well? What's up?"

Elise had been working on a cure for lycanthropy. So far she'd come up with zilch. The only reason I could think of for Edward to rush to *J-S* headquarters in remote Montana was that she'd had a breakthrough.

The idea made me nervous. If Elise found a way to cure them, what would I do with the rest of my life?

"Nothing is up," he said. "Elise thought she might have discovered something."

"Did she?"

"That remains to be seen." He sighed. "But I do not think so."

I let out the breath I hadn't even known I was holding. "Will you be back soon?"

"No. You and Jessie can handle things in Crow Valley."

"But—"

"I am tired, Leigh. I need a rest."

My heart started thudding faster and harder with dread. "You're sick."

"Perhaps. Sick and tired of the blood, the death, the killing. And for what? There are always more."

I'd never heard him so down. Usually Edward was the one buoying everyone else's spirits.

I glanced at Jessie, frowned. He'd never been like this before he'd met her.

"I'll make sure there aren't any more here," I promised, and hung up. "What exactly happened in Miniwa?" I demanded.

"You know."

"Wolf god, totem. Been there, heard that. I meant to Edward."

Her gaze slid away from mine.

"What?"

She shrugged. "He made a few mistakes. Nothing major. Everything worked out for the best."

Mistakes? That didn't sound like Edward.

"What kind of mistakes?"

"He got distracted. We got captured." She shrugged. "It happens."

"Not to him."

"Never?"

Not that I knew of.

I'd considered telling Edward I thought Hector might be here. Until he'd answered the phone speaking German. Until he'd gone all Eeyore on me.

"He's acting so weird," I murmured. "He didn't want to come back."

"Can you blame him? The guy's been hunting were-wolves, and Lord knows what else, for sixty years. I'd be ready for a break."

I suspected she was right, but I didn't like it. I decided to keep my suspicions about Hector between myself and Jessie until I was sure I wasn't seeing things again. Why upset Edward if I didn't have to?

"What about the information from Quantico?" Jessie asked.

"By noon."

"And Fitzgerald?"

"He doesn't recognize the name, but he's sending rogue agent pictures."

"Good. There's not much else we can do until then. I'd better make my rounds. Not that I'll see anything, but I try to at least pretend to earn my second paycheck."

"This place is awful quiet after the sun goes down."

"Creepy, isn't it?"

"Yeah."

Crow Valley after sunset was as quiet as the proverbial tomb. No lights in any of the windows. Not even a cat trolling the streets.

The entire town had a deserted air. As if too many of the citizens had disappeared. We just didn't know how many.

Where there were werewolves, people went missing. Which was usually how the *Jäger-Suchers* ended up be-ing called to the scene. Then we made sure the missing were explained. Our favorite excuse was that they'd walked into the woods and never come back out. It happens more than you'd think.

16

That there were no missing persons reports continued to bother me. Were the werewolves only killing transients? I had a hard time accepting that.

In wolf form, werewolves were hunters, like me. When presented with a weaker entity, they attacked. They might posses human level intelligence, but I'd never known them to be able to pound back the bloodlust.

They saw people in the woods and they killed them. Plain, simple, to the point. I doubt they stopped long enough to ask for a résumé.

I put the thought aside and headed to my apartment. I had more pressing concerns.

The route into the woods was as familiar as the array of cars surrounding the tavern and the wail of jazz through the open windows.

I glanced at my watch. Coming up on 5:00 A.M. Did anyone ever go home around here?

I retrieved a spare .22 from my glove compartment and shoved the smaller gun into the waistband of my jeans. They were too tight to hide the thing, but I wasn't going anywhere without a silver bullet–firing weapon again. I might be slow, but eventually I caught on.

Dirty, hungry, tired, I needed a shower, food, and bed in that order. But before I climbed the steps to my lonely room, I wanted to check behind the Dumpster one last time. Maybe the gun had fallen into a hole or something.

I was grasping. Pretty much anyone could have taken the gun while I'd been inside the tavern. Of course he'd have to have been watching me hide the thing . . . a fact I didn't want to examine too closely.

As I approached the garbage bin, a fat raccoon shot a glare in my direction and waddled away. Better than a rat, though I bet a few of them made regular visits here as well. I wasn't afraid of animals. How could I be? But rats made me shudder. What was with those hairless tails anyway?

I'd brought the flashlight from my car, and I shone the beam back and forth across the front of the Dumpster, across the paper-strewn ground, then behind. Not a single gleam of gunmetal made my life any easier. It was bad enough I'd have to admit taking Damien's gun; I didn't want to tell him I'd lost it, too.

Kneeling next to the wall, I reached into the crack between the building and the steel container. Something skittered out the other side and ran away.

"I did not hear that," I assured myself.

I continued to feel around but came up with nothing.

The shriek of a dying animal shot my heart straight into my throat. Whatever had run from me had slammed straight into something else. Bummer for him.

I retrieved my hand, sat back on my heels, scowled at the scum under my nails. A growl rumbled along my spine like sandpaper. Slowly I straightened, then turned.

"One, two, three, four, five. Shitty odds," I muttered, and drew the gun.

I didn't know how many bullets I had. Not enough. Who'd have thought I'd need more than a clip's worth to get from my car to the house?

The wolves advanced, legs stiff, hackles raised. My first bullet kicked up dirt in front of the lead animal. His lip curled; then he threw up his head as if laughing at me.

I shot a glance toward the staircase that led to my apartment. A wolf sat on the bottom step, tongue lolling as he panted like a great big dog.

I could shoot him and try to get to my apartment, but there were five—I looked back just as several shadows detached themselves from the trees and crossed the parking lot—make that ten wolves behind me. Thank God none of them were white. Still, I was in serious trouble.

The main wolf pack was between me and the tavern. I could yell for help, but the music was too loud. They'd never hear me.

My mind raced as fast as my heart. I cast a glance toward Damien's cabin. Nothing between it and me but grass. That building was the only chance I had.

I fired another shot, actually hit one of them this time. The flames, the stench of burning flesh and fur, the howl of the dying distracted the others long enough for me to achieve a small lead.

I'd take what I could get. They were going to catch me. There was no way I could outrun close to a dozen wolves. Hell, I couldn't outrun one, but I had to try.

A chorus of howls rose behind me, so loud I flinched, stumbled, and nearly fell. Their footsteps echoed mine. The warmth of their breath brushed my calves. The scent of predator after prey cascaded through the night—a sharp and gamy aroma reminiscent of fear and death.

I couldn't recall if I'd locked Damien's door after I'd

picked it. If I had, I was dead or soon to be furry. Either way, I'd take a few of them with me.

I reached for the knob, but the door swung open. I smashed into Damien's chest.

"Oomph," he said, and caught me.

My momentum propelled us inside the cabin.

"Shut it! Shut it!" I shouted, kicking back, managing to catch the door with my heel.

I tensed, expecting bodies to thud against the other side. Glancing at the window, I waited for the shadow, the crash, death.

Nothing happened.

I pulled free of Damien's arms, ran to the glass. The first rays of sun lightened the eastern horizon, threw streams of pink and gray across the hauntingly empty clearing.

"Are you all right?"

I ignored him, stepping to the door, yanking it open, and sticking my gun outside. The wind blew a leaf end over end across the threshold.

"Did you see them?" I asked.

"Who?"

"Couldn't you hear them?"

He didn't answer and I turned. Gently he removed the gun from my shaking hand. "There's nothing there, Leigh."

"Ten. Maybe more. They howled. Chased me. You had to see them."

"All I saw was you."

My head jerked up. Our eyes met and something passed between us that had nothing to do with the situation. We both remembered the last time we'd been together. Remembered it and wanted more.

He was the first to look away. We'd been gazing at each other so intently, the loss of that contact was like a physical break. I took a single step toward him before I caught myself. Now was not the time.

He crossed the short distance to the kitchen table and laid the gun on top. He wore his usual outfit—black on black—his feet were bare, but his shirt was buttoned. For reasons beyond my understanding, I was more turned on by his pale, long feet than I'd ever been by his smooth, muscled chest.

I was dizzy from the adrenaline; fear-induced sweat chilled my skin. I needed to sit down, so I did. On the floor at his feet. Bad idea. I was reaching to run a thumb along the lilting arch before I knew what I was doing.

He fell to his knees beside me. I yanked my hand back and held it still in my lap as he put a palm to my forehead. "You're sick."

I must be if I'm thinking about how your feet would feel all tangled up with mine.

I turned my head, afraid if he kept touching me I'd beg. I wanted him, but not like this. Not when I was sweaty, smelly, not quite certain of my sanity.

"You didn't see them?" I asked again.

"Them who?"

"The wolves."

"Wolves?" He glanced out the door, which I'd left wide open. "No."

"Shit." I rubbed a hand over my face. My palm came away wet. With sweat or tears I wasn't sure, and that scared me almost as much as the wolves had.

"I heard some howls. They—" He stopped.

"What?"

"They came from the woods. I didn't think anything of it. Wolves howl all the time. I like the sound." He shrugged. "Makes me feel less alone."

I snorted. Better to be alone forever than to have company like that.

I didn't know what to think. Had the werewolves run into the woods instead of chasing me? Why? I'd never known them to give up on a sure thing. I didn't like to think what it meant if they had.

The only other explanation was that they'd never been there at all. I liked that idea even less.

"I have to go."

I got to my feet. So did he.

I knew I should stay. I needed to question him.

Who the hell are you? Why are you here?

But right now I wasn't capable of it. I had to get away from Damien. Be by myself. Get a grip.

I looked out the door. The white wolf stood at the edge of the forest, waiting for me.

I blinked and he was gone.

There was no way I could go out there.

Damien must have mistook my hesitation for something else. He came up behind me, shut the door, locked it. Then he put his hands on my shoulders. His breath brushed the bare skin of my neck, and I shivered again for an entirely different reason.

What the hell? I thought. I couldn't go back to my room. I might as well stay here. In the past I'd tried drinking and drugs to make me forget the damned white wolf. They hadn't worked. There was one vice I'd neglected.

I bet Damien could make me forget . . . everything.

I turned and offered my mouth to his.

17

Damien went still. "This is a bad idea, Leigh."

I went on tiptoe, brushed my lips back and forth across his chin, then reached up and licked his bottom lip.

"Fuck me," I whispered. "You know you want to."

He reared back, staring at me as if I'd lost my mind. But I already knew that I had.

"No," he said.

I reached down and cupped him. He was hard and heavy against my palm. "No?" I drew a fingertip up his length.

He caught his breath, closed his eyes. I slipped my hand into his pants, closed my fingers around him, and pumped.

Cursing, he grabbed my wrist. I managed to rub my thumb over his tip; moisture beaded between our skin. I wanted to taste him.

"Leigh," he ground out.

Maybe later.

"Stop talking."

I kissed him the way he'd kissed me earlier. Nothing gentle about it. No giving, only taking. If he kept yapping, I'd lose my nerve, and I didn't want that. I wanted him.

He gave in with a furious rumble from deep in his chest. Suddenly his hands were everywhere, touching everything. His mouth was right behind them.

I fumbled with his shirt. Why now, of all times, had he buttoned the damn thing? I lost my patience and yanked. Buttons pinged against the floor. At last I could kiss the chest I'd been fantasizing about.

He tasted as good as he smelled, an enticing combination of sunshine and shadow. Salt and sweet, clean skin. I licked his soft, flat nipple. It beaded and I rolled it with my tongue, tested the tip with my teeth.

His fingers tightened in my hair, pressing against my skull to a point just short of pain. I suckled him and his hand fell to my waist, but he didn't pull me near. Instead, he seemed to be holding me away. I didn't like it.

I reached for him, stroked gently. He leaped, grew, heated, and at last he drew me closer. It felt so good to be held. No one had touched me since Jimmy and . . .

My mind shied away from the past, clung to the present. *Think of nothing but this, no one but him.*

My hand increased the pressure, the speed. My name erupted like a curse from his lips as he tugged at my clothes. He didn't have much luck. They were too tight to get rid of easily.

I was afraid he'd call a stop again, and if he did, I'd listen to the voice I'd stifled, the one that kept screaming, *Are you insane?*

Maybe. Oh well, nothing I hadn't been before.

To stifle the voice, I yanked my tank top over my head, lost the boots, the socks, the knife, then shimmied out of my jeans. By undressing myself, I could control the situation, control what he saw, what I hid.

I straightened, standing naked and exposed. Suddenly the room wasn't so hot; it was downright chilly.

The gray light of dawn cast a shadow over his face, making his eyes darker than I remembered, closer to brown than hazel. His hair was mussed, the lack of sun hiding the streaks of red amid the chestnut strands. His jaw was dark with stubble. I wanted to feel the scrape against my thighs, my belly, my breasts.

His shirt hung loose, the black accenting his pale, smooth skin. His trousers rode low on his hips. He was slim but toned, every inch honed to perfection. I wanted to see all of him, touch him, too.

I eased the shirt from his shoulders. He shrugged and it fluttered to the ground. He seemed unaffected by my nearness, my nakedness. Standing completely still, he didn't reach out. Did he find me unappealing?

The thought made me frown. I hadn't looked at a man with any interest in over two years, but not because no one had looked at me.

Small, petite, blond—almost. I was flat chested, true, but there were plenty of men who didn't mind, who, in fact, preferred a boyish shape to a voluptuous one. However, Damien might not be one of them.

I stepped forward and laid my palm against his chest, felt his heart pounding like the wings of a bird that had been startled from the trees. He might appear unaffected, but his body couldn't lie. He wanted me.

I hooked my thumbs in his pants, shifted them down his hips, over his erection, then let them fall to the floor. He grabbed me by the shoulders, his touch no longer gentle.

His mouth on mine re-ignited the lust. Everything about him aroused me—his skin, his hair, his scent. My fingers fluttered everywhere, stroking, kneading, discovering.

His bed was across the room. A lifetime away. I was tempted to opt for the kitchen table, but would that label me an overeager slut? Probably.

Did I care? Not really.

The decision was taken out of my hands when he lifted me into his arms and headed for the bed. I didn't argue. Not even when he fell onto his back, letting me sprawl all over him. I felt exposed, naked.

Oops, I was.

I tried to shimmy off, so I could press my back against the mattress. He couldn't see me, couldn't touch me, where no one had touched me since. Panic pulsed in a hot, oily mass at the base of my throat. Then he grabbed my thighs, opened my legs, and arched.

I forgot all about what I wanted to hide as his erection slid against me just right. He kept his palms on my hips; his thumbs glided up and down the sensitive area where my thighs connected to my body. Gooseflesh broke out, making the light sheen of sweat on my skin tingle. I felt alive in a way I hadn't felt since I'd begun courting death.

He pushed me toward the edge. I didn't want to go. Not so fast, not like this. I wanted him inside me. I needed him to fill the eternal emptiness, assuage the burning, aching abyss that was Leigh.

Tightening my legs, I lifted myself, searching for fulfillment. It wasn't hard to find. He slid inside just a bit.

Suddenly I was on my back, his body flush with mine, his hands pinning my wrists to the mattress as I fought him.

"Dammit, Leigh." His forehead pressed against mine. "Wait a second."

"I don't want to wait."

If I waited, I'd think, and thinking was bad. Right now all I needed was him. I wasn't remembering or missing anyone else.

"Neither do I," he muttered, and reached over the side of the bed.

I tensed, uncertain what he was doing. But when his hand became visible again, I understood.

I was much, much dumber than I looked.

He rolled away and in a quick, practiced move sheathed himself in a condom. Watching his clever fingers play over his own skin excited me.

Even if I'd been able to think clearly, I had no time for recriminations. He was back in an instant, sliding between my thighs, stroking my waist.

"No more waiting," he murmured, lips drifting from my ear, to my neck, then back to my mouth.

I wrapped my legs around him and he filled me in a single, driving thrust. He was too gentle; I wanted it rough.

As I urged him with my hands, my hips, my teeth, he caught the rhythm and swept me away—from him, from Crow Valley, but, most important, from myself.

He knew which buttons to push. At least on me. When I was near the edge, panting, gasping, he slowed, then went still.

Circling both my wrists with one of his hands, the scrape of his rough fingers enticed me. He held me captive so I couldn't touch him or hasten him on. Then he let his mouth do amazing things wherever it could reach. My breasts were small, but that only meant they were more sensitive. Having him hard and still inside me while he suckled and bit and played with my nipples made me come in a deep, pulsing wave, but it wasn't enough

"Again," he muttered, slowly drawing himself out to the tip, then pushing in as deep as he could.

"I can't," I murmured, even as I wrapped my legs around his back and pulled him closer.

He teased me until my skin was slick with sweat and

my mind was spinning along with my body. This time when I went over, he came, too, the pulsing ejaculation an added sensation that had me tightening around him, drawing out the moment as long as I could.

But sooner or later all good things must end. There were technicalities to take care of. He went to the bathroom. Water ran; the toilet flushed. The world rushed back like a flood. What had I done?

Screwed a stranger. Big deal. These days everyone was a stranger. What did I expect, that I'd go without sex for the rest of my life?

He'd been good. Make that great. Even if I hadn't been with a man in two years, Damien would still have been amazing.

And why not? He was gorgeous, built, skilled. Of course he was the best fuck I'd ever had. I should have been dancing for joy. Instead I felt like crying.

"Do you have a cigarette?" I asked.

"Leigh." His hand covered mine. I stared at the ceiling as if it were the most fascinating entity on the planet. "Sex isn't going to help."

My gaze flew to his. "Help what?"

His smile was both gentle and sad. Damien's smile. "Help you to forget."

My eyes narrowed. "Forget what?"

"Leigh," he said again, and touched my hair.

My chest ached. My eyes burned. I had to stop him from being nice to me before I cried. I turned my back, then realized what I'd done and slammed my shoulders flat to the bed.

I glanced at his face.

Too late. He'd already seen.

18

His face went hard and still; his eyes darkened to the shade of evergreen smoke. "Jesus Christ, Leigh, what the hell is that?"

"Nothing."

"Nothing?" He stood and took a few short, jerky steps away from me. "It looks like someone dug a furrow in your back with a butcher knife."

I winced. It had felt like that when it happened.

He caught my expression and gritted his teeth. "I'm sorry. It's just—" He moved his hands in a helpless gesture. I understood. My back wasn't pretty. I tried not to peek at it, either.

I hadn't let anyone see me naked since it happened. I could tell myself sex didn't interest me once Jimmy had died, and that was partly true. But nothing increases celibacy like a huge scar that runs from just below your left shoulder to your right hip. My days of wearing bikinis were over. Any hope of a backless wedding gown was as dead as my fiancé. But I'd live.

Bummer.

"Who did that to you?" Damien asked.

I sat up, keeping my shoulders slanted away from him. His hands clenched; his muscles bunched.

"It was an accident," I lied.

As if I'd admit a werewolf had marked me as his forever. Damien frowned. "What kind of accident?"

"I don't want to talk about it."

"Too bad. I do."

I got off the bed, crossed the floor, found my clothes. I didn't even realize I'd presented him with my back again until his fingers drifted over my left shoulder.

I yelped, jumped, spun. How had he followed so quickly and so quietly?

"Don't touch me," I whispered.

I couldn't bear for anyone to touch where Hector had.

"Does it hurt?"

"Of course not. It's been years."

In truth, the thing had been aching on and off since I'd seen, or imagined, the white wolf. But I wasn't going to confess that to anyone, ever.

"If it doesn't hurt, then why can't I touch you?"

"Why the hell do you think? It's ugly. I'm—"

I broke off. I'd wanted sex; I'd gotten it. Time to go.

"I have scars, too," he said quietly.

I glanced up. He pointed to his thigh where a thin white line bisected the skin. I snorted. "That's a scratch."

In truth, his body was damn near perfect. How had he gotten to be . . . twenty-something with only one small scar?

"Is this what you're trying so hard to forget?" he asked.

"I'll never forget."

How could I? The scar would be with me forever, along with the memories.

"Did one of the wolves hurt you?"

In the midst of putting on my shirt, I froze. "What wolves?"

"The ones you're after."

A chill trickled over my skin. How could he know who I was?

Then I remembered what sex had made me forget. The gun behind his toilet tank. The single silver bullet that I'd already used. I might be lying to him, but he was lying to me, too.

I finished dressing. Time to get back to work.

Damien lit a cigarette, stood at the window, naked, blowing smoke through his nose. He offered me a drag, but right now I didn't want to put my mouth where his had been. It might make me want to put my mouth other places.

"Who are you?" I asked.

He shrugged, the movement pulling his muscles tight, then releasing them. "No one."

"Then why were you hiding the gun?"

He frowned. "What gun?"

The complete bafflement on his face slowed me down. "Uh, the one behind the toilet tank."

He lifted a brow, then the cigarette to his mouth. Slowly he drew in, blew out. "When were you in my bathroom?"

Oops. I decided to be honest. About one thing anyway.

"I broke in."

"Emergency bathroom break?"

"Not exactly."

"What, exactly?"

I didn't know how to explain why I'd gone through his things. I'd had good reason, but none I could tell him.

Jäger-Suchers were supposed to be a secret monster-hunting society. *Secret.* As in, need-to-know only. He didn't need to know.

There was a lot of that going around.

"Let me ask you a question," Damien murmured.

"Sure," I said, eager to get off the previous topic.

He pressed his thumb and forefinger together over the glowing stub. I blinked. That had to hurt, but he didn't flinch. I recalled the sensation of his scarred, rough hands dancing over my body. Maybe it didn't hurt anymore.

The cigarette extinguished, he flicked what was left end over end. It landed between my feet.

"Killing and burning wolves. Breaking and entering." He crossed the room, stopping so close I could smell the smoke on his breath. I wanted to lick his teeth. "Searching my room and finding a gun."

He didn't touch me, didn't have to. Just the scent of him, the heat, all that lovely pale skin and rippling muscle. My body remembered and it yearned.

His voice lowered, so soft I had to strain to hear him. "Who are *you*, Leigh?"

Danger, danger. Time to lie a little more.

"I told you. I'm with the DNR. The wolves . . ."

My mind blanked. What was my cover again?

"Right," he said. "That new strain of rabies."

"Yes." I let out a silent sigh of relief.

"Where's the gun?" he asked.

Hell.

"I—um—confiscated it."

"Confiscated? Can you do that?"

"Sure." I wasn't exactly sure, but he didn't need to know that, either. "Is it yours?"

"No."

"Then . . . ?"

"When I moved in, you can bet I never looked behind the toilet tank. Who knows who lived here before me?"

Was he telling the truth? I kind of thought that he was.

If the gun was his, he was a very good actor. If the gun was his, what possible good could a single silver bullet do?

The question now was: Whose gun had it been?

Another job for Jessie McQuade.

"I have to go," I said.

He was still standing so close the hair on my arms prickled. He hadn't touched me since the ill-fated stroke to my back. I wanted him to, and because of that, I headed for the door.

"Wait."

With my hand on the knob, I stopped. He followed, reaching out to place a hand on my shoulder. I tensed, but he refused to let go. When I'd yearned for his touch, I hadn't meant there.

Because I yearned and hated myself for it, hated him, I lashed out. "This was a stupid idea."

"I know."

His quiet admission was like throwing ice water on my anger. I wasn't sure what to say. Sex had made me forget for a little while the realities of my life. But once the madness receded, I could see clearly again.

I was lying to him. He had no idea who I was. What I did. He had no idea how dangerous it was to know me. If he was around when the shit hit the fan—and it would; it was only a matter of time—he'd get hurt. He might get dead.

I yanked open the door. On the threshold I paused. All the cars were still there.

"Does anyone ever go home around here?" I asked.

"A lot of them walk."

I glanced back. Damien stood in the doorway, stark naked and aroused. I wanted him again. So much for self-control. What I felt for Damien reminded me far too much of what I'd once felt for Hector, and it frightened me.

I forced my gaze back to the cars. "They walk home in the dark?"

"Better than driving after you've been drinking since midafternoon."

"But—"

"Most of them live in town. It's quicker getting home as the crow flies."

What was with all the crow references?

"I don't get it," I admitted.

"A crow flies straight from one place to another. They don't care about roads. If you go home as the crow flies . . ." His arm shot past my face, finger extended toward the woods.

"You mean your customers walk home through the forest at night?"

"Why not?"

I could think of several reasons. All of them furry.

"Have any of them disappeared lately?"

"Disappeared how?"

"One day here, tomorrow not so much."

"Of course."

"And you don't wonder where they went?"

"People come and go. They move. They start patronizing a different tavern. I'm not their father. Why?"

"No reason."

"You think they got killed by wolves?"

I shrugged. He was skirting a little close to the truth.

"Wolves aren't aggressive," he said.

"They are if they're rabid."

That much was true. All reports of wolf attacks were by rabid animals—or at least that's what we liked the common folk to believe. If the news got out that werewolves lived all over the place, it wouldn't be pretty.

"What aren't you telling me?" he asked. "Have there

been rabid wolf attacks in Crow Valley? Is that why you're here?"

"Yes."

What was another lie among so many others? I had to make him stop asking questions any way that I could.

"But we don't want that to get out," I said hurriedly. "People will panic. We'll have nuts in the forest with guns, shooting pets, then each other."

"Not to mention the press."

I flicked him a glance. I hadn't thought of that, but he was right. Imagine, if you will, reports of a rabid wolf pack eating people upstate. What a story.

"You can see why I'm being secretive," I said. "We're handling the problem."

"By we, you mean you and the sheriff?"

"Yes."

We *were* handling the problem. Just not that problem.

"You won't tell anyone?" I pressed.

"Who am I going to tell?"

I glanced at the bar, then back at him.

He snorted. "I don't tell them anything. I listen."

"Good. Thanks."

He moved in my direction, and I fled before he kissed me again. One more like any of the others and I might forget everything I should remember.

I hurried up the steps and inside my apartment, then glanced at my watch. Seven A.M. I had to be back at Jessie's by noon so we could go over the Quantico report on serial killers. I could hardly wait.

I took a long, hot shower. By the time I got out I smelled like citrus and honey, not earth and wind. My muscles were relaxed, my brain mush. I went to bed, fell asleep right away, and for the first time in my life I had nightmares in the daylight.

In my dream the white wolf speaks, with Hector's voice. "*Querida,* what did you expect?"

He'd always called me *querida,* even though there'd been nothing of love in what we'd done. At least for me.

I back away, my hands outstretched, but he keeps coming, his stiff-legged gait and raised hackles terrifying, the growl beneath the words making my skin prickle.

"I had to get rid of them so you could be mine forever."

"No."

I hear myself speak in my sleep; the word echoes through my dream. Hector smiles, grins, pants. His teeth are as red as his tongue.

God, get me away from him.

I spin and run up the steps in the home of my childhood. But my childhood is over—beginning right now.

"Mine," Hector snarls at the others, stopping their mad pursuit of fleeing prey in midstep.

Hector is the alpha—there is no doubt, no question. Just as there is no question that he will catch me. Both then and now. It is only a matter of time.

I lock myself in my room, grab the phone, listen for a dial tone, and hear nothing. My cell phone is downstairs, in my purse, useless to me now.

I run to the window, but before I can get it open and scream for someone, anyone, to help me, the door splinters inward, and he is there.

I don't want him near me with the blood of my loved ones still wet on his fur, ripe in his mouth. I look around for a weapon, something, anything, but there is nothing in this pink and white frothy sanctuary of my childhood.

"You'll never die, *querida.* We'll be together always. You'll like it. I promise."

I stare into his eyes and remember how it came to this.

The deaths of my family, of Jimmy, were my own fault. Because I couldn't say no when Hector touched me.

In my sleep I moan, toss, turn. I couldn't stop myself from touching Damien, either. But it isn't the same. I'm not promised to another. I'm not having a last fling. I'm not flirting with the Devil. Damien is just a man. Hector was a beast.

I move as far into the room as I can, cower against the wall, wait for him to strike.

His eyes are so human they make me dizzy. I stared into those eyes while he did . . . amazing things. Things that made me writhe, moan, scream for more. Hector had bewitched me, and now I knew why.

Gunshots erupt downstairs. The sentries howl. The scent of burning flesh and flame drifts upward and Hector snarls.

I think he'll run. Instead he lunges. I turn away, hide my head, wait for the slash of his teeth. My dress tears; cool air caresses my back.

"Wolves mate for life, *querida*."

Worried, disturbed, I straighten, glance over my shoulder just as he strikes—claw, not tooth. But why?

I scream as white-hot agony erupts from shoulder to hip. He leaps upward, muscles flexing, body stretching—both horrible and beautiful at the same time. He crashes through the glass and is gone.

Edward bursts into the room, hurries to the window, curses. As I lose consciousness, he bends over me and whispers, "Everything will be all right."

The phone begins to ring.

I gasped and came awake with the bright light of day shining across my face. How long had I slept? Not long enough.

What a strange dream. Hector the wolf had never spoken, though the words of my dream were real enough. He'd told me things in phone calls that made me weep. It had been my fault my family had died, because I'd let Hector into my life and he hadn't wanted to let me out of his.

He was possessive, obsessive. Freaking crazy. He wanted me for himself, and the only way to keep me was to make certain I had no one to turn to but him.

He hadn't counted on Edward.

I'd traced the calls after I got out—by then, I had the technology—but they'd been placed from pay phones in different parts of the country. It did me no good to report them to the police. Dead men didn't dial long-distance.

I shook my head. My cell phone was ringing *now*. The sound wasn't an echo of the dream.

With a groan, I hoisted myself out of bed and crossed to the kitchen table. "Hello?"

I flinched, half-expecting Hector's deep, musical voice to whisper my name.

"Where the hell are you?" Jessie snapped.

Relief made me smile. "Good morning to you, too."

"It's afternoon."

"Already?"

"I have the report from Quantico."

"And?"

"I think your friend Hector is on it."

19

I went into the bathroom, splashed my face with water, and brushed my teeth. My mouth tasted like something had died in there. My back was on fire.

I turned, twisting awkwardly, trying to see in the mirror above the sink. The long, furrowed mark pulsed bright red, as if infected.

The scar had never bothered me once it healed. Sometimes I even forgot for an hour or two at a time. What was the matter now?

I straightened, rubbed my hand over my face, and looked again. The scar was just a scar. Puckered. White. Healed.

"Shit."

I was losing my mind.

I threw on some clothes, retrieved my weapons, and left the apartment.

The remnants of the nightmare faded as I drove into Crow Valley. It wasn't as if I'd never had one before. I'd just never had one in the daytime.

Which disturbed me. I'd been able to keep the nightmares at bay by sleeping when the sun shone. If that relief was gone to me, would I ever be able to sleep again? I didn't want to think about it.

So I didn't. I'd become very good at pushing aside anything I didn't want to dwell on. If I hadn't been, I doubt I'd be functional at all.

Crow Valley was as busy in the light of an October afternoon as it was empty of an October midnight. Folk of every age, shape, and color walked up and down the picturesque streets. Some even waved as if they knew me. They probably did. In small towns gossip traveled at the speed of sound. One of the reasons I didn't stay long in any one place.

I drove to Jessie's apartment. It was nearly five o'clock. I'd slept, and dreamed, the day away. But since she didn't go on duty until the sun went down, we still had time to do our job.

Jessie opened the door before I even knocked, and shoved the fax into my hand. "About time."

"What's up your ass?"

She turned on me, and I blocked her punch with my forearm. She might have slammed me against the wall once, but that didn't mean I'd let her do it again.

"I'm in no mood to play nice," I warned.

"Bitch, bitch, bitch." She stalked away, plopping onto the couch with a scowl.

"What's the matter with you?" I tried a more pleasant version of the same question.

She glared at me. "Will's not back."

"Did you call him?"

"Cell phone's off."

"Does he forget to turn it on?"

"Every damn day."

"Then what are you worried about?"

"Let's see—werewolves, vampires, zombies, witches,

and all sorts of other things I don't even know about. Then there are car accidents, mass murderers, blood clots, heart attacks, strokes, and various acts of God."

I blinked. "Gee, how do you sleep?"

"When he's not here, I don't."

Now that I looked closer, there were dark circles under her eyes; lines of stress bracketed her mouth. She was really worried, and I couldn't say that I blamed her.

"Did you call any friendly state cops?"

"You think I'm a fool? Of course I called."

"And?"

"Nothing."

This was exactly what I'd been talking about when I said attachments were a bad thing. Jessie wasn't thinking of werewolves and serial killers; she was thinking of Will.

"If anything had happened, they'd know about it, Jessie."

"Then where is he?"

I had no idea. But if I gave voice to any of my thoughts, she'd only try to slug me again, so I glanced at the sheet of paper in my hand.

"*Open Serial Killer Cases Where Cannibalism Is Suspected.*" What a lovely title. There were only two. Herman Reyes and some guy named Louis-François Charone.

"You said Hector was on here."

"Check out the place where they last saw Herman Reyes."

I did. Topeka—in the year my life ended. Hell.

I lifted my gaze. "Then Hector is Herman."

"You tell me."

Jessie held out a photo. Dizziness rushed over me in a nauseating wave.

Querida.

The word whispered through the room. I swayed.

"Hey!" Suddenly Jessie was there, catching me around the waist and holding me up. "I guess I don't have to ask if that's him."

I shook my head.

"Here." She yanked out one of the dining room chairs. "Sit."

I did. She shoved my head between my knees, none too gently. "Now breathe."

I hated taking orders, especially from her. But I hated fainting even more, so I breathed.

A glass of water appeared between my feet. I sat up and sipped. Jessie leaned against the table reading the rest of the faxed report. She lifted her eyes.

I waited for her to ask if I was OK, if I needed to lie down, take a pill, see a doctor.

"I guess he changed his name," she said.

She was going to pretend I hadn't nearly taken a nose-dive onto her carpet. I was going to let her.

"I guess. But why? Hector died in 1977. No one would think the two were the same man."

"Why take a chance?"

"I suppose."

This explained why I hadn't been able to find him anywhere that I'd searched. He'd no doubt changed his name again.

Jessie continued to read. Her lips tightened.

"What?"

She looked at me, then back at the paper. "All of his victims have been the same type of woman."

I knew I wasn't going to like this, but I asked anyway. "What type?"

"Blond, petite."

"Hell."

Had Hector planned on killing me, too? Why hadn't he?

"Let me see that report."

"No."

"I could make you."

She snorted. "I doubt that."

Since I was still dizzy and my hands were shaking, she was probably right.

"He was a serial killer then and is a Weendigo now," she murmured, "satisfying his need for like flesh in both forms."

"But how did he become a Weendigo in the first place? Isn't that an Ojibwe warrior cursed by the great spirit?" I asked.

"The great mystery."

"Whatever. Hector was a lot of things, but Ojibwe wasn't one of them."

"I'm not sure how the whole cursed-by-a-mystery works. We'll have to ask Will."

The reminder that Cadotte wasn't back yet when he should have been caused a shadow of fear to tighten her face.

"Do you think Hector's here?" I blurted.

"We'll know soon enough."

"How?"

She lifted the photo. "I show this to my deputy. El-wood is a nosy old coot. He knows everyone in Crow Valley. If Hector is in town, Elwood's met him. We'll nail Herman/Hector's ass within a day."

I was glad she had confidence, because I didn't. I'd dealt with Hector. He was one scary dude.

And he was up to something. I just knew it.

20

"Let's go out and blast some werewolves," I said. "We'll both feel better."

"I don't think so."

"Really. You will. I promise."

I knew *I* would.

It was probably a mistake. She was worried about Will and I was worried about Hector, but we'd be together and we'd have guns. What could happen?

"We should wait," Jessie said.

I rolled my eyes. "As long as we burn the wolves, like good little *Jäger-Suchers,* everything will be OK."

She shook her head.

"I'm supposed to be training you. You're supposed to be patrolling the town. We're going to blow that off because pretty boy stopped for a few drinks and didn't ask permission?"

"Keep it up," she muttered, "I just might shoot you."

If she was back to threatening me instead of staring at her shoes and moping, I was on the right track.

"Come on. By the time we get back, Cadotte will be

home. You don't want him to know you're sitting around by the phone, do you? Have a little pride."

Her eyes narrowed; I smirked, taunting her. I'd welcome a good fistfight. I wanted my mind off Hector. Off the knowledge that he was here, somewhere, watching me.

I'd been searching for him for years. But I'd never once felt that he was near. Until now.

My scar ached and burned. Was that what he'd meant when he'd said I would never be free of him? And here I'd thought he'd only been referring to my nightmares.

"I got a package from Mandenauer," Jessie said quietly.

I forgot about hunting, about Hector. "The rogue agent file?"

She nodded and handed me a FedEx envelope. They had overnight delivery even in Shit Heel. Amazing.

"I talked to Damien. He said the gun wasn't his."

"And you believed him?"

"Yeah, I kinda did." I hesitated, glancing at the package in my hands. "Did you . . . ?"

"Of course."

"And?" I held my breath. Had Damien lied?

"I didn't recognize Fitzgerald. But then I'm not as close to him as you are."

My breath caught. How could she know? Did my forehead flash *She slept with him!* in orange neon?

"What's that supposed to mean?" I demanded.

"Never mind. Just look at the pictures, Leigh."

I upended the envelope onto the kitchen table. Several photos fell out. None of them were Damien.

"I'd better find out who lived in the cabin before he did," Jessie said.

"Couldn't hurt."

She nodded. "Hold on; I'll get my rifle."

Jessie disappeared into the bedroom. I guess we were going hunting. I couldn't very well renege when I'd just taunted her into it.

She returned with her gun and ammunition. "What if we see the white wolf?"

"Shoot first, ask questions later."

"That would be my call."

We took the squad car. While we'd been chatting, the sun had gone down and Jessie had gone on duty.

"Have you searched for their lair?" I asked.

"A little, with Mandenauer."

I should have known. One of my first lessons had been How to Find a Lair 101. Once you did, the rest was so much easier.

"We checked all the usual places," Jessie continued. "Caves, abandoned buildings, dugouts, collapsed barns. Nothing."

I remembered an earlier conversation with Will. "What about the mine?"

She glanced at me, her eyebrows lifted in surprise. "Let's find out."

We headed out of town.

"What about Elwood?" I asked.

"What about him?"

"Shouldn't you get him the picture, let him know who we're after?"

She glanced at her watch. "He's off the clock. I won't be able to get ahold of him."

"No phone?"

"He's got a phone, but he won't hear it."

"Because?"

"He turns off his hearing aid as soon as his shift ends."

Hearing aid?

I shook my head. "What if you need backup?"

"I don't want it from him. Shakiest gun in the West, remember?"

"Gee, I feel so safe and protected."

"Crow Valley hasn't had a murder since it appeared on the map."

"Somehow, I doubt that."

"Well, none that were reported anyway."

Which reminded me. "Anyone gone missing in the last few days?"

I was thinking about the black wolf—and the nine dead from the other night.

"No." She glanced at me. "It's strange. I agree. But without a report, what can I do?"

"With a report, what would you do?"

"Not much."

We'd know where the missing person had gone— straight down a werewolf gullet, but we couldn't say so. If someone was reported missing, Jessie would call headquarters. They'd make something up, ascertain that their lie held water. That's what *Jäger-Suchers* did.

"I'll show Elwood the picture of Hector in the morning," Jessie said. "He'd be no use now anyway. He gets a little . . ." she rolled her finger around her ear, "when he's tired."

Swell. Werewolves, a psychotic, cannibalistic ex-boyfriend, and a loony deputy. I loved this town.

We reached the southern outskirts. I'd never gone in this direction before. Jessie swung onto a wide dirt path. Was anything paved around here but the highway?

Thirty seconds over another "good" road she stopped. "We'd better walk in."

I nodded. If the werewolves knew we'd found their lair, they'd abandon it. We'd be back to square one.

I checked the wind, adjusted our direction. Werewolves could smell, see, and hear better than real wolves, definitely better than humans. We should stay upwind, keep quiet and out of sight.

I glanced at the sky. The moon became larger and larger with each passing night. Soon it would hang heavy and full. By then we needed to know where they went to change. We needed to even the odds as best we could. We needed to find out what they were up to.

Jessie went first, cutting through the trees, heading away from the road. I followed, just behind and to the left, keeping an eye on our back trail. You never know what might creep up on you.

I was impressed with the way she moved, avoiding sticks, dry leaves, low-hanging branches that could not only blind but also make a helluva lot of noise if they snapped.

I'd heard rumors that she'd been some hotshot deer hunter in her previous life, which must have thrilled all the manly men in Miniwa to pieces.

At least she knew how to walk through the woods with a gun. I wouldn't have to worry about getting my brains blown out. One less thing.

Jessie glanced at me, pointed ahead. I followed her finger. The entrance to the mine loomed from the night. Set into a hill, it was boarded up. Except for a single plank that hung free. By accident? Or design?

Time to find out.

Together we moved out of the cover of the trees, eyes searching the shrubbery for movement, the ground for tracks. There was nothing.

Jessie made for the entrance. I grabbed her arm and she scowled, tugged, but I shook my head. I was going in first.

I held out my hand for the flashlight that hung from her utility belt. She stuck out her tongue, but she gave me the flashlight.

I didn't have to tell her to watch the clearing, make sure we weren't trapped in here. She turned and scanned the woods, rifle ready.

Switching the heavy-duty cop flashlight to *on,* I aimed it inside the abandoned mine. No shining eyes stared back. Nothing jumped out and said, *Woof!*

So far, so good.

I squeezed through the small area left by the lapsed plank and entered the cool, damp interior. The flashlight revealed a packed earth floor, decrepit poles, and beams that had collapsed. No clothes, no shoes, no wallets or purses. Double damn.

They hadn't been here. At least not today.

The lack of a lair was beginning to disturb me nearly as much as the lack of missing persons reports. There had to be a lair somewhere. It didn't take a genius to find it, just patience and time. Neither one of which I had in abundance.

"Leigh?"

"Yeah?" I whispered. "I'm here."

"Anything?"

"Not yet."

"Hurry up," she said quietly. "This place gives me the creeps."

I had to agree, though I wasn't sure why. There was nothing out of the ordinary. Abandoned mine, middle of the forest. Deserted, dark. Big deal. As long as there weren't any werewolves out for my blood, it was a good day.

I inched farther inside, flicking the flashlight back and forth across the floor in front of me. The earth tilted downward. The air grew cooler. I kept walking—until something crunched beneath my boot.

I froze and aimed the beam onto my toe. I'd stepped on a femur. As in human leg bone.

Ugh.

There were a lot more bones scattered in a descending trail of white down the path in front of me.

"Jessie?" I called. "You'd better come see this."

She didn't waste time. In less than ten seconds she was at my side.

"Looks like you found a few missing persons."

"Looks like."

"Hell. Now what?"

"I don't know. We can find out who they are, but it'll take time and raise a ruckus."

"Ruckus? Good word."

"This makes no sense." I shook my head. "Why would they drag their kills here? They've never cared before who they killed or where they left them."

"They've never eaten one another before, either."

"Good point."

"No body, no proof," Jessie murmured. "If they kill transients, hide what's left when they're through, no one's the wiser. They could keep hunting until they clean out the town. Except that might be suspicious."

"Wouldn't it, though?" I shook my head. "This makes no sense. A werewolf is smart, but it's a werewolf. People are food. Any people. I just can't see them picking and choosing like they're at a buffet line. Can you?"

"I don't know. You're the expert."

I was, and I was stumped.

"This *could* be their lair. If we set up outside, waited awhile, we should be able to pick off a few."

"Won't they smell us?"

"Maybe. Depends which way they approach." I shrugged. "I don't know what else to do."

"Can't hurt to try."

I agreed and we headed for the entrance.

"I hate to leave them here like this." Jessie glanced back at the trail of bones.

"They won't know."

"I will."

I understood her unease. Humans buried their dead—in a nice cemetery. Or kept their remains in a pretty urn on the mantel. They did not leave their werewolf-gnawed bones in an abandoned mine forever. And we wouldn't, either.

"When this is over, Edward will send in a team," I said. "They'll identify everyone, and if they have any family, they'll be notified."

And lied to, my mind mocked.

"If they had any family, I doubt they'd be in here. It's sad, don't you think? Disappearing and no one even knows that you're gone."

I kind of thought it was nice. No one to mourn. No one to cry. No one to wish that they'd died, too.

"You know we have to leave them here, Jessie," I said quietly. "Dragging them out will alert the werewolves. Letting the world know that there's a pile of human bones in Crow Valley will end any hope we have of finding out what's going on and stopping it."

"I know. But I don't have to like it."

She stalked ahead of me and I let her go. I shouldn't have.

"Oomph," was all she said when the wolf leaped through the entrance and hit her in the chest.

The animal went straight for her throat, no fooling around. An excellent clue that this was a werewolf. Wolves just don't attack people. It's against their nature. Werewolves, however, are unnatural from the get-go.

The beast snarled and snapped, lunging with all he had as he tried to end Jessie's life. He was seriously pissed. I suppose we'd stepped on sacred ground or something. Who knows with them?

Jessie was quick, and she'd dealt with werewolves before. She grabbed his neck and levered the snapping jaws away from her skin.

I shot him in the head. Fire blazed through the cavern, highlighting Jessie's pale, shocked, blood-spattered face.

She heaved the wolf to the ground and rolled away. I stepped past them both and glanced outside. He'd been alone. At least for now.

I hurried back, grabbed her elbow, and tugged. "Let's go."

She got up, retrieved her rifle, which had flown into a corner when he hit her, then followed me out of the mine.

"You OK?" I asked.

Jessie nodded. A quick glance at her hands revealed red streaks on her palms but at least no blistering burns from the exploding werewolf.

"Back to your place."

"We were going to hunt."

"I think we already did."

"But—"

"Forget it, Jessie. We can come back, but I have a feeling they're on to us."

Since a werewolf and not a person had attacked, I didn't think the mine was where they went to change. I'd found no evidence of that—no clothes, no shoes, no underwear.

The mine might not be their lair, but it was something. I'd have to ask Edward just what.

Jessie could walk, even talk. But she was pale, brain

spattered, and her hands clenched the rifle too tightly. I made her go first. I didn't trust those hands on that gun behind my back right now. Accidents might happen, but I didn't plan on letting them happen to me. At least not here, not now.

We reached the car, and I slid into the driver's seat. Jessie didn't argue. But when I started the engine, she suddenly reached over and switched it off.

Her expression was as serious as I'd ever seen it. Her eyes huge, pupils dilated, her face was ghostly white beneath the drying blood.

"If I'm ever bitten," she said, "shoot me."

"Jessie—"

She grabbed me by the throat, squeezed my windpipe just enough to shut me up. My fingers circled her wrists. I tried to break her hold, but she was strong and a little bit crazed.

"I don't want to be one of those things. And Will . . ." She cursed and let me go.

I thought it was mighty big of me not to beat her silly. Instead I rubbed my throat and let her talk.

"Will would say it didn't matter. That he loves me no matter what I am."

"He would."

"I know. I loved him, too, even when I thought he was one of them."

I didn't get that. However, now was not the time to bring it up.

"I should have shot him, but I couldn't."

"Lucky you didn't, since he wasn't."

"Shut the hell up," she said, though there wasn't much heat behind her words. "I know he'll never do it. I probably couldn't off myself either. I wouldn't want to leave him."

"You'd rather turn furry, howl at the moon, and eat raw people than leave him."

She stared me straight in the eye and said, "Yes."

"Fine. You get bitten, I blow your head off." I held out my hand.

"With silver."

I shrugged. "Goes without saying."

She put her palm against mine. "I'll do the same for you."

I guess that made us lifelong pals.

21

We remained quiet all the way home. I don't know what *she* was thinking, but my thoughts were full of what would happen if one of us got furry.

Would I be able to shoot her as she'd asked me to? Yes.

Would she be able to shoot me? It didn't really matter, because I'd be able to shoot myself.

Jessie let us into her apartment. She went straight to the message machine in the kitchen.

"You have no new messages."

Her sigh of disappointment plucked at something too near my heart. I'd been in love once. I'd lost him, badly. I understood where she was coming from.

Will wasn't back yet; he hadn't called, and she was even more worried.

I glanced at my watch. Three A.M. Not good. I was starting to worry myself.

"Take a shower," I told her.

"Kiss my ass."

She's baaack, my mind taunted. I'd been waiting for Jessie to snap out of her zone. It figured that she'd do so cursing me.

"I'll pass," I returned, "but thanks anyway."

"I don't want to take a shower," she said mulishly. "I'm still on duty."

"And I bet the people you've vowed to serve and protect will be thrilled with your new look. Blood and werewolf brains are such a fashion statement."

"Do you have to be right all the time?" She stomped into the bathroom.

"That was a rhetorical question, right?"

She slammed the door in my face.

I opened her refrigerator and helped myself to a can of soda. Then I sat on the couch and I considered what we'd learned.

Not much.

We still didn't know where their lair was, and I had no idea what they were up to, hiding human bones in the mine.

Hector was here. I was certain of it. But what was he planning? And how was the brown wolf involved? What about the power eater legend Will had been mumbling about? I had to think we were hip deep in something serious.

A tap on the windowpane made me jump so high I nearly levitated. I spun around, gun in my hand, and came face to beak with a crow on the windowsill.

The thing tilted his head, first one way, then the other, as if trying to figure out what I was.

"Take off." I set my gun next to my cola, then made a shooing motion, to no avail.

Caw, he returned, then stretched out and tapped the glass again.

I was so preoccupied with the damn bird, I didn't notice the scratching at the door until it was too late. The lock clicked free.

I've been set up, I thought.

Crows and wolves work together in nature. Who's to say they don't work together unnaturally, too. Had the pesky bird drawn my attention away from the door long enough for one of the bad guys to get inside?

I sprinted across the room, pressed my back against the wall, waited for the intruder to show himself.

He did, and I jumped him. In a quick, professional movement, he flipped me onto my back, hard, then pressed a knee into my chest.

"Oh, hi, Leigh."

Cadotte was back.

He stood, then held out a hand to help me up. I couldn't breathe.

"You OK?"

I shook my head.

The bathroom door opened. "Leigh?"

Cadotte's face lit up from the inside out. He left me on the ground to die and ran to Jessie.

"Will," she whispered; then she slugged him.

"Ow." He rubbed his stomach. "What the hell was that for?"

She grabbed his cell phone from his belt and waved it in front of his nose. "Turn it on once in a while, dick weed. You scared me to death."

Jessie tossed the phone upward. He snatched it from thin air as she stalked past him and into the living room. Observing me on the floor, she smirked. "Did he flip you?"

I nodded.

"He thinks he's Jackie Chan."

Right now, I kind of thought he was, too.

Jessie spun toward Will. "Where's my gun?"

"In the trunk of my car."

"Fat lot of good it's going to do you there."

"Getting stopped with a loaded firearm would not be healthy, Jess."

I managed to get off the floor under my own power; then I collapsed in a chair. "Why not?"

Will pointed a finger toward his face. "Indian. Gun. Too many cowboys."

"I still don't get it."

Jessie made an impatient sound. "The civil rights movement hasn't gotten here yet. There's still a lot of prejudice against Native Americans."

"A loaded gun in the car *is* illegal," I pointed out.

"True. But there'd be a whole lot more than arresting going on if Will was stopped with one." She glanced at him. "Sorry. I wasn't thinking past your being safe from the werewolves."

He shrugged. "I'm fine. But why are you home, in the middle of your shift, wearing a towel?"

Jessie gave me a narrow-eyed glare, which I took to mean, Shut up. So I did.

"Never mind me," she said. "Where have you been?"

"Madison."

"You were supposed to be back eight hours ago."

He shrugged, his face sheepish. "I got distracted."

Neither one of them paid any attention to me.

"What was it this time?" Jessie asked.

I waited to hear what his vice was—drinking, drugs, gambling. Considering Jessie's short fuse, I doubted it was women.

"The book was ancient, Jess. Written practically on papyrus. You should have seen it." His face went all dreamy. "Remarkable."

She rolled her eyes, shook her head, then looked at me with a shrug. I tried not to laugh.

Cadotte's vice was books.

"Never mind that, Slick. What did it *say*?"

"Right." He pulled his glasses out of his shirt pocket and a sheaf of papers out of his pants. "I had to write all this down. They wouldn't even let me use the copy machine. Can't blame them. Who knows what artificial light would do to something so old?"

"Steady, boy." Jessie put a hand on his shoulder. "Don't start mumbling and drooling on me now. I need that info."

He nodded, shuffled papers, shoved his glasses up his nose in an absent gesture that made Jessie's face soften and her fingers tighten on his arm. "From what I can gather, the power eater is an obscure legend—"

"Again?" Jessie said drily.

He lifted his gaze from his notes and winked. "Stick with me, kid; I've got a million."

"The wolf god was an obscure legend, too." Jessie faced me. "You know how well that went."

Will held up one finger. "But I know the whole legend this time. No missing pages."

"Then get on with it."

"A Weendigo becomes a power eater by eating power."

"Hence the name," Jessie drawled.

"Let him finish," I snapped.

She shot me a glare, but she closed her mouth.

"Werewolves are very powerful," Will continued. "Taking their life destroys the power forever unless—"

"They eat it," I guessed. "By eating the werewolf."

He nodded, then stared at his precious papers some more. "A human becomes a beast, a Weendigo, by practicing cannibalism, then being cursed. A Weendigo becomes a power eater by being a cannibal—of a different sort."

"Could a non-Ojibwe become a Weendigo?" I asked, remembering my earlier question in regard to Hector.

"Of course. *Weendigo* is an Ojibwe term for 'werewolf.' A general word, not necessarily race specific."

"Uh-oh."

"What?" he asked.

Will didn't know about our Hector theory yet. I waved his question off for now.

"You said the first Weendigo was cursed by the great mystery. What about the ones since then? How did they get to be the way they are?"

He glanced at Jessie, frowned. "I thought Mengele—"

"Yeah, yeah," I interrupted. "But not every werewolf was created by him. Obviously, since the Weendigo legend predates the rise of the Reich and all the subsequent good times."

"True." He shuffled his papers again, found one, began to read. "Humans who develop a taste for human flesh are cursed. They become the beast that lives within them."

"How?"

He shrugged. "*Poof!* They're a beast."

Well, stranger things had happened.

"What does the blood moon have to do with any of this?"

"That's where it gets fascinating."

"I bet," Jessie muttered.

He ignored her and so did I. "Beginning on the night of the harvest moon the Weendigo hunts his own. He eats their power, night by night, gaining strength and ability, until the eve of the blood moon, the hunter's moon, when the power eater becomes the supreme alpha."

"Yada yada," I said. "So what?"

Will's lips twitched. He really was a nice guy. Most people would be sick of my mouth by now. But then look who he was in love with.

"The power eater is the ultimate werewolf. A shape-shifter beyond anything the world has ever known." He lowered his notes and stared at Jessie, then me, in turn. Any trace of amusement was gone. "The power eater can do anything."

"He's already a shape-shifter; what more is there?"

"I don't know."

"Thought you knew everything."

"Everything there is to know from the book. Unfortunately, it was a little vague on the specifics."

More like a lot, but what can you do?

"The ultimate werewolf," I murmured.

As if we didn't have enough problems with the regular ones.

"What, exactly, is a supreme alpha?" Jessie asked.

"I think that means he's in charge of all the other werewolves."

"Let me guess," she continued. "They're his army. He's the head man-wolf. He gets to rule the world."

"Appears that way."

"What *is* it with wanting to rule the world?"

"Got me." Will shrugged. "Sounds like a pretty lousy job."

I had to agree. "How does the power eater become the supreme alpha?"

"By eating the power of a hundred werewolves before the hunter's moon."

"Yuck."

"You asked."

"What should we do?"

Jessie was staring at me. I was kind of surprised. But then again, I was supposed to be in charge.

"Kill them," I said. "Kill them all."

22

I waited for Will to argue, but he didn't.

"The fewer werewolves for the Weendigo to kill and eat," he said, "the less power he accumulates."

"And if he doesn't have a hundred by the night of the blood moon, I'd say he's screwed." I glanced at Jessie.

"Works for me," she said.

I glanced at the window. The sun was coming up. "Too late today. But tonight—"

Jessie nodded. "Tonight we have some fun."

Neither one of us noticed Will going into the bathroom, but we saw him come out. He held Jessie's blood-spattered uniform in his hands.

"What the hell is this?"

We exchanged glances. I shrugged. He was all hers.

"What does it look like?" Jessie headed for her bedroom. I assumed to get dressed. I know I never like to argue while wearing a towel.

Will followed her. "What happened?"

"Relax, Slick; it's not my blood."

"I'm so relieved."

He didn't sound relieved. He sounded pissed.

I retrieved my gun and slipped out the door.

I didn't want to listen to them argue. I definitely didn't want to be around when they made up. Just the thought made my body remember what I'd been doing with Damien about twenty-four hours ago. I wanted to do it again.

That I couldn't only made me want to more.

I drove home as daylight burst over the horizon. I enjoyed sunrise, the end of night. All the dangerous beings with fangs gone to sleep or returned to human form. What wasn't to like?

For the first time I could remember, I pulled into an empty parking lot. Where was everyone?

I climbed out of the car, taking my guns along. Upstairs I set the weapons on the table, took a quick look-see around my apartment. Didn't appear that anyone had been in here lately, except for me. I considered taking a shower and climbing into bed. Then I heard the music.

The notes flew on the early-morning breeze and shot through my window. Not jazz for a change, but a hoof-stomping country tune. Toby Keith singing about the red, white, and blue. I loved that song.

I loved country music. I liked the slow ones and the fast. I liked the easy southern cadence of the words and the long-drawn-out stories they told.

Who was playing country music in an empty bar? Only one way to find out. I went downstairs.

The door was open. I stepped inside.

Half-afraid I'd find Cowboy, I wasn't any happier to see Damien. Well, who had I expected? Elvis?

A huge boom box perched on a table, a stack of CDs at its side. Damien swept the floor with his back to me. I tried to inch out, but he straightened. "Wait."

Toby was informing the world we'd put a boot in their

ass; it was the American way. You can see why I like him. He's a man after my own heart.

"I . . . can't." I kept moving backward. He turned. The anguish on his face stopped me in my tracks. "What's wrong?"

He shook his head. "Nothing. You're right. You should go."

I should, but now I couldn't. He was upset. Seriously upset. I'd planned to avoid him, as best I could living in his front yard. I'd definitely decided we shouldn't be alone together. I knew what would happen if he came anywhere near me. I had no self-control around him. I'd already proven that.

But he was hurting, badly. I couldn't just run upstairs and go to bed. Even if he did turn down the music.

I inched closer. Toby wanted to talk about me, I, number one. I wanted to talk about Damien.

"Bad night?" I murmured.

He shrugged and returned to sweeping, though the floor seemed pretty damn clean to me.

"Not really. I accomplished what I set out to."

I frowned. "What? Selling more whiskey than rye?"

"No, more beer than tequila."

I couldn't tell if he was joking or not.

"Why are you still here?" I asked.

"Nothing better to do."

Damien and I had a lot more in common than I cared for.

He glanced up. "Where did you take off to in such a hurry before?"

I'd torn out of here after Jessie's call, which had followed my horrible daymare. Just the memory of it made me cold and clammy.

"I had to meet the sheriff."

The truth. Wow. I could tell it.

The music changed. Toby was done and a sweet, swaying ballad began. Trisha Yearwood wondered how she could live without him. How would she ever survive?

I used to love this song as well. Until it hit too close to home.

Suddenly Damien stood directly in front of me, without his broom. He was close, invading my space. I took a step back and stumbled over my own two feet.

His hand snaked out; his arm pressed against my spine. Now I couldn't breathe along with Trisha.

"Damien—" I began.

"Dance with me," he whispered. "Just once."

I could have refused, should have. But he smelled so good—like wind and trees and summertime, with a hint of tobacco that should have been unpleasant but was, instead, tempting.

His skin was warm, his breath balmy against my cheek. When he touched me like this I remembered everything that had happened between us. It had been sex, not love, but I could pretend, and right now I needed to.

I melted against him and we began to move with the music. He was a good dancer, unusual in a man his age.

My grandfather had shown me the waltz, the polka, the fox-trot. No one knew how to dance like a civilized human being anymore. Except Damien. Someone had taught him, just like my grandfather had taught me.

The music swelled, seemed to both surround and fill me. My feet moved next to his in perfect rhythm. As I laid my head on his chest, he pressed his cheek to my hair.

I hadn't realized how lonely I was. My life was full. Of death, sure, but that's the way I wanted it. I didn't have time to miss all I'd lost. Not much anyway. Whenever I did, I moved to another town, shot a dozen more werewolves, and refused to listen to the sobbing little girl inside of me who missed her mama. I was heap big were-wolf hunter; I didn't get to cry. So why did I want to?

Because here, in Crow Valley, I had caught a glimpse of what I lacked. Not only friendship but also companionship, love, sex, anything that made life worth living, except killing—which made me one sick cookie. And I called Hector psychotic.

I was being tempted back to another world, and I wasn't sure I could live in it. Seeing Jessie and Will, so in love, holding Damien close, so sexy and . . . aroused.

I stiffened, but he tightened his arms and wouldn't let me go.

"Please," he whispered. "Don't leave me yet."

A thick, warm feeling settled just below my heart. I didn't want to leave. Not him. Not yet.

It was daytime. The werewolves were human again. We were safe—for a little while. And I needed him now. Even more than I'd needed him yesterday.

I lifted my head. He was watching me with an indecipherable expression on his face. I wasn't sure what he was thinking. Was I ever?

A new song began—a boot-stompin' two-step. We continued to slow dance as Trisha informed us that her lover could smile like an angel, lie like a rug.

"Too bad you're no good," I murmured.

Damien's lips lifted in the closest thing to a smile I'd ever seen on his face. Was that an omen?

Suddenly he twirled me out, then yanked me back and started a fancy double-step I was barely able to follow. By the time the song ended I was breathing heavily and laughing. Damien stared at me with an odd expression.

"What?"

"I've never seen you laugh like that."

I quit. I had no right to laugh, to smile, or to be happy.

He touched the corner of my mouth with his fingertip. "Don't stop."

I shuddered, fighting the urge to capture his finger in my mouth and nibble. What was the matter with me?

Jimmy and I had had sex, and it had been good. Hector hadn't been bad, either. Well, what did I expect, fucking the Devil?

But Damien . . . Everything about him exuded sexuality. I couldn't be in the same room with him and not want him—even before I'd had him. Now that I knew what lay beneath those black clothes, I had a hard time remembering why never again had seemed like a good idea.

His finger skimmed my jaw, feathered down my neck, slid along my collarbone.

"Damien—"

"I never should have touched you."

The pain in his voice, on his face, made me go silent.

"It was a mistake. But I can't help wanting you again." His hands closed around my upper arms; the grip was just short of painful. "I don't care if it's wrong."

He let his head fall forward until our foreheads touched. His hair sifted over my face and I caught the scent of the trees.

"I don't care if you shoot me." His breath tickled the corner of my eye as his hands gentled, and his thumbs stroked the soft, sensitive skin at the inside of my arm. "I don't care about much of anything right now except being inside you."

Suddenly I didn't care about anything else, either.

I tilted my head, brushing my lips across his. My tongue flicked out, teasing, taunting, tormenting.

He tensed. "Leigh."

I loved how he said my name. Softly, almost reverently, as if the word were torn from somewhere deep within him.

I didn't want to wait. I didn't want to think. I raised on tiptoe, leaning into him, my fingers busy with the buttons of his shirt, my palms spreading across his chest, satisfying my desire for warmth, strength, sensation.

I needed to feel alive, and in the past two years I hadn't. Not until I'd met him. As he'd said, it was wrong, but right now I didn't care.

I wanted to feel his life in me, and I knew exactly how.

Replacing my hands with my mouth, I kissed his smooth chest, traced my teeth across his belly, laved a circle around his navel. By the time I reached his waist, I'd unhooked his pants. They slid to the floor just ahead of me.

"Leigh?"

He came back to himself long enough to reach for me. I batted his hands away and took him in my mouth.

I'd never gone down on anyone before, not that I hadn't heard all about it. I'd been to college.

He was smooth, hot, and hard. I rolled my tongue over his tip. He tasted like the earth, the wind, the water. I scraped my teeth gently across his skin.

His hands on my head, his fingers threaded through my hair, and he showed me the rhythm. Moaning, he thrust into my mouth, faster and faster. I was so excited, I was afraid I'd be too rough. But that didn't seem to be a problem.

He pulled me away and I struggled to take him back. "Leigh, wait; we should—"

I licked him. His breath hissed in, sharp and quick. He glared at me. "Let's go up to your room."

There was no way I could wait that long. I tugged on his hand until he knelt next to me; then I leaned over and nipped his lip.

"Now," I whispered. "Here."

"Here?"

"You just cleaned the floor, didn't you?"

I startled a laugh out of him. The sound caused my belly to tighten with a hunger that had nothing to do with food. Laughing, he was more beautiful than ever before.

I had to have him.

Now. Here.

I yanked off my shirt, then tore at the rest of my clothes. He didn't help. Instead he watched. Having his sober hazel eyes drift over me in appreciation was nearly as arousing as the touch of his lips and his hands.

Nearly. When he bent and flicked a nipple with his tongue my legs wobbled and I clung to him.

"I can't wait," I panted.

He moved away, yanking protection from his pants—did he have a spare condom everywhere?—then lying back on the floor.

"Come here." He held out his arms.

I shook my head. "Why don't you—?"

"You're not lying on the floor. Not with me. Not ever. Come here," he repeated.

From the determination on his face, if I wanted him, I could have him. But only like this. Who was I to argue?

I straddled him, took him deep inside. His hands on my hips, he guided me. We were both so close to the edge, it didn't take long. I watched his face as he came. For an instant I wanted to touch his cheek and kiss the lids of his sad, sad eyes. But I knew better.

Then my own release took me, hard and fast, a near-painful explosion that left me gasping.

When I came back to myself I was draped all over

Damien, his body still buried deep within. But that wasn't the intimacy that made my heart lurch, then thunder.

No, it was the way he ran his long, clever fingers up and down my back.

23

"Don't," I said.

I tried to get up, but Damien held on. He was taller than me and a whole lot stronger. Besides, it was hard to fight someone while buck naked and sexually languid. Though my head said run, my body said walk, or perhaps lie here and do it again.

"Let me go."

"No."

He continued to rub my back. Fingers drifting along my scar, thumbs sliding against my spine. One movement relaxed me; the other made me want to jump out of my skin.

"Why are you embarrassed by this?" he murmured.

I didn't answer, couldn't speak. My eyes burned and my throat went tight. The scar would forever remind me that I had been the one to bring disaster down on everyone I loved.

It was fitting that Hector had made me as ugly outside as I was inside. What kind of woman slept with one man when she was engaged to another?

That was a rhetorical question. I can spell slut as well as the next guy.

When I got up, Damien let me go. When I went to get my clothes, he followed. I tensed, expecting him to touch me again. Instead, he kissed me—right on my scar.

I spun around and slapped him. The sound of the blow was crisp in the silence of the early morning. A red slash rose on the pale skin of his cheek.

"I'm sorry," I whispered, horrified that I'd struck him.

He ignored my apology, ignored what I'd done, what I'd said, to take me in his arms and lay his palms all over my back again.

"Do you think this makes you ugly?"

"I don't need a scar for that."

His eyebrows lifted and he tilted his head.

I pulled out of his embrace. I'd said too much. I had to get out of here before I blabbed every secret in my head.

I put on my pants, reached for my shirt, and his fingers circled my wrist. "Leigh, talk to me. I'd like to understand."

His gentle voice did me in. Tears seeped from my eyes. I had to make them stop. Big, bad werewolf hunters did not cry. Petite, blond girlie-girls did. They also got their families murdered before their eyes while powerless to do anything about it. I was no longer that girl; I was the hunter.

I tore away from his touch, threw on my shirt, and ran out of the bar, then up the stairs.

Once in my room I shut and locked the door. I was alone. I should be happy. Instead, the sadness, the loneliness, pressed at me.

I needed to see Jimmy. To remember what it had felt like to love and then lose him.

"I can't live through that again," I whispered.

I was tearing through my suitcase, tossing clothes onto the floor, desperate to find the only snapshot I'd kept of him, when the door behind me clicked open.

I spun around. Damien stood in the doorway. There was a key in the lock.

"You can't just come in here."

My brave words would have sounded better without the tears on my face and the wobble in my voice.

He removed the key, tucked it into his pocket, and closed the door.

"Talk to me," he repeated.

"I can't."

He was half-naked again—loose black pants, no shirt, no shoes. He'd get very little service here.

"You think you're ugly because of a scar. You don't know what ugly is."

Actually, I did. I'd been killing it for two years now. But I couldn't share that with him any more than I could share anything else.

"There's such ugliness in this world, Leigh. So much sadness, so much loneliness. I've seen some pretty awful things, moving around like I do. Met some truly ugly people."

He thought I was upset because I was maimed. I was, but not because of the mark, because of what it represented. Hector was coming back for me. It was only a matter of time. And if Damien was in his way, he'd end up just like Jimmy.

"This can't happen again," I blurted.

Only a foot away, he reached out and yanked me against him. Shocked, I let him.

He kissed me—mouth open, tongue searching, teeth clashing.

Lifting his head, he murmured, "You mean that?"

"Y-y-yes."

"Maybe it can't, but it will. You know it, and I know it. I can't stop touching you. You can't stop wanting me to."

I'd have accused him of being arrogant if he hadn't been right. Which only made me more panicked. More frightened. More desperate.

"No." I shoved him away with both hands to his chest. He barely moved.

Grabbing my forearms, he dragged me onto my tiptoes. With my feet off the ground and my hands captured I could do nothing but stare at him.

"Yes," he insisted, and his eyes deepened from hazel to brown. "You want this to be just sex? Fine. It's just sex. If that's all you can give me, then that's what I'll take."

He licked a tear from my cheek. I shuddered as my body cried out for his. "Damien—"

He kissed me again. This time I struggled. He was right. I wanted him beyond all reason, and that terrified me.

The door crashed open. Suddenly Damien was gone. I stumbled and nearly fell. Then I could only watch as Will socked Damien in the jaw.

I opened my mouth to shout, "No," but Damien's fist shot out almost too fast to see. It was certainly too fast to avoid. Will's chin snapped back.

The two shook their heads like dogs who'd been doused in water, then circled each other.

I took a step forward just as Will did some fancy Oriental round kick. Damien caught Will's foot right before it connected with his nose. I blinked, impressed. Then Damien shoved and Will tumbled to the floor.

I grabbed Damien's arm. He shook me off. His face was set, his eyes wild. This was not good.

Will flipped from his back onto his feet in a lithe gymnastic movement. He jabbed, feinted, and knocked Damien's legs out from under him.

Damien went down hard. Will advanced, lip raised in a semisnarl. What was the matter with these guys? They were no better than animals. I jumped on Will's back.

"Stop," I panted.

Will kept going, and I cocked my arm around his throat, tightened just a little. He choked and froze, giving Damien a chance to get to his feet. He appeared extremely pissed.

Jessie chose that moment to walk in my door. "What the—?"

She yanked me off the boyfriend by my hair—a neat trick, considering the length of it.

I'd known we'd go round and round; I just hadn't expected it to be like this. We were adults, law enforcement officials, comrades in arms. We shouldn't be screeching and scratching and fighting like girls. But we were.

I was angry—at myself, the world, you name it. She was pretty mad, too. I guess I couldn't blame her. She'd seen me jump on her boyfriend and try to choke him. What did I expect? A present?

What I got was a scratched cheek, a bruised wrist, and a kick in the shin. The last really hurt.

"Bitch!" I snarled, and I went for her eyes with my thumbs. Someone hauled me back.

Jessie came after me with her hands crooked into claws. Will caught her around the waist. The two of them crashed to the floor and rolled around.

I was having enough trouble of my own. An iron band was choking off my air. I glanced down and recognized Damien's arm. He was holding me off the ground. I was kicking him in the knee.

"Relax, Leigh. Calm down."

"Easy for you to say," I wheezed.

He kissed my neck, just below my ear. "Hush," he whispered, and amazingly, I wanted to.

I went limp in his arms and he set my feet back on the floor.

"Let me go," I demanded.

"I don't think so."

He kept his arm around my waist, though he loosened his grip so I could breathe. My entire back was pressed to his front, and he appeared awful glad to see me. No wonder he didn't want to let me go. In those pants of his, everyone would know how very much he liked me.

Jessie was still cursing, so Will sat on her. "Jeez, Jess, if you're gonna have a catfight, at least tear off some clothes, fall in a lake."

"Find a vat of Jell-O," Damien muttered.

Will glanced at him and smirked. "Exactly. Make it worth our while."

I frowned. The two of them had been bent on killing each other only moments before; now they were pals?

Jessie and I exchanged glances. "Men," we said at the same time, with the same disgusted inflection.

They ignored us.

"I take it you know Leigh," Will said.

"And you appear on good terms with the sheriff."

"I thought you were hurting her," Will explained.

"We were having a minor disagreement. I appreciate your taking care of her."

"Her is right here," I growled. "And she can take care of herself."

"Of course she can," Damien said easily, and released me.

I spun around with narrowed eyes. His words had

sounded suspiciously patronizing. The red mark on his jaw made all the fight drain out of me. I wanted to touch him, to hold him. Behavior from days gone by when I'd been a nurturer and a caregiver. I was neither any longer, so I tucked my hands into my pockets and turned away.

Jessie tried to throw Will off her back but had no luck. "Get off me, Cadotte; you weigh a ton."

"You promise to play nice?"

"Hell, no."

"That's what I thought."

He got off her anyway.

Jessie bounced to her feet and sent me a glare. I raised my hands. "I surrender."

"Good. I don't want to give the two of them any more stiffies." She lowered her gaze to Damien's pants. "Although he doesn't seem to need any help." Her eyes flicked to me. "What have you been up to?"

"Jess, mind your own business," Will said.

"She *is* my business."

"You wish."

Jessie ignored me. "Who the hell *are* you, Fitzgerald? Where did you come from?"

"Around."

"You're working for cash. That's illegal."

Damien held out his wrists. "Arrest me."

Jessie's lips tightened. "Maybe later."

He turned his attention to me. "You had her check me out?"

I shrugged. "Better safe than sorry."

"And what did you find?"

"Not one damn thing," Jessie interjected. "No one's that perfect. You've got secrets, Fitzgerald, and I want to know what they are."

"Get in line," he muttered.

The room went silent. Jessie glared at Damien. I glared at Jessie. Damien glared at me. Will was the only one who didn't seem upset. Anymore.

"So where did you study?" Will asked.

Damien blinked and turned to him. "Study what?"

"Self-defense."

"The school of hard knocks."

"You've never had formal training?" Will appeared shocked. "I've been doing tai chi for quite a few years. You're as quick as anyone I've ever seen."

"Thanks."

Damien didn't elaborate. Another little secret to add to the pile. I couldn't throw stones. I wasn't going to tell him about my past, either.

"What are you two doing here?" I asked.

The last time I'd seen them they'd been fighting. Right about now they should be . . . making up.

"I had a call from Elwood," Jessie said.

For a minute I had no idea who she was talking about. Then I remembered Elwood was the deputy. Jessie had given him the picture of Hector. If Elwood had called, then—

The blood drained from my face and I swayed.

"Leigh!" Damien caught me, but I shoved him away.

"I'm all right."

Jessie and Will were staring at me as if I'd sprouted two heads. "What's the matter with you?" she demanded. "We need to check out a new wolf kill. I can't have you puking in the bushes on the way."

"Wolf kill?" I said faintly.

"Yes. Elwood came across—" She broke off and glanced at Damien. "You mind?"

"Uh . . . no. Sure." He squeezed my shoulders. "I've

got to get some sleep." He kissed my forehead and I resisted the urge to cling. "I'll see you later."

The sound of his footsteps clattering down the steps receded far too quickly. Why I suddenly associated Damien with safety I wasn't sure, but I needed to stop. The only person I could depend on was myself—and maybe Edward.

"Elwood didn't recognize Hector?" I blurted.

"What?" Jessie had been scowling at the door. "Oh, that's why you went white. I haven't shown him the picture yet. I was going to when we reached the site."

Will sighed. "Sorry, Leigh. Jess gets focused on one thing, to the exclusion of all else. She didn't mean to scare you."

Obviously Jessie had told Will about Hector. Or at least as much as she knew.

"I can apologize for myself." Jessie glanced at me. "I wasn't thinking."

I shrugged. It wasn't her fault I was crippled by the thought of Hector Menendez anywhere near me.

"You think this guy could be the one we're looking for?" Will asked.

"I don't know."

"Who else could it be?" Jessie demanded. "Herman is Hector. He's a cannibalistic serial killer. Hector is the white wolf."

"I don't know if the white wolf I saw was Hector. I never got close enough to see this one's eyes. Besides, I've seen white wolves before when they weren't really there." I frowned. "Just not lately."

"He's here," Jessie said.

"But—"

"No buts. He's here somewhere. We're going to find him and cut out the bastard's heart."

"She likes you," Will murmured. "I can tell."

Jessie gave him a narrow-eyed glare before returning her attention to me. "You're not crazy, Leigh, not anymore."

I wished I could be as certain of that as she was.

24

Though Jessie's belief in me helped, I still had doubts about my sanity. Maybe I always would. But until I was sitting in the corner talking to myself again, I had a job to do.

"Where are these dead wolves?" I asked.

"Close. You ready?"

I nodded.

I was tired. I'd been up all night. But time was growing short. Less than a week until the hunter's moon, and the tally of dead wolves was growing. There was no way to know how many the power eater had already killed and consumed. We could be fighting a losing battle. Hell, we probably were.

But I couldn't give up. I doubted Jessie could, either. Giving up wasn't in either one of us.

I followed her down the steps, Will at my heels. There was no sign of Damien anywhere. I glanced toward his cabin, but the curtains were drawn.

"Sorry I kicked you," Jessie said.

"I shouldn't have scratched."

"I pulled your hair."

"The biting was uncalled-for."

"Stop," Will said. "I'm getting excited again."

Jessie and I rolled our eyes; then we laughed and she slapped me on the back. All was forgiven.

"Women," Will muttered.

The three of us headed into the woods. Cadotte lagged behind.

"Don't worry about him," Jessie said. "He's in the zone. Trying to figure this out."

"Won't he get lost?"

"Nah. He's not that easy to get rid of."

"I heard that!" Will called.

Jessie grinned. I wanted what they had so badly, I could taste the longing at the back of my tongue—an unpleasant flavor like ashes mixed with lemon juice.

"You know what you're doing?" she asked.

"Following you."

"I meant with Fitzgerald."

"Not a clue," I admitted.

"Sex is one thing, Leigh, but . . ."

"But what?"

"Attachments." She shrugged. "You can't have them if you're going to be a *Jäger-Sucher*."

I flipped her off, but I knew she was right.

"He could be anyone, Leigh. Anything."

"It's just sex," I assured her.

"Any good?"

"Oh, yeah."

"I figured. He looks like he knows what he's doing."

I glanced behind us. Will had stopped a hundred feet back and was staring up at the sky. "Cadotte doesn't seem like any slouch in that department."

Although right now he appeared to be a prime candidate for Forrest Gump of the year.

Jessie's smile became secret. "He's not. He also isn't a werewolf."

"Neither is Damien. Ring, remember?"

"Super-duper shape-shifter, remember? For all we know, silver don't mean shit anymore."

I stopped dead on the path. Jessie did the same.

"Hadn't thought of that, had you?"

I hadn't. *Damn.*

"Come on." Jessie tugged on my arm. I followed obediently. "I called the tavern owner again."

"And?"

"The bartender who worked there before Fitzgerald, Abel Smith, lived in the cabin. He took off one night and never came back."

"There seems to be a lot of that going around."

"I'll say. I ran Abel's name. Got nothing. Mandenauer never heard of him, either."

"What does that mean?"

"I have no idea. Abel could have left the gun—or anyone before him. Who knows? Your good pal Damien might even be lying."

She was right. We were no further along than we'd been before.

The two of us walked in silence for a minute; then Jessie cast a quick sidelong worried glance my way. "When I fell in love with Will I wasn't sure who or what he was."

"How could you do that?"

"You've seen him. I was a goner the first time he said my name."

"What if he'd turned out to be a werewolf? Would you have killed him?"

She hesitated, then shook her head. "I'd have protected him. I'd have done whatever I had to do to find a cure."

"Cure?" I snorted. "Right. That's been going well so far."

I thought of all the years there'd been werewolves— too many to count. I thought of the genetically engineered ones, as well as the Weendigos, cursed by the great mystery. Those were just the werewolves we'd encountered. Who knew what lived out there in the night?

There were plenty of legends and beasts but no cures. Elise Hanover had devoted her life to the project, and as far as I knew she'd gotten nowhere fast.

"I loved him," Jessie said quietly. "I'd never loved anyone before."

"I have. And a werewolf killed him. I can't forget that."

"No?"

"Should I?"

"Maybe. I don't know."

"Maybe? The answer is no. Hector murdered my father, my mother, my sister, my brother, and my fiancé. You know why? Because I slept with him and that made me his. I tried to break it off, but he only wanted me more."

I'd never told anyone that. I held my breath, waited for the recriminations. Instead, Jessie shrugged. "Some guys are like that."

"He was a monster. He was going to turn me into a werewolf, too. So we could be together forever."

I shuddered as the memory slid through my mind. Hector's voice on the phone, calling me at odd hours, telling me everything he'd planned for me. I think.

"What happened?" Jessie asked. "Why didn't he bite you?"

"Edward came. Hector knew Edward would kill me if I was bitten. So he—"

I broke off. No reason for Jessie to know how Hector had marked me or why.

"He's been waiting for the perfect time to come back and finish what he started."

"I wondered why you became a *Jäger-Sucher.*"

"And you think you know?"

"What better way to protect yourself than by becoming a hunter of the thing that's hunting you?"

I'd become a hunter for vengeance. But no matter how many of them I killed, it would never be enough. I was going to have to kill *him.*

The thought sent a shaft of panic through my chest so painful I found it hard to breathe.

Will caught up with us. "I was thinking—"

"Gee, that's new," Jessie drawled.

He continued to speak as if she hadn't. "Leigh, your family was killed by the white wolf on the night of the blood moon?"

Jessie had been blabby, but I couldn't fault her for it. We had to work together, as much as I'd rather work alone.

"Yes," I answered.

"Why that night, I wonder? Is there something special about it?"

I shrugged. "You're the paranormal expert."

"Not really. But I know someone who is."

"One of those elders you mentioned?"

"I talked to them. No one's ever heard of the power eater. But they knew a woman of great rank in the Midewiwin."

"English, please," Jessie instructed.

"The Grand Medicine Society. Once it was a secret religious fellowship devoted to healing through knowledge of the spirits. According to the elders, Cora Kopway has spent her life studying old texts and meeting with the spirits in her visions."

"Wouldn't being a scholar preclude being a visionary?"

Will smiled. "Not to an Ojibwe. Everything relates to everything else. Life is a circle—"

"Yeah, whatever," Jessie interrupted. "When can we see this chick?"

"We?"

"That's right. I'm not letting you out of my sight until this is over."

He frowned. Opened his mouth as if to argue, then shut it again.

"She likes you," I said. "I can tell."

A voice hailed Jessie. We turned in that direction. A heavyset elderly man waved to us through a gap in the trees. He was a big guy, but his skin was so wrinkled and his shoulders so stooped he gave the appearance of shrinking.

The three of us entered a clearing. Three dead wolves littered the earth. I could tell without getting any closer that none of them had been eaten. What was up with that?

Jessie introduced me to her deputy as being from the DNR. Elwood shook my hand with more enthusiasm than anyone else ever had. I was half-afraid he'd dislodge the hearing aids tucked into both ears.

"You know what's going on here?" he asked.

"Rabies," I answered. "New strain."

"Never seen wolves kill their own like this." He shook his head as he stared at the bodies. "Kind of sad."

It could get a whole lot sadder, but I kept my opinion to myself.

"Tell us what you know," Jessie instructed.

"I received a call from Joe Elders. His dog took off, and he found the mutt gnawing on that one." Elwood pointed to the gray and white wolf nearest to me. "Dog was up on his shots, so we're kosher there."

I nodded. If we were dealing with rabies, I'd be happy, as it was, didn't care. "What about the others?"

"When Joe looked around a bit, he found 'em nearby."

"They weren't together like this?"

"No. I pulled them over myself. Sorry. I shouldn't have done that?"

I shrugged. Hard to make a fuss about the crime scene in this case. How would I explain what the crime was?

"The first one was here. One there." He pointed to the east. "About ten feet. Other one that way." He switched his arm to the north. "About twenty feet. Almost like the wolf was waiting around to pick 'em off one at a time." He frowned. "But wolves don't do that, either. I ain't never seen such a thing."

"Thanks, Elwood," Jessie said. "We'll take it from here."

He started to move away.

"Wait." Jessie pulled the picture of Hector out of her back pocket. "You seen this guy in town?"

The old man took the photo, frowned, squinted. I held my breath. Did I want him to have seen Hector, or didn't I?

Finally he shook his head. "Can't say that I have."

"Positive?" Jessie asked.

"I'm good with faces. Fellow like that would stand out."

I let out the breath I'd been holding. Now what?

"Why don't you ask around?" Jessie said.

"Sure." Elwood put the photo into his pocket. "Whad he do?"

"Nothing. Yet."

The old man shrugged and left.

Jessie turned to me. "He's got more contacts than I do. He'll check with the owners of the cabins in the woods and on the lakes. If Hector's anywhere near here, Elwood will hear about it."

I didn't like leaving the search to someone I didn't know, but if Jessie trusted the man, I discovered that I did, too.

All three of us knelt next to the dead wolves. They'd been killed, violently. Throats torn out, bite marks on the bodies. But they hadn't been eaten.

Had the man and his pet disturbed the Weendigo before he could accomplish his mission? I had a hard time believing a being that didn't flinch at cannibalism in both human and werewolf form would mind killing an intruder and his puppy dog. So what had happened here?

"You said the brown werewolf killed another one," Will murmured. "He didn't eat him."

"Not while I was there."

"So maybe one is killing, the other is eating."

"We thought about that," I said. "But I don't recall two wolves in the power eater legend."

"If the white wolf is the most powerful, and getting stronger with every bit of power he eats, he could already be controlling the others."

"But does it work if one wolf kills and a second eats? Doesn't one have to kill, then eat, to capture the power?"

"I'll have to read my notes," Will said, "but I don't remember anything that specific. Using the locals to help him would make sense. He needs to reach a hundred."

"If he's powerful enough to control the others, if he's the ultimate werewolf, how are we going to stop him?"

Jessie asked. "What if silver doesn't work on the power eater the way it works on everyone else?"

Will scowled. "That would suck."

I had to agree.

25

"We need to make an appointment with Cora," Will said.

"An appointment?" Jessie asked. "She's that busy?"

"You'd be surprised."

"Call her then."

Will unclipped his cell phone from his belt. "No service. Again."

Jessie glanced at her phone and growled. Sometimes cell service was lost this deep in the woods.

"Why don't you two go on," I said. "I'll finish up here."

Jessie frowned. "This is my job—"

"Is it? I thought it was mine."

"You two could arm wrestle for it," Will suggested.

I'd tangled with Jessie once. In a fair fight, she could kill me. A dirty fight was another matter. But I'm sure a dirty fight—as in mud wrestling—was just what Will had in mind.

"I'll pass."

"Me, too." Jessie considered for a moment, then gave in. "Fine, Duchess, you burn the fanged and furry; we'll go back to town and set up an appointment with the voodoo priestess."

"Grand medicine spirit woman," Will said. "Eighth level."

"Whatever."

"Jess, she's old and very well respected. You have to behave."

Jessie looked at me. "Don't I know how to behave?"

I glanced at Will. "Am I supposed to answer that?"

"No. Give us a call," he glanced at his cell, then hooked it back on his belt, "when you get to your place. Maybe we can see Cora today."

He took Jessie's arm and tugged her back the way we'd come. Amazingly, she went without argument. Probably figured they'd have time for a quickie—I glanced at the three wolves—maybe even a longie, before I was finished.

I dragged them into the center of the clearing, as far away from trees and bushes as I was able to get, added accelerant, then pulled out a match. I'd done this so many times, I wasn't really paying attention. Instead, my gaze drifted to the forest, absently watching the flicker of Jessie's and Will's clothing fade away.

I struck the match, and a sudden flash between me and them made me freeze. I stared in horror at what appeared to be stealthily moving white fur. I couldn't take my eyes off the sight or figure out what it might mean.

Then the match burned down to my fingertip and the pain caused me to curse, then drop it on the ground. I stomped the flame into oblivion and glanced back in the same direction.

The flash of white was still there.

I lifted my face to the sky. The sun shone brightly in

the middle of the day, though the rays did not penetrate into the deep forest. Nevertheless, I drew my gun and ran.

I should have shouted right away, warned them, something, but I wanted to kill him. I wanted to end this before I had to see someone else I cared about die.

Time seemed to slow. They couldn't have gone far, yet I seemed to run forever without getting any closer.

The brush cleared and I saw him. Or thought I did. Poised to spring, he was still too far away for me to hit with a handgun.

"Jessie!" I shouted. "Wolf!"

A gunshot rang out. I frowned at the weapon in my hand. I hadn't fired it.

Another shot brought my head up. The gunfire was coming from the other direction, and the white wolf was gone.

I ran toward Jessie and Will, heedless of the sniper. The shots had stopped. Because they were hit? Or because the shooter was gone?

I burst through the trees, saw them on the ground, and my heart lurched. Jessie had thrown her body over Will. Her gun was drawn and aimed toward the shots, but when she heard me the barrel swung in my direction.

"Get down!" Jessie snarled.

I hit the dirt.

Will struggled to get up. Jessie shoved his head into the ground. "Don't," she warned.

We lay there for five minutes at least, ears straining for the sound of approaching footsteps—or padding paws. Nothing happened.

Eventually I motioned toward the west. Jessie nodded and I crawled into the brush as she covered me. I scouted the area all around us. Ten minutes later I returned to the clearing.

"Nothing," I said. "Not a track, not a calling card. Zip."

Jessie scowled and allowed Will to sit up. Her hands fluttered over him checking for injuries.

"Knock it off." He pushed her away. "I'm fine."

"What happened?" she asked me.

I hesitated. It was broad daylight. I *couldn't* have seen the white wolf.

Besides, a gun had been fired. No matter how super-duper a shape-shifter this guy was, a wolf didn't have the opposable thumbs necessary to fire a weapon. Usually didn't need to, since his teeth and claws, speed and agility, were weapons enough.

In other words, if there'd been a wolf, he would have attacked, not changed into a human and shot at them. I'd been seeing things again.

"Leigh?" Jessie pressed. "What, exactly, did you see?"

"Nothing."

"You shouted wolf," Will pointed out. I glared at him and he held up his hands in surrender. "You said it."

"Yes," Jessie murmured, "you did. Was it Hector?"

"Look at the sky!" I shouted. "Any moon? I couldn't have seen what I thought I did."

I sat down in the trampled grass and dirt, then wiped my hands across my face. "I'm losing it again," I whispered. "I should go back to the padded room where I belong."

Jessie grabbed my upper arm. Her fingers dug into my flesh hard enough to make me wince. "You're not crazy. He's fucking with you."

"But it's daytime."

"Everything we believe about werewolves seems to be coming apart. For all we know, a power eater can shift any damn time that it wants to."

I blinked. She could be right. For some reason, the thought cheered me.

Jessie's hold gentled. "You saved our lives, Leigh."

"I doubt that."

"You yelled; we hit the ground; a bullet whizzed through the air where my head had been."

"Mine, too," Will added.

"I should have called out as soon as I saw the white flash behind you."

Jessie released me. "No harm, no foul."

"Why didn't he come after you?" Will asked. "We left you by yourself back there."

I shuddered at the thought of being alone in the woods with my nightmare. "He doesn't want me dead," I said, "just furry."

"There has to be a reason he let you go this time." Will frowned as if an idea had just occurred to him. "He must be saving you for the blood moon."

"Gee, thanks, I hadn't thought of that yet."

"Sorry," Will muttered.

We clambered to our feet.

"Guess I'd better go back and finish what I didn't even start," I said.

"I think we'll go with you." Jessie grabbed Will's hand and tugged him into the lead.

"I'll be OK."

"Sure you will."

Cadotte glanced over his shoulder and shrugged. I gave up and followed them to the wolf pile. In truth, I didn't want to be alone in the woods, day or night, anymore.

Jessie and Will stopped so fast I plowed into them. "Shit," she muttered.

I went on tiptoe and peered over her shoulder. Pieces of the wolves I'd left behind were all over the place.

"Chalk up three more for the bad guys," Will said.

"He was trying to draw me away from them, and I let him."

"He was also trying to kill us. Those bullets meant business."

"Moves awful quick, even for a wolf," Jessie observed.

"And changes quick, too. Between the time I saw a wolf, then someone shot at you, couldn't have been more than a minute."

"Could have been two of them again."

She was right. Most likely the white wolf drew me away from the kill, then circled back. Someone, or something else, had shot at Jessie and Will.

"Let's burn what's left and get the hell out of here," I said.

"I'm with you."

Pulling the body parts back into a pile was one of the least pleasant experiences of my life. Thankfully, I had help doing it. By unspoken agreement, Will did the physical labor along with me while Jessie stood guard. We'd been surprised once. None of us planned to be surprised again.

I had just dumped more accelerant on the pyre and thrown on a match when Will exclaimed, "Oh, my God!"

I spun, gun already in my hand, but nothing was in the clearing save the three of us and what was left of the dead wolves.

Will ran across the damp, trampled grass toward Jessie. She scowled at him. "What is your problem?"

He ignored her question, grabbing her by the shoulder and yanking her around. A bright red splotch of blood marred the back of Jessie's uniform shirt. Since she hadn't touched a single wolf body part, this concerned me.

"You're hit." He turned her to face him and tried to unbutton her blouse.

"Get a grip, Slick." She smacked his hands away. "Not now."

"Let me see." He tried to undress her again.

"A scratch. Forget about it."

My heart thundered; my mouth was dry. She'd been wounded because of me. I'd worried that Will would be hurt, maybe killed, and Jessie would be unable to cope. In reality, it was the other way around.

The anguish on Will's face, the blood on Jessie's clothes . . . I was having a hard time thinking straight. I *had* to get them out of the line of fire.

"Take her to town and clean her up," I ordered.

Jessie threw me an annoyed glare. "Who put you in charge?"

"Edward."

"This is my town. I'm not going anywhere until we're done here."

"You're done."

She stepped forward until we were toe-to-toe. Since she had a good six inches on me, I had to crane my neck to meet her gaze. This made some of my authority go straight down the toilet.

"I'm done when I say I'm done."

I quivered with rage—at the one who had hurt her, at myself for getting them into this, at Jessie for being so damned stubborn.

All of a sudden the tension drained out of her and she glanced at Cadotte. "Watch the fire while I talk to Leigh."

He hesitated, then nodded and moved off. Jessie turned to me.

"I can handle this myself," I began.

She snorted. "Right. You need us. We need you. Get used to it."

"I'll call Edward. He'll come back."

All I had to do was tell him that Hector was here, he'd be on the next plane. Up until now I'd avoided that conversation. Edward had saved me once. This time I wanted to save myself. But not at the cost of Jessie and Will.

"You'll call Edward and tell him what? That I'm incompetent? That Will's a pansy?"

I frowned. "No. . . ."

"I chose this. So did Will. We knew the risks."

Did they? I had a hard time believing that. If they knew their chances of surviving this job were forty to two, would they stay? Maybe I should tell them.

"You have each other. What do you need a dangerous job for? What if—?"

"We die? I've asked myself that question a hundred times. I could get hit by a truck tomorrow. Will could get shot by an overeager redneck today. That's life, Leigh. At least we're trying to save the world before we go."

A crusader. Who'd have thunk it?

"It's not like we *plan* on dying," she continued. "I did kill the wolf god—all by myself." I lifted a brow. "Kind of."

"Hector is bad news." I looked around the bloody clearing. "And getting badder."

"Oooh, I'm all a-shiver."

I started to think ahead. I'd go out hunting alone. Ditch them whenever I could. Maybe I could end this without ending them.

"I'm gonna stick to you like glue," Jessie murmured.

My eyes went to hers like a magnet drawn to metal. Amusement lightened her face, but her voice was stone-cold serious.

"You're not running around like Dirty Harry. We're together now. All for one, one for all."

"Mix metaphors much?"

"Bite me."

"If Hector gets to me first, I just might."

Jessie glanced over her shoulder at Will, who was still amusing himself with the bonfire. "Remember what you promised me and I promised you?" she whispered.

How could I forget a promise like that? I nodded.

"We're partners now."

I scowled. I'd never had one of those, and I wasn't sure what to do. Hug her? Shake her hand? Knock her out, tie her up, and keep her somewhere until the danger was over?

"I've never had a friend like you before," she admitted.

Aw, hell. Now I couldn't tie her up.

26

We returned to my apartment about midday. The parking lot remained deserted. A good thing, too, since Jessie's shirt was a mess. Will and I looked like we'd bathed in red paint to our elbows.

The three of us hurried to my place. I dug out my first-aid kit. After washing myself, I cleaned and bandaged Jessie's "scratch" while Will called Cora Kopway.

"You should probably have stitches," I said.

"Slap a butterfly Band-Aid or two on there and shut up."

I followed her advice, though none too gently. She didn't flinch. What a woman.

Her shoulder would match mine. If her furrow had been thirteen inches instead of three.

"She'll see us at four," Will said.

I finished my lame attempt at medical assistance. "How far away is it?"

"About an hour."

Great. I could catch a nap. Sadly, the two of them didn't seem in any hurry to leave.

When Jessie said she was going to stick to me like glue, I hadn't thought she meant while I slept.

"Aren't you two going to go back to your place?"

"What for?" Jessie asked. "I like it here."

She settled into a chair, put her feet on the coffee table. She'd appear relaxed if she'd been wearing a shirt. The bra and khaki trousers just didn't say "laid back."

"You need to change," I pointed out.

"Don't you like me just the way I am?"

"Get out."

"I don't think I will."

My eyes narrowed. "Listen, McQuade, I was doing just fine before I met you."

"That was against your average, everyday werewolf."

"You can't move in with me."

"No?"

"I don't need a babysitter."

"Come on, Jess," Will murmured. "You could use a shower, new clothes, a little nap."

"See? You guys need a nap. So do I."

"I can imagine who you'll be sleeping with."

I hadn't even thought of that. I had truly planned on a nap, but maybe I needed to get tired first.

"Get lost." I threw her bloody shirt into her lap.

Her mouth tightened mulishly, and I hurried to reassure her. "I'll be fine. I promise. No walks in the woods. I'll go directly from my apartment to my car with my gun drawn."

"We'll pick you up," she said. "It's on the way."

I decided to let well enough alone.

Jessie stood. Her shirt was really disgusting.

"I'd loan you one of mine," I said, "but I think you'd burst the seams."

She tilted her head. "Was that you being nice? Because you weren't."

"Here." Cadotte drew his T-shirt over his head and tossed it in her face. "Wear mine."

I couldn't help but look. All that smooth, toned, tanned muscle should have made me drool. Instead I could only think of another man's chest—one that was just as smooth, equally toned, but marble pale.

Jessie glanced at me and sighed. "You'd better keep yourself covered, Cadotte. You might cause an accident on the road."

"No more than you will with a uniform shirt that looks like something out of *Night of the Living Dead*. Put the thing on and let's go."

Will stalked out the door. Jessie shrugged and put on his shirt, which fit her pretty well. Smoothing her palms down the front, she rubbed her cheek against the neck, inhaling deeply. Her face went dreamy; then she saw me watching and stiffened. I smiled. They really were very sweet together.

"We'll be back in a few hours. Be here. And try to be in one piece, OK?"

"I'll do my best."

I waited until I heard the motor start; then I listened to the gravel crunch, the sound becoming softer and softer until it disappeared altogether. An instant later, I was out the door, gun drawn as I'd promised. I hurried downstairs and across the wide yard that separated the tavern from Damien's cabin.

The air was warm, the sky sunny—the kind of lazy day referred to as Indian summer; I'm not sure why.

I knocked. No one answered. Damn. So much for afternoon delight.

A glance at the tavern revealed a CLOSED sign in the window. Maybe Damien was still asleep. Would he be mad if I let myself in?

He was a guy. He wouldn't care if I torched the place as long as I crawled in bed with him afterward.

I tried the door. Open. How convenient.

Stepping inside, I called his name. He didn't answer.

The room was dark. The bed tousled. I couldn't see if he was in it.

I crossed the short distance and laid my hand on the lump in the middle of the mattress. Nothing but pillows.

Slowly I turned in a complete circle. I didn't see him in the single living/dining/sleeping area. The door to the bathroom was open. I took a quick look-see inside. Empty.

I had just decided to creep back out when the thunder of footsteps erupted on the porch. The door burst open and Damien stumbled inside.

He was dressed as he'd been when I met him. Black pants, no shoes, no shirt. His chest was slick with sweat; his hair glistened. His skin was pale, and his eyes gleamed almost yellow. He appeared feverish.

He slammed the door and leaned his back against it. Despite the sweat and the signs of exertion, he wasn't even breathing hard.

I drew my gun and hurried to the window. "Where are they?"

"They?"

"Who's chasing you?"

He gave me an odd glance. "I was jogging."

"In your bare feet?"

"Yeah."

My eyes scanned the clearing, but no one, nothing, appeared. I set my gun on the table nearby.

"Paranoid, Leigh?"

"Actually, paranoid is my *middle* name."

His smile was weak, and that worried me even more than his pale, damp skin. I took one step toward him, and he crumpled to the floor.

"Damien!" I went to my knees next to him. "What is it?"

"I did too much. I'll be OK."

"How long were you jogging?"

He shook his head, didn't answer.

I put my palm to his forehead. He was cool to the touch. Nevertheless, I went into the bathroom and wet a cloth with cold water. Then I bathed his face, his neck, his chest. His heart pounded beneath his skin, far too fast for the ease of his breathing. He had me worried.

He started to shiver. I wasn't sure what to do, so I yanked the sheet off his bed and wrapped it around his shoulders; then I urged him forward, crawled behind him, and let him lean against me.

Wrapping my arms around his middle, I rocked him until the chills went away and his heart rate leveled off.

"Thanks," he whispered. "It was hotter than I thought. I went farther than I should."

Holding him in my arms, comforting him as I'd once comforted little children, changed things. I recalled all I'd ever wanted—husband, home, family. Suddenly I wanted Damien, forever.

My whole body tensed. I had to make this about sex again, so I ran my fingers through his damp, silky hair. His sigh was filled with pleasure. He turned his head and I gave him a kiss. He stiffened.

"*Shh*," I murmured against his mouth.

"I'm all sweaty, Leigh. I smell."

"I don't care." He should know what I'd been wading in an hour ago—or not. "We'll take a shower after."

"After?"

I scooted out from behind him, knelt between his legs. Then I ran my tongue over his chest. He tasted great— like a hot summer night, sand, surf, energy. My mouth moved lower.

The muscles of his stomach danced against my lips. I

rubbed my face against the growing interest in his pants, then mouthed him through the black cotton.

"OK," he ground out. "Shower after."

"Glad you see things my way."

As I got to my feet I lost the boots, the knife. Walking to the bed, I lost the rest. By the time I was there, I was naked and so was he. I didn't realize until I lay on the crumpled sheets that I'd bared my back to him without a thought.

He stood next to the bed staring down at me. The expression in his eyes said he knew what that meant. I trusted him; I cared about him. I shouldn't, couldn't. But I did.

I shot up like a jack-in-the-box and took him in my mouth, drew my teeth down his length, made him forget everything but now. This was just sex. It had to be.

Once, oral sex had been more personal than intercourse. But nowadays it meant next to nothing. Thank you, Mr. President. Everyone did this, just about everywhere.

I sucked Damien hard, felt him at the back of my throat. He groaned and the sound inspired me. I grabbed his hips and pumped him back and forth, but he wouldn't let me make him come.

His hands on my shoulders held me away; then he pressed me onto the bed and covered my body with his. In the state I'd coaxed him into I expected fast and furious. What I got was a slow, gentle embrace.

He didn't plunge into me. He didn't enter me at all. Instead, he lay nestled between my legs as he ran his fingertips all over my face.

"Damien," I growled.

"Shh," he repeated. "Shh."

Then he kissed me, and he kept kissing me for a very, very long time.

There's an art to the kiss, one he'd studied well. I remembered necking in my boyfriend's car—junior year, at the park. We'd done nothing but kiss, and I'd been so turned on I could hardly sit still.

That's what I felt like when Damien kissed me. As if I'd have an orgasm just from the flicker of his tongue along the edge of mine.

I kissed him back, twined my fingers through his hair again, reveled in the taste of his mouth, the sensation of his skin, the scent of him and me together.

By the time he slipped inside, I was so wet I hardly felt him, until he flexed and I cried out, nearly orgasming at his first thrust.

"Look at me," he said. "I want to see your eyes when you come."

I didn't want to, but he stopped moving, and when I wiggled he pinned me to the mattress with his weight. My body screamed. I was on the edge of something wonderful, and all I had to do was open my eyes.

So I did.

What I saw in his made me go still. My heart thundered and my chest ached. He kissed me, long, lingering, and when he lifted his head a tear ran down my cheek.

"I didn't mean to make you cry," he whispered.

"Too late."

He licked away my tears as he had once before. I shuddered as my skin tingled from the contact. His breath brushed the wet trail, turning the tear track from hot to cold. He began to move, and as my body convulsed, so did his. We stared into each other's eyes and we knew.

This wasn't just sex anymore.

When it was over and the sweat on both our bodies had

cooled, he rolled to the side, pulling me along with him. I started to get up, but he held on tight. I should leave, but having him near felt too good, too right.

He kissed my forehead and he didn't say a word.

My dreams were back—the good ones where I had five kids, a ranch house in Topeka, and a husband who came home at six. Pathetic, but that's what I'd always wanted. Since the day I'd received my first doll.

The dreams were laughable in the face of my present life. I was a werewolf hunter. I bathed in blood. I baptized by fire. I survived through the gun and the knife. But that didn't make my dreams any less real.

Damien wasn't the settling type—obviously. For reasons of his own he was a drifter and probably always would be.

But when I closed my eyes I saw little blond girls and dark-headed boys frolicking on a lawn circled by a white picket fence.

You see why I hadn't allowed myself to have sex since Jimmy had died?

For me sex was associated with love, commitment, a lifetime together. That's the way I'd been brought up. The only time I'd veered away from that path I'd brought nothing but death and destruction to everyone I loved.

Damien kissed my hair. I snuggled against his chest. What if I gave it all up and started over?

I blinked at the thought, one I'd never had before. Since Hector my life had been focused on one thing and one thing only: killing the monsters, then dying. But dying didn't hold much appeal anymore, and that had started when Damien walked into my world.

I'd have to kill Hector first, of course. I couldn't go back to a regular life when he was out there waiting for me. But once he was dead . . .

Anything was possible.

27

A sudden thought made me stiffen and push away from Damien's embrace. Anything just might be possible much sooner than I'd thought.

"You didn't use a condom," I said.

He didn't so much as blink. He didn't curse or cry or run or exhibit any of the other typically male reactions to such a statement.

"I know."

"You . . . know?" I sat up. "What the hell is that supposed to mean? You could have gotten me pregnant, stud boy."

"No." He sighed. "I couldn't. I mean I can't. I won't."

Now he cursed, then ran his fingers through his hair and got out of bed. "I'm sorry. This probably isn't the best time to tell you, but I can't get you pregnant."

"Why not?"

"They tell me it's medically impossible."

I wanted to ask, *Who told you? When? Have you seen a specialist? What* exactly *is the problem?*

But the way he held his shoulders, as if he expected questions and didn't want to answer them, made me hesitate. I didn't like to talk about the scars on my back. Maybe Damien didn't care to discuss the scars within himself. I could respect that.

"Well, there goes my white picket fence dream," I quipped.

It had been a stupid dream anyway.

Damien's eyes narrowed; his head tilted. He was too damned perceptive. Before he could question me, I blurted, "Why did you use a condom in the first place?"

"Pregnancy isn't the only concern."

Well, duh. Now I cursed.

"You don't have to worry about me," he said quickly. "I'm clean. I swear."

"Me, too," I whispered.

Silence settled between us. Clinical conversations appeared to be a great mood killer. Fancy that.

"Leigh?"

"Mmm?"

"I love you."

I could only stare at him for several ticks of the clock. "You . . . you can't love me. You just met me."

He smiled sadly. "I've been waiting my whole life for you."

"That's nuts."

"I know."

"You're blinded by great sex."

"No, Leigh, I'm blinded by you."

I didn't know what to say, so I said nothing at all. Damien sat down on the bed and ran a palm over the shorn ends of my hair.

"I always knew that when I met *the* woman for me, I'd look at her once and think, 'Here she is.' I was right."

"You know nothing about me."

"You're wrong. I know you're brave and strong, loyal."

"You make me sound like a Labrador retriever."

He ignored my mutterings. "You're sexy and sweet, caring. Beautiful, and a little bit sad. I wish you'd trust me with what makes you sigh when you think no one's listening."

Did I do that? Probably. I wished I could trust him, too. But if I told him my secrets, I'd have to kill him.

Ha-ha.

"You've got secrets of your own, Damien."

"Yeah, I do."

"Are you going to trust me with them?"

"I can't."

We were in the same boat. Figures.

I took his hand. Ran my thumb over his silver ring, remembered what Jessie had said about the power eater. How could I ask him if he was a werewolf? It wasn't like asking him if he was married, divorced, or currently single.

He didn't feel like a werewolf. I know that sounds odd. But werewolves have evil hearts. They don't start out that way, of course. They start out like you and me. When they're bitten, the virus changes them, both physically and mentally. Sure they seem like people, but inside there's a demon panting to get out.

I'd researched this, countless times during long nights when I shouldn't sleep. Demons lived—everywhere.

How could Damien love me if his heart was full of hate? He couldn't. But I'd recognized love in his eyes. I'd seen the expression once before. An expression I'd never thought to see again.

I wished I could tell him I loved him, too, but I couldn't. Not until my old life was dead.

"I—"

He put his fingers over my lips, shook his head. "How about that shower?" he asked.

My mouth curved. I kissed his hand, then took it in my own and led him to the water.

I left Damien asleep on the bed. We'd made love in the shower. He had scratches on both his shoulders and an imprint of my teeth on his neck. I guess I couldn't sneer at Jessie and Will anymore.

I managed to make it to my apartment and change out of my dirty clothes before Will pulled up in a Jeep. I squeezed into the backseat.

"Not taking the official Crow Valley cruiser?" I asked.

Will shook his head. "Cora wouldn't appreciate a cop car in front of her place. All the neighbors would wonder what she did this time."

This time?

I looked forward to meeting Cora Kopway more with every passing moment.

"So what were you up to while we were gone?" Jessie asked.

"Sleeping."

She glanced over her shoulder, winked. "Us, too."

I couldn't help but smile. It had been a long, long time since I'd had a girlfriend. Jessie and I would probably never have met or become close in my other life. That would have been a big loss. I liked her more than I would ever say.

"How's the shoulder?" I asked.

"I'll live."

"Sore?"

"Yeah. But at least it's not my gun hand."

Trust Jessie to worry about the important things in life.

She turned so her back was to the window, wincing a bit at the movement. "I talked to Elwood."

Uh-oh.

"He checked with all his cronies. Talked to the gas station attendants, real estate agents, anyone who might have noticed a new guy in town. No one's seen Hector."

I frowned. That was weird.

"Which doesn't mean you're crazy," Jessie hastened to assure me. "It just means he's keeping a low profile."

For the first time in a long time I didn't feel crazy. I felt . . . good. I kept thinking: What if?

What if I killed Hector?

What if Damien really loved me?

What if I loved him?

He couldn't give me children. Or so he said. But there were new advances in medicine every day. What if he could be cured?

Then everything I'd ever wanted could come true.

"Leigh?"

I focused on Jessie. She appeared concerned.

"You wanna stay with me here?"

"I'm sorry. Did you say something?"

She rolled her eyes. "Get your head out of the bedroom and listen. Even if the white wolf isn't Hector, we still have to find and kill it."

"I'm in complete agreement."

"And if it isn't him, we'll just keep hunting until we find the right white wolf. Wherever it is, however long we have to search."

"OK."

She faced the front, shaking her head. "And she says *I'm* gaga."

Her words would have made me angry once. Now I just wanted to laugh.

We reached Cora's house. The tiny log cabin set between towering evergreens made me think of Hansel and Gretel. I hoped she wasn't a witch.

The door opened before we even knocked. Cora Kopway looked like no witch I'd ever known. As if I'd known any.

She was tall, willowy, with long, flowing black hair that held only a trace of silver. Her face possessed a beauty that defied age. She'd seen many things—some good, some bad, some in between—and all of them had marked her.

She wore a blindingly white T-shirt, tucked into a long colorful skirt. Each finger sported a ring. Silver sparkled around two of her toes. Three earrings hung from one ear, two from the other, and bracelets jangled about her slim wrists.

She didn't smile, just stared at us with solemn, dark eyes. Then she turned and disappeared into her home, leaving the door open behind her.

"I thought she was old," Jessie whispered.

"She is," Will whispered back. "My people age well, unlike yours."

Jessie kicked him in the ankle, then followed him inside.

The cabin was a museum. Indian art graced the walls, stocked the shelves and the tables. I was unfamiliar with the artists, but most of the paintings and the sculptures were of animals—bear, moose, birds, coyotes, and, of course, wolves.

On one shelf I caught a glimpse of a kachina doll, which I knew wasn't Ojibwe. I assumed Cora's collection represented all the North American tribes. I'd love to go through everything, but we didn't have the time.

Candles burned here and there. Something smoldered in a pottery bowl. The room smelled of fresh-cut grass and, at the same time, new snow on a crisp winter night. How could that be?

She motioned for us to take seats on furniture that reflected the colors of the earth and the sky at sunset. Mahogany, sand, azure, burnt orange—the room both eased and energized.

Cora sat in a straight-backed chair on the opposite side of an oak coffee table, its only adornment a smoking salmon-shaded bowl. Now that I was closer I observed a tiny flame in the center with what appeared to be grass all around it. A definite fire hazard.

She continued to peer at us with that same solemn expression. I had a feeling she could see into my head and discern my thoughts. I tried like hell to make them pure. But the more I tried, the more impure they became.

What did I expect after the way I'd spent my afternoon?

"I hear you know all about woo-woo?" Jessie blurted.

Will's sigh was long-suffering. "Jess," he admonished. "Don't speak until spoken to."

She stared down her nose at him. "You have *got* to be kidding me."

He narrowed his eyes. Amazingly, she sat back on the couch, crossed her arms over her chest, placed one knee over the other, and shut up.

"I'm sorry, *n'okomiss*. She doesn't understand."

Cora acknowledged the apology with an infinitesimal nod. Her earrings swayed and tangled in her long black hair. The room became silent again.

"You have been marked," she murmured, turning her gaze on me.

I started and my scar began to ache. It had been blissfully silent since morning.

"Marked by the demon. You are his. He has come for you."

Jessie cast me a quick, worried glance. I couldn't do anything but peer into Cora's eyes. How could she know?

"You never said she was a psychic, Slick."

"I am what I am," Cora intoned, still staring at me. "You would do well to listen."

"I'd be happy to," Jessie said, "if you told us anything fresh and new. She's marked by the demon; he's coming. We got that already."

"William, your woman needs to learn silence."

"Good luck," he muttered.

Cora reached into the pocket of her skirt, then made a flicking motion toward the bowl at the center of the table. The flame shot nearly to the ceiling.

Jessie started coughing. When she finished, she opened her mouth, but no sound came out.

"Uh-oh," Will said.

Cora just smiled.

Jessie grabbed at her own throat, shook her head, pantomimed, badly.

"Your voice will be returned when you leave my house. Until then, be still or I will make you."

Jessie froze, then sat back on the couch and took Will's hand. His fingers tightened on hers.

"What is it you wish to know?" Cora asked.

"Have you heard the Legend of the Power Eater?"

"Of course. The Weendigo that becomes so much more."

"What else?"

She shrugged. "The power eater craves power. He can never have enough. He is the ultimate shape-shifter."

"What, exactly, does that mean?" I asked.

"The more power the Weendigo eats, the greater his abilities. He can shift to any form, any time, any where."

"That is so not good," I muttered.

Will motioned me to silence. "You mean the power eater can become something other than a wolf?"

"Of course."

"In the daytime?"

"Most certainly."

Jessie, Will, and I exchanged glances. That explained how I'd seen the white wolf in the daylight. A thought occurred to me.

"Could a power eater change the color of his fur?"

Cora tilted her head and considered. "I have not heard of this, but I don't see why he could not."

In other words, our two killer wolves could really be one.

"Can you explain, *n'okomiss,* how the man becomes the beast?"

"He is cursed by the great mystery."

"Is there any other way?"

"Possibly."

She stood and moved—or rather flowed; her gait was too smooth to be called mere movement—to the bookcase, where she removed a huge tome. Will leaped to his feet and hurried over, taking the book from her hands and carrying it to the table.

No title graced the cover, which appeared to be real leather. When she opened to the middle, the pages crackled with age.

"If a man wished to become a Weendigo he would eat the flesh of his enemy."

I frowned. Petite blond women were Hector's enemy?

Suddenly it hit me. His mother. She had been blond; she had left him. He had never forgiven her.

"Then what?" I asked, my voice hoarse.

"Then he would call on the powers of darkness to transform him into a beast."

"How do you call the powers of darkness?"

"There are many ways, but the most common is the five-pointed star."

I sat up straighter. "A pentagram?"

"Yes."

Jessie glanced at me with wide eyes.

"What about a pentagram?"

"The one who wishes to become would draw the star on his body. Somewhere vital."

As if by magic I saw Hector's chest, the black shiny pentagram stark over his heart.

"And then?" I whispered.

"Then he calls on the evil ones to make him Weendigo."

"The Evil Ones?" Will broke in. "Matchi-auwishuk?"

"Perhaps. There are many evil ones in this world and the next."

"And the evil ones," I pressed. "They would make him Weendigo? Just like that?"

"If he offered them a sacrifice."

"What kind of sacrifice?" I asked, but I already knew.

Hector had become a Weendigo by promising to kill my family.

28

"The sacrifice must be blood, death, tears."

"The usual," I muttered.

"Obviously you aren't asking these questions for an afternoon's entertainment," Cora said. "There is a power eater on the loose and the blood moon is coming."

"Yes, *n'okomiss*."

"You wish to know how to destroy it?"

"That would be very helpful—".

"Wait," I interrupted. "Why the blood moon? Why that night then? Why the same night now?"

Cora turned her solemn gaze to me. "Like time has power. He became more than a man on that night. On this one he will become more than a beast."

"I don't get it," Will said. "Weendigos are only made on the night of the blood moon?"

"It is the best time for that sort of thing."

"Why?"

"Do you know the history of the hunter's moon? Why it is called the moon of blood?"

I did. I'd spent countless nights researching the full moon that blooms in October.

"In ancient times people would hunt," I began, "then preserve meat for the winter. The hunter's moon was the blood moon because of the amount of blood spilled on a single night."

"And when so much blood is spilled, the earth cries out," Cora continued. "So many souls released to the great mystery. Though necessary for life, the amount of death creates a perfect aura for evil deeds."

"Peachy," I muttered. "So how do we kill him?"

"Will silver work?" Cadotte asked.

"Silver always works."

All three of us let out a sigh of relief.

"But sometimes not as well as others."

Jessie made a rude gesture with one hand. Will caught her fingers and squeezed.

"I don't understand," he said.

"Silver will kill the Weendigo. It should kill the power eater. But the supreme alpha? I do not know. There has never been one before."

"Never?" Will asked.

"The requirements to become such a thing are intense. Human becomes monster becomes beast. Beast becomes stronger and stronger until he is ultimate, then supreme."

"Sounds like a pizza," I muttered. Jessie snickered.

Cora reached into her other pocket, and I clapped my hand over my mouth.

"What happens on the night of the hunter's moon?" Will asked.

"If the power eater attains all the power that is required—"

"One hundred werewolves."

"Yes. Then he becomes the supreme alpha."

"How?"

She frowned. "He becomes."

"Poof?" I asked.

Cora turned to Will. "What is *poof*?"

He shrugged. "Magic. One minute he's the power eater; the next he's supreme alpha? He doesn't have to do a ritual? Another sacrifice?"

"Oh, yes. There must be another sacrifice."

"Blood, death, tears? Again?" I asked.

Cora's brow wrinkled. "One would think so, but I have not seen it written. I will search the records and call if I find anything useful."

Jessie made an annoyed sound. Everyone ignored her.

"I would appreciate that, *n'okomiss*. I don't mean to rush you, but the moon grows large."

"I understand."

We rose, and she followed us to the door. Once on the porch, I thanked her. She smiled and put a hand on my bad shoulder.

"This means nothing," she murmured. "By giving it power, you are letting him win."

She was both spooky and right. However, when the scar ached and burned like a freshly torn wound it was a little hard to forget.

Jessie cleared her throat, pointed to her mouth. I wanted to toss her a Scooby snack.

Cora snapped her fingers and Jessie started speaking in midsentence.

"—think you are anyway? What's the deal?" She turned to me. "I thought you were on my side. And you." She rounded on Cadotte.

"Do you have any more of that powder, *n'okomiss*?"

Cora smiled and turned her pockets inside out.

They were empty.

. . .

"Was she scary?" Jessie asked. "Or was that just me?"

"Scary," I agreed.

We were on our way back to Crow Valley. Jessie had railed on Will until he'd said, "I told you to behave."

That shut her up as quickly as the powder had. If there'd been any powder. I wasn't quite sure about that anymore.

"What did we learn, children?" Jessie asked.

"The night of the blood moon will not be fun."

"I knew that already."

So had I.

"Hector became a Weendigo two years ago by promising to give the forces of evil the lives of your family."

I'd known that, too, but hearing it out loud made me wince. Since Jessie was gazing through the windshield and not at me, she didn't notice. However, Will's eyes met mine in the rearview mirror.

"Jess," he murmured.

"Huh?"

"I'm fine," I said hurriedly. "We need to work this out."

Jessie glanced at me over her shoulder, frowned, then shrugged and kept talking. "Killing them all still sounds good to me."

"Me, too," I agreed.

"Who knows? We might get lucky and pop Hector without even trying."

"We might." But I doubted it.

"Anything else occur to you while Sister Spooky was talking?" Jessie asked.

I told them my theory about Hector's enemy—petite blond women.

Jessie considered for a moment. "That makes sense, except for one thing."

"What?"

"Why didn't he kill you?"

An excellent question.

"I guess we could ask him when we find him. Or just kill him and forget about it."

"I choose the second thing."

"Me, too."

We went over everything Cora had told us, but we came up with no brilliant ideas for ending the power eater's plans before the hunter's moon. Unless Cora got back to us with something better, we were just going to keep shooting wolves and hope we got lucky.

Not the best plan, but the only one we had.

When we arrived at the tavern, the moon was up and the place was swinging. Jazz poured out of the windows, as usual. Lucky I slept in the daytime. Once in a while.

"I'm going to go back to our place and do some research," Will said.

Jessie retrieved her rifle and ammo from the trunk. "Leigh will give me a lift home, right?"

I nodded. Will drove off in a puff of dust and gravel.

I glanced at the tavern door, resisting the urge to go in, say hi, kiss Damien. With Jessie on my ass, that would be hard to do.

"I'll get my things." I ran upstairs and into my room.

Jessie followed. "One of us should tell Mandenauer what's up."

She was right. I called but got no answer. So I left a message outlining the visit to Cora. I also gave him the details on the mine, asked if he knew what that was all about, and finished with a question: "We still haven't found their lair. Any ideas?"

When I hung up, Jessie lifted a brow.

"What?" I asked.

"You didn't tell him."

"Yes, I did. You heard me."

"You didn't tell him about Hector."

"We aren't sure it's him."

"I am."

Well, that made one of us.

"You should tell him, Leigh," Jessie said quietly.

"No. And I don't want you telling him, either."

I'd gone from wanting Edward to come back and help me to suddenly wanting him to remain far away from here. If our power eater was Hector, he'd like nothing better than to kill, slowly, the man who'd taken me from him.

"Edward told me to handle this. I will."

Jessie stared at me awhile longer; then she nodded. I had a feeling she knew exactly what I'd been thinking without my saying anything. And she called Cora Kopway spooky.

Moments later, Jessie and I headed into the woods. I was supposed to be training her, but in truth, she was ready to go. She was a better tracker than I ever hoped to be. She'd dealt with werewolves before. I couldn't tell her much she didn't already know. When we were through here, she could handle her own assignment with ease.

The night was uneventful—if you call four kills and a couple misses uneventful. But we didn't see the white wolf or the brown one.

We'd been trailing a few females we'd seen from afar for over an hour and gotten nowhere fast. The trail ended less than a half a mile from the tavern, so we decided to call it a night though dawn had not yet come. Jessie and I climbed into my car and I headed toward town.

"Five days until the full moon," she said.

"I can count."

"Cranky from lack of sleep or need for sex?"

I didn't bother to answer.

"Remember what the witchy woman said—this thing can shift in ways we don't even know about."

"Meaning?"

"Damien could be Hector."

I nearly drove off the road.

"Hadn't thought of that, had you?"

"She said he could be different animals, different shades of wolf, shift in the daytime. She never said he could be two different people."

"She never said he couldn't."

What Jessie was suggesting was impossible, wasn't it?

Not really.

"I stared into Hector's eyes. There wasn't anyone home. Back then, I didn't know what that meant. I do now."

"Hector wasn't a werewolf until the night your family died. Before that he was just a man."

"He was a serial killer. A cannibal. How can evil like that not show in someone's eyes?"

"Ever seen a picture of Bundy? Dahmer? Such nice-looking young men."

She had a point.

But in Hector I'd seen the face of evil. I know I had. The truth did not live only in my nightmares. In Damien's eyes I'd seen love—as well as sadness, regret, a little bit of guilt.

Hell.

We reached Jessie's apartment. "Be careful," she said.

"Always am."

She lifted her brows but remained blissfully silent on that subject. I watched until the door to her apartment building closed securely behind her, and then I went back to mine.

I wanted the hunter's moon to be tonight. I wanted this to be over. I wanted to go on with my life. Or at least know that I couldn't.

I shut off the motor and something thunked onto the hood of my car. I glanced up and found a wolf staring back at me.

A thud on the roof, then one on the back end, signaled he wasn't alone. More wolves filtered out of the trees; hackles raised, they stalked stiffly toward my car.

I reached for the rifle in my backseat. The wolf on the hood, a huge gray beast, snarled.

"Too bad, so sad," I muttered.

He smashed his snout through the windshield. Shards erupted inward. The others attacked at the same time, and glass shattered all around me. I flinched, ducked my head reflexively, then remembered the gun.

I shot the gray wolf in the chest. Fire blazed, blinding me. I sensed movement to my right. Another wolf was crawling through the passenger window. A quick glance into the rearview mirror revealed one coming in through the rear.

I'd left my Glock in the trunk. No need for a handgun hunting in the woods. Now I cursed the long, unwieldy rifle in my hands. But the weapon was all I had—until it came down to the knife in my boot.

Hot breath brushed my neck, I turned, and a wolf snarled through a too-small hole in the driver's side window. He reared back to smash the glass again and I shot him. Sadly, that broke the glass. Could things get worse?

Another thud on the hood. The brown wolf straddled the center. Hector? Or someone else?

Hard to tell; he was staring at something above my head. How many wolves were on the roof?

The beast lifted his head and howled. The others froze.

What was he telling them? That I was his? He might think so, but I'd already vowed never again. I checked my ammo. Plenty left for a few more of them and one for me.

The brown wolf clambered onto the roof. The rest ran. The parking lot was deserted, except for the cars. Jazz still blared from the tavern. No one would have heard the wolf's call. Even if they had, they wouldn't have cared. Wolves howled in the forest every damn day.

Suddenly the brown wolf leaped from the roof. He hit the ground running and disappeared into the trees in the wake of the others. I was alone, with a smashed car and a full rifle.

What else could I do? I shoved open the door and followed him into the woods.

Probably not one of my better moves, but as I said, I wanted it over.

Dawn was just a hint in the sky. The wolves were no doubt headed for their lair. Maybe that's what the brown wolf had told them.

Not *Leave her alone*. But *Get your butts back before you change*.

Excitement made my breath hitch. What if I found their lair, killed them all? I could save myself, my friends, the world. Not bad for a night's work.

I could hear them ahead of me. They were moving fast. If they wanted to lose me they could. I'd never be able to keep up on foot.

After a few minutes, the sound of them panting, growling, pushing through scrub faded. All I could hear was the wind through the leaves and the birds waking up with the sun.

Suddenly they stopped twittering. Icy cold dread skittered down my spine seconds before a caramel-shaded wolf rocketed out of the trees to my left. I only had time to shift my weight before he hit me and knocked me on my back.

I let the gun go so I could use both arms, but the thing was huge and pinned my hands beneath me with more skill than a professional wrestler. I braced, expecting my throat to be gone the next instant. Nothing happened.

Slowly I opened my eyes. The wolf lay on my chest, tongue lolling, grinning into my face like a big, dumb dog. Then he licked me—one huge slobber from my neck to my forehead. His breath smelled like blood. Now I did.

A howl drifted toward the descending moon. The wolf tensed; his attention shifted toward the fading melody. When he looked at me, his expression had changed. He snarled, pulled back to strike. This was it.

Aarp!

He yelped as he was dragged away. I scrambled to my feet the instant I was free. The brown wolf killed him in a single vicious yank at the throat. He was really very good at that.

Blood sprayed the ground like in an out-of-control Monty Python skit. I turned, searching for my gun, pouncing on the thing as if it were a buoy in the middle of a vast ocean. When I spun around, rifle at the ready, the only animal in the clearing was dead.

Blood trailed into the woods.

A few hundred yards away the trail petered out. But I could hear him crashing through the trees in his haste to retreat. Time was against him.

I burst into the clearing, got him in my sights, and the sun sparked auburn highlights through his fur. He howled as if in pain, and I hadn't even shot him yet.

I'd seen plenty of men change into wolves, but I'd never seen one change back. It wasn't a pretty sight. The contortions, the grunting and the gurgling, the snapping of bone and stretching of muscles. I stood there, fascinated, amazed, horrified.

I knew that ass.

29

Damien Fitzgerald straightened from quadrupedal to bipedal. Completely naked, he glistened in the early-morning sunshine. I was unimpressed.

My hands shook. My heart raced. My eyes blurred. I'd done it again. Fucked a monster.

What was the matter with me?

"Leigh—" he began, and took a step in my direction.

I fired, the bullet kicking up dirt at his feet. He hesitated but only for an instant. His long bare legs ate up the distance until he was standing far too close.

Why didn't I shoot him? He was the enemy. He could be anyone. He could be *the one*. My finger tightened on the trigger.

Damien grabbed the barrel and put it against his chest, exactly where his heart would be, if he had one.

"You think I care? Shoot me. You'd be doing me a favor."

I frowned, remembering the behavior of the brown werewolf the first night I'd seen him. I'd thought then that the wolf had wanted me to shoot him. Guess I'd been right.

"If you hate me, then kill me, Leigh. The only thing I've ever found worth living for is you."

I stared into his eyes and saw the love again. It terrified me. Was it real or just another lie?

All my silly dreams rose up and choked me. I'd envisioned a life with this man. Family. Children.

I gagged. He hadn't used a condom last time. What did that mean?

Suddenly I was running—through the trees, back the way I'd come. Away from him and all the confusing, heartbreaking things he made me feel. I reached my car. The thing was trashed.

I had nowhere to go, except to my room. So I did.

No messages on my phone, no E-mail to answer. I drifted around the place trying to find something to occupy my mind. But I couldn't.

All I could think about was Damien. The werewolf.

I waited for the hate and loathing that usually filled me whenever I thought of the beasts. They didn't come. Instead, I remembered touching him, holding him, kissing him. I'd loved him. Why?

Desperate, I pulled out the picture of Jimmy, then the ones of my parents, my brother, my sister. I touched their faces with a fingertip. I said their names out loud.

"Emily, Greg, Carol, and Dan Tyler. James Renquist."
Gone because of me. Because of the monsters.

I'd sworn to kill them all. But I hadn't. Not yet.

I tugged a chair even with the door, took a seat, placed my rifle over my legs, and waited. I didn't have to wait very long.

The lock clicked; the door swung open. Damien's silhouette filled the opening. At least he'd found his clothes. Would his body have distracted me even now? I didn't want to know.

"Damn you," I said.

He stepped inside and shut the door. "Too late."

His words reminded me of the nature of werewolves. They were damned, cursed, inhabited by a demon. So what was wrong with him?

"Who are you?" I asked. "*What* are you?"

"I've told you who I am. You saw what I can become."

"You lied to me."

"Not really. You knew I had secrets. Now I don't."

I snorted. "Splitting hairs, Damien."

"Making jokes, Leigh?"

"Are you Hector Menendez?"

He raised his eyebrows. "Do I look like a Hector to you?"

If he was lying, he did it very well. But then so had Hector.

"You're a shape-shifter," I accused.

"I never said I wasn't. What's your excuse?"

"I don't know what you mean."

"The DNR? Rabies? Please. You're a *Jäger-Sucher*."

Well, so much for our *secret* society of monster hunters. Not that the werewolves didn't know someone was after them; they just didn't know who. By the time they saw a face, they were seconds away from being dead. Of course there were always a few that escaped—and after the debacle in Miniwa, who was to say how many of them knew more about us than we'd like?

"Everyone here knows what I am?" I asked.

"Of course not. They'd have killed you. I told them you were who you said you were. Besides, who'd believe a *Jäger-Sucher* would sleep with the enemy?"

"Not me," I muttered. "How long have you known?"

"The first day you showed up. Jessie's one, too." He tilted his head. "I'm not sure about Cadotte. He doesn't smell like guns and death. But he's up to something."

"Why haven't you tried to kill me if you know I'm here to kill you?"

He leaned against the wall, crossed his arms over his chest. His shirt was unbuttoned again. There was a cigarette sticking out of his pocket. I guess he didn't have to worry about cancer. Lucky him.

"I figured if you were nearby," he continued, "I could keep an eye on you. Better the enemy you see than the one you don't."

Enemy? For some reason that hurt, even though it was true.

"Besides," he continued, "why would I kill someone who's doing the same thing I am?"

"Which is?"

"Killing them."

The words fell between us like a boulder through a sheet of glass. My hands tightened on the rifle in my lap. "You say that like you're different from the others."

He shrugged.

My gaze went to his ring finger. Maybe he was.

"How many did you have to kill before you became powerful enough to wear silver?"

Damien frowned. "Silver? Oh!" He lifted his hand. "This? Platinum. My mother's."

Platinum? I'd heard of it, of course, just never considered one metal could so resemble another. I never thought being jewelry-challenged would be a problem in my line of work. Wrong again.

"Give it to me," I demanded.

We'd just see what it was. At *J-S* headquarters. If the thing was made of silver . . . I didn't want to think about what that meant.

He pulled off the ring and crossed the short distance to

drop it into my palm. I kept the gun ready. I still didn't trust him.

He stared at the barrel, lifted his gaze to my face. "I meant it when I said that I loved you."

"Save it," I snapped.

I couldn't think of that now. There were too many other problems to solve.

"I don't understand what you meant about becoming more powerful," he began.

"I'm asking the questions."

I motioned with the rifle for him to back up. He was too close. I could smell his skin, feel the heat from his body. It made me want to touch him, made me wonder, again, if he had bewitched me somehow.

He retreated to the door, closed it, and sat on the floor with his back against the wood.

"Why are you killing them?" I asked.

"Why are you?"

Hadn't I just said I was asking the questions? He didn't take orders very well. Big surprise. I decided to answer anyway.

"I'm killing them because they're evil. Possessed. Murdering, demonic, soulless entities."

"Ditto."

I blinked. "What the hell is that supposed to mean?"

"I agree. That's why I'm killing them."

"But . . . so are you."

"I was. Now I'm different. You were right."

I kept the gun pointed at his chest. But he didn't move from his position in front of the door.

"Start talking," I muttered.

"I was in the war—"

"What war?"

"*The* war. World War Two. What other war is there?"

Damien had been in World War Two? I looked him up and down. I'd been told that werewolves lived forever appearing exactly the same age they had been when they were bitten. Of course I never had much of a chance to chat with them and discover if what I'd heard was true.

"There've been quite a few wars since then," I pointed out.

"None like that one."

He was right. Since the last war to end all wars, combat had changed. No more whole-scale invasions onto beaches. We had fighter jets, aircraft carriers, smart bombs. The face of modern warfare. Americans didn't see their enemy up close and personal anymore. Except for me.

I motioned with the gun. "Get on with it."

"I was a part of the D-day invasion. Seen any film of that?"

"Saving Private Ryan."

He made a face. "From what I heard, the movie was close, but the reality was much, much worse."

"You didn't see it?"

"I couldn't."

Damien was a werewolf, had done unimaginable things, but he couldn't bear to see a movie reenacting a battle. I wondered if the sadness in his eyes reflected more than werewolf guilt.

"I made it past Omaha Beach and started through the French countryside. We were in a race to Berlin. Americans on one side, Russians on the other."

"I know the drill."

"Right. Anyway, there were Germans all over the place. Snipers. Panzers. Damn circus. More so than I realized. We had just moved into Germany when they attacked."

He shifted, looping his arms around his knees and hunching his shoulders. Staring at his hands, he continued. "Hundreds of werewolves came out of the trees and swept over us like . . . like—"

"A werewolf army," I whispered.

I'd heard the story of Hitler's monster legion, but I'd never met anyone who'd seen it.

"We didn't have silver bullets. No matter how many times we shot them, they kept coming. They killed everything in their path. It was a slaughter."

"And you? How did you manage to survive?"

His light eyes flicked to mine, then away. "I was young. Foolish. I wanted to live. I didn't realize what that meant."

Damien took a deep breath as if bracing himself. "When I saw what was happening, I ran and hid. The guns didn't work. Our tanks were too far behind to help. I'm not sure if they could. No silver ammo in them, either." He emitted a short bark of laughter. "One of the werewolves found me. I . . . I . . . begged for my life."

He refused to look at me. I waited for him to continue. What could I say?

"I'd seen so many of my friends die. On the beach, the march, in that forest. I was twenty-three, and I didn't want to die. So I begged. A mistake I've paid for over and over again."

"What happened?"

"The wolf wasn't hungry anymore. He granted my wish and made me like him."

Silence settled over the room as Damien remembered what that meant and I considered it, too. If he had been a werewolf since 1944, how many had he killed? The possibilities boggled the mind.

"I became possessed. The bloodlust is like nothing you

can imagine, especially when you first become. You're out of control. Being in Germany, during that time, I had no problem feeding the hunger. With my entire company wiped out, and pretty much strewn in pieces all over the countryside, disappearing wasn't a big deal. I was listed as killed in action. I never saw my family again." He took a deep breath, let it out slowly. "How could I when I was like this?"

Sympathy sparked in my chest and I squashed it ruthlessly. "I'm not hearing anything that makes you different from all the other murdering scum I've put a silver bullet into over the years."

"I'm not. I killed—first in Germany, then all over Europe and Russia. Back then it was easy. So many people, nobody noticed. It wasn't that much different from when I'd been a soldier. Except now the enemy was any human. It didn't matter what uniform they wore or which flag they waved.

"At first I liked being a werewolf. I'd been afraid for so long. I was a kid when I went into the army. I'd worked on the docks in New York." He glanced down at his hands—calloused, scraped, rough. "It was hard work, but the war was worse. I was terrified of dying, but I had to go. Back then we had little choice. The world was being decimated. We had to save it or kiss everything and everyone we'd ever loved good-bye. I did anyway."

"Wah, wah, wah," I sniped.

His lips lifted into his usual ghost of a smile. "When you're bitten, you change. And I don't mean just the transformation. The virus—or whatever it is that does this—makes you selfish. All you care about is your next meal, how to survive, how to thrive. *Me, me, me* pounds in your head like an anthem. That's the demon, Leigh. Complete and total self-absorption."

"Sociopath," I muttered.

"Exactly."

I made a note to mention this to Edward. Although I doubted very many werewolves went in for psychiatric advice on their psychosis, it couldn't hurt to check out anyone with sociopathic tendencies.

"I stayed in Europe until the last of my family was gone. I didn't want to run into anyone who knew me. How would I explain being alive?"

"Wouldn't your mother have loved you no matter what?"

"Of course. But I no longer cared about my mother, about love, family, or anything that's truly important; I only cared about me."

I frowned. This didn't sound like the Damien I'd come to know and lo— I mean hate.

"When everyone who'd known me then was dead, I came back to America. I missed the place. As much as I could miss or care for anything. Besides, Europe was getting dangerous. All the monsters that had been released by the Nazis—"

I jolted. "You know about that?"

"Of course. We have our fairy tales, our legends, our history, too. The beings Mengele had fashioned in his lab were causing problems. You see, Europeans believe in things Americans don't."

"Like what?"

"People who've lived next to the Black Forest for centuries have watched some unbelievable creatures come out of those trees. They buy silver ammo as easily as we buy a cheeseburger. But in America, a country that's only a few hundred years old, the citizens are modern. They only believe what they see, hear, and touch. Do they sell silver bullets at Wal-Mart yet?"

I saw his point.

"I came back in 1968 to a world gone crazy. People hitchhiking all over the place. Free love. Drugs everywhere. It was the perfect time for monsters. With all the drifting around the country, folks disappeared without a trace."

"And now?" I asked.

"Now it's tougher. But people still disappear. You know that as well as I do."

He was right. Despite the computers, the technology, the numbers and requirements necessary for daily living, people still disappeared. Both Damien and I knew why.

"You haven't told me one damn thing that makes me want to put a slug of silver between your eyes any less."

"I don't kill people any more. I kill werewolves."

I wasn't sure I believed him, but I'd give him the benefit of the doubt. "Why?"

"Because something happened that made me understand what I was doing. Made me agonize over every life I'd taken. Made me remember all the pain I'd caused. The faces of the ones I've killed haunt me, and the only way to make them fade for even an instant is to end the existence of others like me."

"I've never heard of a werewolf with a conscience before."

"Never been one that I know of. I'm cursed—or blessed." His lips twitched. "Depending on how you look at it."

I wasn't sure how to look at it, because I found all of this pretty hard to believe.

30

"About a year ago," Damien continued, "I was in Arkansas."

"You get around."

"Have to. People disappearing is one thing. A whole bunch of them disappearing in the same place is another."

I shrugged, conceding the point.

"Werewolves crave human flesh. Most feed a few times a month, more often if they have a wound to heal. But there's one night we have to feed."

"The full moon."

"Yes. Strange things happen on that night. Ask any cop, ER worker, any third-shift waitress or bartender. Full moon equals a very busy night. A year ago I was in the Arkansas hills. There was a woman. . . ." His voice faded and he stared at his feet again.

"Don't worry; I won't be jealous."

As soon as the words were out of my mouth, I wanted them back. I sounded like a scorned lover, a pathetic, needy girlie-girl. Everything I'd never wanted to be.

Sighing, he ignored my jibe. "It's just . . . hard to remember how I was. What I did."

I doubted I wanted to hear this, but I had to. "Go on."

Damien took a deep breath. "I'd done some work on her place. She was alone. Her husband took off. She had four kids."

My eyes widened. He really was a pig.

"I'd planned on staying awhile. I could get several full moons' worth."

His voice flattened; his eyes went distant; his face was the mask it had been when I first met him, devoid of emotion and life.

"They lived alone. Existed hand-to-mouth. They were perfect, and they were mine."

"What happened?" I whispered.

"The full moon came, so beautiful and bright. The harvest moon. September. Warm days, cool nights, clear skies. I changed and ran, the wind in my fur, the grass beneath my feet. I ran until I was starving, and then I went back."

His voice shook on the last word. He scrubbed his fingers through his hair and his hand shook, too.

"Damien—" I began.

He ignored me. "She always sat outside once she got the kids to bed. A little 'lone time, she called it. I walked right onto the porch. She didn't even move."

He stared straight ahead as if he could see his past. "The youngest child opened the door. The mother cried out, tried to push her back, but the little girl took one look at me and—" Damien shook his head. "She couldn't have been more than five or six, and she knew what I was going to do. She squirmed out of her mother's hold shouting, 'No, Damien,' threw her arms around my neck, and whispered, 'Take me. Mommy needs to be a mommy for the others.'"

"Sacrifice," I murmured. "You didn't—"

"No. But I would have. I didn't give a shit about sacrifice, mother's love, anything but meat."

I flinched.

"I'd have killed them all, but for one thing. The child said my human name while I was in wolf form."

"That doesn't work—"

"Not to change a werewolf's form, but it works pretty damned well to curse him. If there's an Ozark Mountain magic woman nearby."

"What?"

"Mommy knew magic."

"Magic." I resisted the urge to snort. "Right."

His lips lifted, just a little. "We're discussing werewolves and you're rolling your eyes about magic? There's a saying in the Ozarks—if you throw out the witch, you'd better throw out the Bible, too."

"What the hell does that mean?"

"If you can believe in supernatural evil, why can't you believe in supernatural good?"

He had a point. "So what did the Ozark magic woman do?"

"Not much. The most important thing had already been done. Sacrifice."

"But you said you didn't—"

"Just because I didn't kill that child doesn't make her sacrifice any less heroic. I could have run, but I was paralyzed, confused. A being that thrives on selfishness is confronted with total sacrifice. I might have been a wolf, but I still had my brain and it was on overload. I stood there while the mother yanked her child away from me. Her face was wet with tears as she cut her own wrist—"

"Blood, tears, sacrifice."

"The usual," he murmured, echoing words of my own

that he'd never even heard. "Then she cursed, or maybe she blessed, me. I'm still not sure. She said, 'Damien, from this day on your soul is yours again.'"

"Huh?"

"When I became a werewolf, my soul was possessed by evil. I was myself but not myself. She gave me back my soul and my conscience."

"Ah."

"It's a terrible thing to remember what you've done and know how wrong it was."

I understood why his eyes were always sad. Why he never smiled and rarely laughed. Understood but didn't forgive.

"You chose to be one of them."

"I know."

"When did you start to hunt your own kind?"

"I left Arkansas for obvious reasons. Went to Florida, hid in the Everglades. I was haunted by fifty years of faces. Yet the next month, when the full moon came, I hunted. I had no choice. The hunger is a burning, painful thing. You can't think past it."

"Why didn't you shoot yourself before the next full moon?"

He lifted a brow. "I wasn't quite that desperate. Yet."

"Yet?"

"What do you think the gun behind the toilet tank was for, Leigh?"

"I thought it wasn't yours."

"I lied."

I blinked. He'd lied about the gun. But what was one more lie? What disturbed me was how well he'd lied. I'd believed him completely. As completely as I'd believed he loved me.

"Where is it now?"

"Somewhere safe. In case I need it."

"I used the bullet."

He shrugged. "I can always get more."

"But you can't touch silver."

"That doesn't mean I don't know someone who can."

The idea of a hidden gun with a single silver bullet, just in case, disturbed me, and I wasn't sure why. I still might shoot him myself. I pushed the thought aside for later analysis. I had enough on my plate already.

"So you went hunting in the Everglades—"

"Miami, actually. A lot more people. But despite the hunger, I couldn't do it. The very thought of killing and eating a person suddenly nauseated me. Then I came upon another like me and the sickness disappeared. I could kill *them*. With every werewolf destroyed I'd be saving lives, and maybe I could atone a little bit for all the deaths."

I wasn't sure if I believed him. What if he was the power eater? What if he was the white wolf and the brown? What if he was Hector? What if he wasn't? I wasn't truly certain my nemesis was here—except for the weird stinging of my back. Which just might mean I was halfway to crazy again.

I decided to try a frontal assault. "You won't get away with it."

"OK. Whatever *it* is."

He seemed as confused as I was, but he'd seemed a lot of things and none of them were true.

"Why are you here?" I asked. "There has to be a reason you came to Crow Valley instead of any other burg on the planet."

He blinked. "You don't know?"

"What?"

"I figured that was why you were here, too."

I started to feel uneasy. "What the hell are you talking about?"

"*Crow* Valley. You don't know why it's called that?"

"Because there are a lot of crows, though I've only seen one."

"There *were* a lot of crows, back when the town began. Because this place was wolf haven."

"So?"

"Now it's werewolf run."

"I don't get it."

"When this town was founded there were a lot of crows and wolves. But when werewolves move in—"

"Real wolves move out."

"And the regular folks don't notice the difference. Until it's too late."

"You're saying that Crow Valley has a higher than average population of shape-shifters."

"That's exactly what I'm saying."

Which would explain why the power eater was here.

"Tell me how you get more powerful from killing them. How can you eat your own kind?"

"Eat my— What?"

"Don't bullshit me, Damien. I'm here because there's a werewolf killing other werewolves—"

"Me."

"And eating them."

His face went blank. "Not me."

"You said you no longer crave human flesh."

"That doesn't mean I crave werewolf meat."

"Well, what do you eat?"

"Cheeseburgers."

I'd think he was kidding, but he so rarely was.

Damien glanced away as if embarrassed. "The blood-lust seems to be satisfied by killing them."

"You're saying you aren't trying to become the supreme alpha on the night of the hunter's moon."

His gaze returned to mine. "I have no idea what you're talking about."

"Right. There are two of you running around these woods killing other wolves."

Something flickered in his eyes.

"What?" I demanded

"There've been a lot of disappearing lycanthropes. More than I've killed. I figured some of them were scared off, or just took off, but . . ."

"But what?"

"A few times when I've been hunting I could swear there was another wolf following me."

Was he lying again? I had no idea.

"I'd circle around, try to get a scent, but it would change. Appear. Disappear. Lap over other scents. I couldn't catch up to him. I never saw another wolf, except the ones I killed."

Had the power eater been trailing Damien, eating his kills, stealing their power? Or was Damien working with him and lying to me?

I didn't know what to believe. I didn't know what to do. Could I kill him—right here, right now, when he was doing nothing but talking to me? I didn't think so.

"Are you going to tell me what's going on?" he asked.

"No."

"Maybe I can help."

"Maybe you can kiss my ass."

"Leigh." He got to his feet and started toward me.

I aimed my rifle at his head. "Stay over there."

He stopped walking, but he didn't sit down. "We need to talk."

"About what?"

"Us."

Suddenly I was out of my chair, the barrel pressed to his throat. Stupid, really. Werewolves, in both forms, can move more quickly than the human eye. He could take the gun away from me. He had before. He only had to want to.

I was angry, scared, hurt. I'd dreamed things about him and now those dreams were as dead as all my others.

"There isn't any us, Damien."

"I'm still the same man you slept with."

"No, you're the monster who lied to me."

A flicker of hurt passed over his face and for an instant I almost felt bad. Then I remembered something I'd chosen, for a little while, to forget.

"The last time we—" I broke off. I couldn't make myself say it.

"Made love?"

"That wasn't love."

"It was for me."

"What did you do to me?" I gave him a little shove with the barrel of the gun.

"I thought I made you come."

He was pissing me off. Shooting him didn't seem so bad anymore, but I needed some answers first.

"You didn't use a condom. Does this mean I'll have puppies? Cubs? What?"

Damien sighed. "I meant it when I said I couldn't get you pregnant. Cross-species impregnation is impossible. I'd think you hotshot *Jäger-Suchers* would know that."

I frowned. Yeah, why didn't we?

"You didn't give me what you have, did you?"

"Lycanthropy?"

"Or anything else disgusting?"

"The werewolf virus can only be passed through saliva while in wolf form."

I knew that.

"Any disease I might have would be healed the first time I changed. Just like any wound that wasn't inflicted with silver."

Huh, learn something new every day.

"If that's the case, then why did you use a condom in the first place?"

"Wouldn't you have wondered if I didn't?"

Maybe. If I'd been able to think beyond having him inside me.

"I was trying to pass for human," he said. "Especially with you."

"Why especially?"

"I didn't care too much about living, but I didn't want to die. I've got too many of them to kill yet."

I remembered the sentiment, from my own head. That we thought alike disturbed me. I lowered the gun from his neck. "Move back."

He did, but not far enough. Right now, Venezuela wouldn't be far enough.

I sat down. My legs didn't want to hold me upright much longer.

Werewolves have evil hearts, possessed souls. They'd kill their own mother. Lying would be kid stuff. I couldn't believe anything Damien told me.

So why did I want to?

31

Because I was pathetic and needy. I missed love. I needed sex.

Pathetic. See?

My cell phone rang—the sound shrill in the sudden silence. Both of us jumped. I got up to answer. Damien was so close, I shoved him back as I went by, and he let me.

If he was a big, bad werewolf wouldn't he have killed me by now? Why wait? Avoid the rush.

I was grasping at straws and I knew it.

"Hello?"

"Liebchen."

I gripped the phone more tightly, calmed by Edward's voice. My eyes met Damien's and I hesitated. I knew what Edward would want me to do, and I couldn't. Not yet.

"I received your message," he continued. "Any more information for me?"

"Wasn't that enough?" I asked.

"I would say no. The native woman—"

Edward, ever politically incorrect—what can you expect from an eighty-year-old-and-then-some former spy?

"Her information was interesting, but we still do not

know what the power eater plans for the night of the hunter's moon. You do not know where their lair is."

"Any clues on that?"

"Search for a gathering place. Isolated. Protected."

"Been there, done that. Found nothing."

"I cannot help you, Leigh. I am here; you are there. Do the job."

"Why don't you come and help me?" I blurted, then wished I hadn't.

Edward might look like anyone's great-granddad, but he wasn't. He'd blow Damien's brains out without a second thought. Step on the remains, grind them into dust, and never flinch. Once I'd been that way, too. Suddenly I wasn't, and it left me floundering and alone.

"I can't," he answered.

I frowned. Edward had been saying that since I'd gotten to Crow Valley. It wasn't like him to avoid the action. "Why?"

"You've been trained for this job. You do not need me."

His voice was clipped, angry. Something was going on, but I knew Edward well enough to know he wasn't going to tell me what it was.

"Have you done any further investigation of the odd dwelling with the human remains? I have never heard of anything like it."

Which couldn't be good.

"I haven't been back. What should I look for?"

"I have no idea."

This from the man who knew everything.

I continued to study Damien as I spoke to Edward. He leaned against the wall and stared right back. His odd, changeable, unblinking eyes should have made me leery. Instead they made me hot. I was crazier than even I thought I was.

Why hadn't I recognized Damien's eyes in those of the brown wolf? I'd taken one glance at Hector in wolf form and known him for what he was. Damien . . . not so much.

His eyes were strange—changing hue depending on the light and what he was wearing. Still, I should have known. Unless, maybe, I hadn't wanted to see.

Edward mumbled something on the other end of the line.

"What was that?"

"I have to go, Leigh."

And he did. Just like that.

"Now what?" Damien asked.

Exactly. Now what?

Was there a way to check his story? Maybe.

"Do you have a Social Security number?"

"I did." At my frown he continued, "I died in Germany, remember?"

"So you say."

Damn. How was I going to check out his story without tipping off every *Jäger-Sucher* in the country that I was investigating someone who was already dead? I had no idea.

The question disturbed me so much, I let my guard drop. The next instant Damien stood right next to me. I tried to bring up the rifle, but he snatched it away and tossed it on the bed.

The heel of my hand shot toward his nose. Old habits are hard to break.

He blocked the blow with a lightning-fast movement that nevertheless appeared lazy. How did they *do* that?

He yanked me against his body, and he wouldn't let me go. My heart thundered in my ears, warring with the harsh, panting sound that at first I thought was him but instead turned out to be me. I was panicked, frightened, and so turned on my skin seemed to be dancing around on top of my bones.

Was he going to kill me? Or worse?

I struggled, but that only seemed to excite him more. His erection pressed against my stomach, pulsing and shifting, as if it had a life of its own.

He pressed his face to my neck, inhaled as if memorizing my scent. Hell, maybe he was. My hands were trapped against my body; my feet dangled above the floor. I could do nothing to stop him, and in truth, I didn't want to.

His tongue blazed a hot, wet trail from my collarbone to my ear. His teeth grazed the throbbing vein at the curve. I shuddered as he nibbled and laved.

My hands were free. Instead of socking him in the eye, I pulled him closer, my fingers tangling in the dark, curling strands of his hair.

When had my legs wrapped around his waist? When had his palms cupped my ass?

He nuzzled the tops of my breasts. I yanked my shirt down and his mouth closed over a nipple, his tongue pressing me against the roof of his mouth, once, twice, again. I tightened my legs. I was going to come. He lifted his head and whispered, "I love you, Leigh."

My body went ice-cold. I didn't have to struggle; this time when I pulled away he let me go. My breasts were still exposed, wet from his mouth, aching with arousal and frustration. I covered myself and fought the urge to take a shower.

Hurt flickered in his eyes; his face hardened. "It's OK to have sex with you but not to love you?"

I lifted my chin. "That's right. I seem to recall a deal that involved taking what you could get."

"I've been taking most of my life. I've finally found someone I want to give something to."

"I'm not buying."

"I'm not selling. I'm *giving*. I love you."

"Stop saying that!" I shouted.

Jimmy had loved me. It had gotten him killed.

Damien could take care of himself, like Hector. Who had also loved me. Sick son of a bitch.

Which man did Damien most favor? Sweet Jimmy who'd wanted nothing more than for me to be happy? Or demonic Hector who'd only wanted me to be like him?

Shit.

"Leigh," Damien whispered, his fingers caressing my arm, his breath in my hair. "What can I do to make you believe me?"

I was swaying toward him before I realized it. Since I'd lost my family, my future, and my mind, I'd prided myself on my self-reliance. I needed no one. In that way I could never be destroyed again when someone I loved died.

How many days had I known Damien? Already my body accepted his nearness, trusted him above my head and my heart. Stupid body.

I wanted to lean on him, believe in him, but I couldn't.

I inched away, stood on my own again, even though my hand lingered on his arm, slid through his palm, fingers clinging for just an instant to his.

"I have no idea," I answered, which was true.

How could I prove he wasn't an evil werewolf when, as far as I knew, there'd never been a nonevil one before? Asking Edward would raise too many questions. Same thing with Jessie and Will.

The door burst open and Damien shoved me behind him. Impressive. But was the move real or had he heard Jessie pounding up the stairs with his superwolf powers? More than likely.

"Knock much?" I asked.

She ignored me. Her face was eager; she was practically dancing on the tips of her toes. "I have to talk to you," she blurted. "Alone."

Damien shrugged and headed for the door. I reached for him and caught just the tail of his shirt. The silk slid through my fingers and was gone.

I didn't want him out of my sight. What if I never saw him again?

"Damien?" He turned. "Don't—uh—go anywhere, OK?"

He lifted a brow. "Where would I go?"

Was he trying to be a smart-ass? I couldn't be sure.

"Jeez, Leigh, you can hop back into the sack with him later."

I winced. Thankfully she didn't notice, but Damien did. His eyes went sad and he slipped out the door.

Why did I feel as though I'd kicked a puppy?

The analogy almost made me laugh until Jessie spoke. "We've got two more half-eaten wolves."

"Where?"

"Elwood found them near his house about forty-five minutes ago. He lives a good thirty miles on the other side of town."

Thirty miles from Crow Valley. Ten miles from the tavern to town, which made forty miles away.

"Had they been dead long?"

"That's the best part. Elwood saw the wolf eating them."

Our eyes met. I didn't even have to ask.

"White," she said. "Just like we thought."

"That doesn't mean much with super-duper shape-shifter powers."

"Doesn't hurt, either."

I thought about what she'd said. The white wolf had been seen forty miles from here at the same time I'd been saved by a brown wolf, which I knew to be Damien.

It didn't mean Damien couldn't have killed those wolves; he could even have had a nibble or two. But he couldn't *be* the white wolf. This was good news and made me feel a little bit better about not telling Jessie the truth.

"You ran all the way out here and burst in like a kid on Christmas morning to tell me this?" I asked. "You couldn't use the phone?"

"You shut it off, dip wad."

I frowned, crossed the room, glanced at my cell. I had. Chalk it up to having my life come apart at the seams again.

"I was talking to Edward," I said.

"Anything interesting?"

"Not really."

Jessie nodded as if she'd expected as much. "Cora called."

"And?"

"*She* found something interesting."

"Where?"

"In her *Textbook of Witches and Werewolves.* How the hell should I know? Cadotte was practically prancing when he got off the phone. Couldn't wait to tell you all about it."

"Where is he?"

Jessie opened her mouth, then shut it again, shrugged.

"I pointed out that this information might be easier coming from a girl."

Aw, hell.

"Spill it, Jessie."

"Why don't we sit?"

"That bad, huh?"

"You aren't going to like it. That much I know. But Will's on the job. He's searching every Internet corner and every book that he has to find a way to stop this before it happens."

"Stop what?"

Jessie sat on the couch. I perched on the edge of a chair. She sighed and spilled it.

"Remember what Sister Spooky said about the night of the hunter's moon?"

"Sacrifice. Blood, death, tears. Yada yada."

Jessie smiled. "There's a little more to it than that."

"Isn't there always?"

"Yep. Did you know that only the alpha pair in a wolf pack can mate?"

"I seem to recall something about it in *Wolf Behavior 333*."

Jessie lifted a brow.

"Hell. Supreme *alpha*. The ritual involves sex?"

"So I hear."

"With who?"

"His mate."

My back started to burn as if someone had doused it with kerosene and struck a match.

32

"Fuck me," I muttered.

"I think that's what he has in mind."

"Now what?" I asked, which seemed to be the question of the week.

"Now we keep blasting wolves whenever the opportunity presents itself, search for their lair, keep an eye out for Hector night and day, and dig, dig, dig some more for a way to end this before the moon gets full."

"Because if we don't?"

"You get to do the dirty in front of every werewolf in town."

I wanted to say something flippant, but my voice betrayed me. All I could do was move my mouth. No sound came out.

Jessie appeared concerned. She moved closer and patted me on the back, hard enough to make me choke, then cough. At least it was something.

"I'm OK," I managed.

"Will wants to go back to Cora's. Borrow some of her books. Wanna come?"

She was babysitting me. I wasn't going to let her.

"No. I've got things to do."

Jessie frowned. "But—"

"If what you say is true, I'm safe until the full moon. If it's even Hector."

"We both know it's Hector, Leigh."

I shifted my shoulders. Pain flashed across my skin. Yeah, we did.

"I need some sleep," I said. "Why don't you come back here with the books. I'll order pizza. We'll brainstorm, then go out and kill things. It'll be a girls' night out."

She hesitated. "You promise you'll stay inside until we get back?"

"Yes, Mother."

Her eyes narrowed, but she got off the couch and moved toward the door. She seemed to have no ill effects from her own shoulder wound. I was glad.

Jessie paused with her hand on the doorknob. "We know what they're up to, Leigh. That means we're one step ahead of them. I've got a good feeling about this."

"Well then, everything's gonna be all right."

Her lips twitched. She almost laughed. "Keep on being a smart guy. You know how I love that."

The door shut behind her. I looked around the rented room, took in my bag and my laptop. I had no address but .com, no closet but a suitcase. I was suddenly sick of having nowhere to call home. When had that happened?

I lay down, tried to sleep. Drifted in and out. But every time I closed my eyes I saw the mine, those human bones. There was something weird about that. They were almost like a warning.

I sat bolt upright in my bed. We'd never gone past those bones and suddenly I wanted to.

I glanced at the window. Night was falling. I must have drifted further than I'd thought.

I'd promised Jessie I wouldn't go outside, definitely shouldn't at this time of night. Oh well, I'd never been very good at keeping promises. Remember the one I'd made to Jimmy?

I got dressed, grabbed a few guns, some ammo, then walked downstairs.

Damien's cabin was dark. However, the bar was lit up like a major-league baseball field during the seventh-inning stretch.

I headed in that direction. Even Jessie couldn't get mad at me for investigating with Damien at my side. What better backup than a werewolf? Too bad I couldn't tell her that.

Stepping inside the tavern, I frowned. The place was empty, except for the shoes, wallets, purses, keys, and little piles of clothing.

My fingers tightened on my rifle. Their lair had been here all the time.

Damien had to have known. Why hadn't he told me?

Of course, I hadn't asked. Who'd have suspected they were changing right underneath my nose? Talk about hiding in plain sight.

My plans changed. I'd just sit down and wait for them to come back.

I thought of how many I'd kill tonight. Maybe even Hector, though I doubted it. He wouldn't be dumb enough to show his face here.

So why was my scar burning as if it were a fresh, new wound?

"Waitin' for someone?"

I gasped and spun toward the bar. Cowboy stood on

top, leering, snarling, or whatever the hell it was he did with his lip.

"Uh, yeah, well, I was looking for Damien."

Cowboy narrowed his eyes. "He ain't around."

"I see that."

"Yer not gonna ask why everyone's clothes are all over the floor?"

"Why?"

He snorted. "You know why."

Cowboy jumped off the bar, his boots clicking on the wood floor as he meandered toward me. I kept my hands on my guns, my eyes on his face. I'd crossed him off as a werewolf long ago, but maybe that hadn't been such a bright idea. I'd figured if he was a shifter he'd have cured whatever ailment had made him a midget in the first place. But maybe he hadn't. Maybe he liked being small. Maybe it got him ignored.

He stopped only a foot away from me. "I got somethin' to show you."

He began to unbutton his shirt. I backed toward the door. "Uh, no thanks."

He smiled. "You don't mind seeing Damien's chest, but you don't want to see mine?"

"That about sums it up."

"Believe me, Leigh, you're gonna want to see this."

Somehow I doubted that. I reached for the doorknob. My hand touched the brass just as Cowboy's shirt fell open.

The pentagram tattoo on his breastbone gleamed black against his pale, smooth skin. I couldn't move. Couldn't breathe.

I lifted my gaze from his chest to his face. His eyes were weird—water flowing under dark ice. I stood there staring as Cowboy's black irises turned blue.

"Oh, God," I whispered.

His face was flowing now, the skin rippling like Silly Putty. I could see another face beneath, fighting to get out.

Was he getting taller? Broader? When had Cowboy grown a goatee?

The tavern spun. Tiny black spots flickered in front of my eyes. I fought the weakness, but it didn't do any good.

"*Querida,*" he murmured. "I've missed you."

I passed out cold at the toe of itty-bitty boots, which had suddenly burst open at the seams.

33

I woke up in the dark. Someone was carrying me. I knew who that someone was, even without the aching, burning agony of my back.

I wanted to struggle, but I fought the urge. Better to let him think I was still out. Maybe I could surprise him and . . .

I wasn't sure what.

The air was cool on my face. We were inside, but not a building. I heard a shoe scrape dirt, then crunch something dry and old.

Like a bone.

Hell. The mine. I guess I was going to see what lay behind that pile of human bones.

"You can stop pretending. I know you're awake."

His voice slid out of the night like a slowly slithering snake. I lifted my head, but I couldn't distinguish anything in a darkness so complete it pressed against my skin like velvet.

His voice had always been seductive, soothing. Even now, when I knew the truth, that voice could still make me want to do things that were illegal in several southern states.

I gave myself a mental slap. He had bartered the lives of everyone I'd ever loved. He had sold his soul to the dark side.

I wished I had a light saber and a good connection to the force.

I'd have to make do with my hands and my wits. I didn't think they were going to be enough.

A light flickered up ahead. Dim, wavering, like a candle around a corner. I could see the low ceiling, the ancient wooden pillars, the dust, dirt, a few bones. If I wanted to, I could turn my head and see his face. I just didn't want to.

"Put me down," I ordered.

He ignored me and kept walking toward the light, which grew bigger and brighter, illuminating an arched doorway. We went through and into a room with a bed, suitcase, table, and chairs.

Someone had been living here. I knew who.

I struggled and he laughed, then let me go. I tumbled onto the floor, gained my feet, and scrambled away.

Hector Menendez appeared exactly the same as he had two years ago. Handsome, exotic, suave. Except now I recognized the beast hovering at the back of his eyes.

"You aren't going to get away from me this time, *querida*. It is your destiny to be my mate."

"I don't think so."

He shrugged, unconcerned. "It's still three nights until the full moon. Jessie will find me before then."

His thin lips lifted. "Jessie and her Indian lover will not return from their trip to see Cora Kopway."

I blinked.

"The idiot I sent to kill them in the forest was no better than the one I sent to bite you. I thought if they were dead it would confuse everyone, give me more time to do what I had to. I should have ripped their throats out myself."

I winced as memories threatened.

"You think I'm a fool?" he continued. "I know everything you've done. *Everything*."

I certainly hoped not.

"A bartender, Leigh? An Irishman, no less. You insult me."

"He's one of you."

"He's a peon. A weakling. I'm going to be a god."

"You wish."

"I don't have to wish. I am more than halfway there."

I had to get out of here. Save Jessie. Save Will. Myself while I was at it. Sadly, Hector stood between me and the door. I had no weapon, and he was stronger than me, even without the super-duper shape-shifting shit.

"You think I don't know what Damien has been doing?" he asked. "He thinks he's thinning the pack, but he's only given me more power with every death. I've been stalking him as he's been stalking the others, gaining the strength of those he kills under the moon."

Well, that cleared a few things up.

"How did you discover the Legend of the Power Eater?" I asked.

I couldn't imagine Hector, who despite his own minority heritage had very little patience for any others', studying Ojibwe folklore.

He sat on the bed. He was wearing something different than Cowboy had been. I recalled the boots splitting open as he changed. His clothes must have, too.

We'd been right about shifting between human forms.

Gee, give us a cigar. I wondered what else he could do, then decided I really didn't want to know.

"Once upon a time, I was a lowly half-breed." At my confused frown, he shook his head. "Half-Hispanic, half-white. I fit in nowhere. Not even my mother loved me enough to stay. I decided I wanted power. I wasn't going to get it through money or politics, but I could get it through death and destruction, which worked out well for me, because I liked it."

While he spoke, my gaze darted around the room, searching for a way to escape. I didn't find one, so I needed to keep him talking.

"How did you learn of the legend?" I repeated.

"I've traveled most of my life. Seen many things. When people stumble on something they can't explain, their mind rationalizes. Mine did not. I looked for the truth. There's another world that exists after the moon rises. I wanted to be a part of it. I hired someone to find out the best way for me to do that."

"And then?"

"I ate him."

I gaped at his matter-of-fact tone. "But he . . . I mean, uh—"

"He wasn't an enemy?" Hector shrugged. "Consider him a freebie. Practice, if you will, for the main event."

"Which was?"

"You know what I did, Leigh."

"Petite blond women, flesh of the enemy, sold your soul, sacrifice."

"Very good."

"One thing I don't understand. Why didn't you kill me?"

"*Querida,* how could I kill the woman meant to be my mate?"

"But—" I pointed at my hair, or what was left of it.

"It is a shame you felt the need to disfigure yourself, but when you are Weendigo, like me, that will not matter."

I tried again. "If petite blond women were your enemy, then why not me?"

"Because I knew from the moment you spoke to me that you were destined to be mine."

"Why?"

"You came to me. No one else ever had."

No one? I found that hard to believe. Hector was nuts, but he was handsome. Was I the only idiot who hadn't seen the rot beneath the flower?

"And because you came to me," he continued, "I knew you saw past my heritage, my poverty and shame. I knew you loved me, even when you said you did not."

"You thought I wouldn't care that you were a serial killer, a cannibal, the murderer of my family?"

"Those things were means to an end. So I could become Weendigo. So I could make us the alpha pair. We will live forever, *querida*. Together."

Not.

"How did you find me?"

"Were you hiding?" He appeared amused.

"*Jäger-Suchers* are . . . I mean we—"

"Are supposed to be a secret. True. To the general public. But the werewolves know you exist. Your friend Mandenauer is something of a legend, maybe a bogeyman. So are you, Leigh. When I make you one of us, werewolves all over the globe will cheer."

"I'm so glad they'll approve," I muttered.

"Ever sarcastic. It's one of your charms."

I chose to ignore that. If he found my sarcasm charming, I was in big trouble. Oh, wait. I *was* in big trouble.

"I still don't understand how we ended up in the same town. At this time of year."

I needed to keep him talking until I figured out what to do or someone found me. Which could take quite a while.

"I *brought* you to Crow Valley." He tilted his head and the light caught his blue eyes. For an instant the irises appeared red, as if a camera flash had gone off or a demon waited inside. "I thought you knew that."

"Brought me?"

"It wasn't hard. I control this town. I am the alpha here already. I tell them who to kill. They bring the bones to this place."

Ding, ding, ding. The light went on.

"No human remains, no FBI," I murmured.

Hector just smiled.

"But dead wolves would bring the DNR at the least."

"*Jäger-Suchers* eventually," he agreed.

"How did you know they'd send me?"

"You are the best, *querida*. Who else would they send?"

Gee, it paid to be at the top of my field.

"I don't understand why the other werewolves would follow you. You're murdering your own kind for power."

"Oh, they don't know it's me."

"What?"

"Any wolf that's seen me kill one of them is dead."

"How are you going to explain becoming supreme fur boy?"

"By the time they figure out what I'm up to, I'll be unstoppable, and they'll be happy about it."

"You think?"

"Of course." He winked. "Because I'll be giving them you."

"Excuse me?"

"The most successful werewolf-hunting *Jäger-Sucher* next to Edward Mandenauer will be the werewolf queen. You won't be killing them anymore. They'll lie down at my feet and roll over."

"And if someone figures this out before then?"

"I'll just give them Fitzgerald. He's going to have to go anyway."

My heart stuttered and seemed to stop. "W-why?"

"He touched you. He dies." Hector shrugged. "I need a sacrifice for the night of the blood moon. Damien will do nicely."

I'd wondered how much I cared for Damien; now I knew. The thought of him dying practically paralyzed me.

The entire time Hector and I had been talking I was desperately searching for, frantically trying to think of, a way out. My heart thundered and my hands shook. But at least I no longer felt like fainting.

Until Hector got off the bed and came toward me. I did *not* want him touching me.

"Are you ready?"

"F-for what?"

"To become."

My mouth fell open. I must have looked like a supreme idiot. "But—but the ceremony takes place on the night of the hunter's moon."

He strode closer. I took a step back. "Of course it does."

"Then what—why?"

His slim manicured hand reached out and grabbed me so fast I didn't have time to run. As if I could. His breath brushed my face and I shuddered. The black lights flashed again. So much for not feeling faint.

"Come here."

He drew me forward. I had enough sense left to hold back. Hector made an impatient sound. "I must tie you up, *querida.*"

He tugged me to his bed and shoved me onto it. I struggled, but in minutes I was bound hand and foot. My judo expertise was worthless. Boy, did I miss my gun.

Since the only weapon I had left was words, I used them. "You have to tie me down to do me. Pretty pathetic, Hector."

He merely smiled. I hated that smile.

"You are under the mistaken impression that I plan to *do you* tonight."

I blinked.

"But as much as I might enjoy it, that would be wasteful. I will take you under the full moon, as every werewolf watches. But before that happens, we must address one minor point."

"What's that?" I aimed for a strong, confident voice; what I got was near to a whimper.

"As kinky as it might be for you, there is no cross-species mating."

Remembering my conversation with Damien, I started to get an idea of what Hector was after. I tugged at the ropes, but it didn't do me any good.

"For the ceremony to take place on the night of the blood moon, you must already be one of us."

Oh, hell. I hadn't thought of that.

Hector needed to bite me *now*.

34

"First I sent Bob and his pals, but you ran them off."

At my blank expression he elaborated. "Big gray wolf and several others?"

Ah, the ones that had attacked my car.

"Then I sent Teddy."

Which I assumed to be the caramel-shaded drooler Damien had dispatched.

"Bob and Teddy were fuckups in life. They weren't any better as wolves. If you want something done, you just have to do it yourself."

The last word descended into a growl. Hector unbuttoned his shirt, shrugged the garment off, and shucked his pants. I tried to avert my eyes, but the pentagram tattoo glistened black in the lamplight, catching, then holding my attention.

His chest was smooth, unmarred, except for that. I wondered for an instant why the tattoo didn't heal every time he changed. But then he changed, and I didn't care about anything else.

I'd seen a hundred, a thousand, men go wolf, but never one as quickly as Hector.

Only the very old or the very powerful could change like that, or so I'd heard. Take a guess which one Hector was.

He changed so fast my brain had a hard time keeping up with my eyes. One instant his nose and mouth were there; the next they were a snout. White fur sprouted from his pores; hands and feet became paws; a tail sprouted from his butt. I blinked and he was on all fours. The next instant he let out a howl that echoed off the enclosed space, making my ears ring.

His head swung in my direction and his mouth opened in a doggie pant. Too bad his teeth were all werewolf.

I pulled on the ropes, but I'd been pulling since Hector had tied me to the bed. He knew what he was doing. I wasn't going to get away.

The mattress dipped as he leaped on top. The slightly gamy scent of wild animal washed over me. His fur brushed my arm. I fought not to retch. I certainly didn't want to lie in my own puke. But then again, once he bit me, what difference did anything make?

The white wolf straddled me. Right paws on my left side, left paws on my right. He seemed to be uncertain where to bite me. His snout snuffled my legs, my arms, my crotch.

"Hey!"

He lifted his head. His tongue lolled and drool dripped onto my chest.

"Get on with it," I muttered.

He tossed his head, yipped, and nuzzled my breast. I cringed.

A growl reverberated around the room. Hector froze. So did I. Together our heads turned.

Damien stood in the entranceway. Or rather, a brown wolf did.

Hector snarled. I expected him to jump off the bed, off

me, and chase Damien into the woods. Somehow I'd have to get free. Somehow Damien would have to win a fight to the death against an extremely powerful shape-shifter, How was he going to do that?

I was so preoccupied with the problem, I didn't see it coming. When Hector's teeth sank into the fleshy part of my upper arm, I shrieked.

Hell, I'd have shrieked even if I'd seen it coming. Being bit hurt!

Without so much as a backward glance, Hector leaped off the bed. Damien braced himself for the attack. I wanted to shout, *No, save yourself! I'm already dead!* But my mouth was too dry to form the words, my throat too thick to make a sound.

But instead of smacking into Damien or launching himself with claws and teeth, Hector shifted into a crow and flew out the door.

For an instant I thought I was delirious. I closed my eyes, hard, opened them again. Damien sat on his haunches, nose tilted up as he searched the ceiling for Hector.

No such luck. The bird, the wolf, the man, was gone.

I'd never seen anything like it—except in a vampire movie. *Bam,* he's a bat. In this case, *wham,* he's a crow.

I'd only seen one crow in this town. On Jessie's windowsill. No wonder Hector had known everything we'd done. No wonder we'd been unable to find him or the white wolf.

This was going to be a helluva lot more difficult than I'd thought, and I'd thought it would be damn near impossible.

I glanced at my arm. Ugh, that wasn't right. A flap of skin hung free, and blood dampened the sheets. It burned like a son of a bitch.

How long did I have before I got furry? Less than twenty-four hours. I needed to find Jessie and Will, preferably before whoever or whatever Hector had sent to kill them succeeded. Then I would tell them all that I knew and bite the bullet. So to speak.

I turned my head, whistled to Damien. He trotted over.

"Can you get me out of this?" I asked.

He licked me from chin to forehead.

"You love me. I know. Thanks."

If I'd wanted a dog, I'd have bought one. Having the man I'd slept with panting with passion was one thing. Having the man I slept with drooling werewolf slobber all over me was another.

I heard his bones crackle before I saw him shift. He was faster at it than a lot of shifters I'd known, though not as fast as Hector. Of course, Damien was over fifty years a werewolf. The change had to get easier with practice.

A few minutes later he crouched next to the bed. His gaze immediately went to my arm. "Oh, Leigh, I—"

"Save it," I snapped. "Cut me loose. We have to find Jessie and Will."

I'll say this for Damien; he could take orders. He freed me, grabbed some of Hector's clothes, which were too big on him, but naked guys can't be choosers, and helped me off the bed.

He tried to treat my wound, but I shoved his hands away. "Forget it."

I yanked a pillowcase off a pillow and tied the thing around my arm. It wasn't easy with only one arm. This time when Damien helped, I let him.

"You should have that cleaned and stitched," he said as he tightened the bandage.

"Won't matter."

Our eyes met. "No," he murmured. "It won't matter. Not to me."

I ignored the implications. Didn't have time for them right now. Or anything else.

"We have to get to a phone."

I stood and swayed. Another scene played before my eyes—earth, trees, blue sky. I smelled the dirt, heard the leaves rustle, felt the sun hot on my fur.

Fur? Ugh!

Suddenly I was back in the abandoned mine. I touched my arms, my face. Skin. Whew!

"Whoa, what was that?" I muttered.

"Flashback?"

"I've never been able to smell so well, hear so distinctly. I don't recall having fur."

"Flashback," Damien stated more firmly. "Collective consciousness. It happens once you're bitten. Gets worse and worse until you change for the first time."

Well, wasn't that just *peachy*?

Damien scooped me up and started for the door.

"Put me down."

"Uh-uh."

"I can walk. Pretty soon I'll be able to lope."

Why I was making jokes I had no idea. Defense mechanism, I guess. If I didn't laugh or try to, I'd cry. Maybe shriek, scream, beat on the wall a little. I didn't have time for any one of those things.

"I know how this goes. You'll keep having flashbacks. They'll get stronger and longer."

He spoke as he walked out of Hector's hidden room, up the hill, past the bones, and toward the entrance.

"You'll get dizzy, weak, feverish, and then—"

"I'll get furry. I know."

"What you don't know is that the more you run around, the faster it happens. The smaller you are, the faster it happens. Back when I first . . . became," he ducked through the opening and into the night, "I liked to watch the ones I'd bitten."

I must have made a face, because he sighed, and the sound held an acre of sadness.

"Evil likes to watch what it creates and marvel. Why do you think there are more and more werewolves instead of less and less?"

I hadn't thought about why. I'd only been glad of the job security.

"When we first change we're like kids in a candy store. Not only do we kill more than an older werewolf; we make more like us, too." He stopped walking and stared into my face. "You won't be able to help yourself," he whispered.

Oh, yeah, I would. I'd help myself just fine. With a silver bullet. And if I couldn't, Jessie certainly could.

I let Damien carry me back to the tavern. Why make things worse by being stubborn? Not that I hadn't been in the past, but maybe I'd gained a little sense along the way. Maybe.

"Hector is Cowboy. Or Cowboy is Hector."

"Who's Hector?"

I hesitated. I'd never explained the power eater legend to him fully. I'd certainly never explained my personal connection to the entire fiasco. And I didn't want to. I settled for a partial version of the truth.

"Hector is the power eater we've been searching for. Obviously he can shift into just about anything or anyone. He's eating the werewolves. Gaining power to become supreme alpha. It's a long story."

"And you really shouldn't talk, Leigh."

Probably not, but I wanted to know a few things before it was too late.

"How did you find me?"

"I came to work. I could smell that you'd been there."

"Smell?"

"My nose is pretty good, even in human form. I smelled Cowboy. The two of you went into the woods. That bothered me, so I followed. His scent changed. Like the one I'd been searching for, which makes sense now, I guess. Since I didn't know what I'd be up against, I shifted, then kept following the scent of you."

We stepped into the clearing. The moon reflected brightly off the hoods of the cars in the lot. For once the bar was silent.

"Why didn't you tell me this was their lair?" I asked.

"How was I supposed to explain that I knew what a lair was? If I'd told you that, wouldn't you have known what I was? *I* wanted to kill them."

"Then why didn't you just blast them like I do?"

"Besides the problem of loading silver bullets—"

"I thought you had a friend for that."

"A single silver bullet is one thing; magazine after magazine is another. Besides . . ." he trailed off.

"What?"

"This is going to sound foolish."

"Say it anyway."

"Well, it didn't seem fair to shoot them."

"Fuck fair," I snapped.

"I told you it would sound foolish. But I felt better meeting them on equal terms. Most of them didn't ask to become werewolves. They had no choice."

I could see his point, which disturbed me. Maybe I was changing even faster than I thought.

"Didn't you worry that one of these days one of them would be stronger than you?"

"I hoped for it. I wanted to die, until I met you."

"And then?"

"I wanted to live, at least until you found out the truth and hated me for it."

I could feel his gaze on my face. Did I hate him? No. Far from it. But I couldn't tell him that. Not now. Not when I planned on dying myself.

He took the steps to my room with me in his arms as if I weighed no more than a kitten.

Suddenly I had a flash of rolling in the grass. The blades brushed my fur. The mosquitoes buzzed around my face. I snapped at them, caught several in my mouth. I wanted to run. Feel the miles fall away beneath my paws. Chase a rabbit or maybe something bigger. Like a little girl.

I started. Shook my head. Slapped myself right between the eyes.

"Leigh?"

We were in my apartment. Damien set me on my feet. "What did you see?"

I did *not* want to talk about it. I stumbled across the room, found my cell phone, and dialed Jessie's number.

There was no answer.

35

"I've got to go," I said.

I took one step toward the door and fell to my knees as the room became a forest again. Damp earth seeped through my pants legs, chilling my skin. The air was musty. I smelled moss. In the distance a wolf howled. I lifted my mouth to call out . . .

And ended up coughing, choking, in Damien's arms.

"I don't think you're going anywhere."

"Stop me."

"No problem."

He scooped me up again and took me into the bathroom, where he dumped me onto the toilet seat.

"I'm cleaning that wound, and I'm calling a doctor."

"Damien, it won't do any good. You and I both know that."

He hung his head. "Just let me clean it then. OK?"

"If I do, will you let me find Jessie?"

"No. But I will."

I glanced into his eyes. This was the best deal I was going to get.

I yanked the pillowcase bandage off my arm. "Knock yourself out."

His smile was the same smile I'd come to love. Sweet, sad, infinitely beautiful. I was going to miss him.

My arm was bloody and gaping, made me nauseous just to look at it. I turned away, and he dampened a cloth and began to wash away the gore.

After a few minutes Damien made an impatient sound. "This isn't going to do any good, Leigh. It just keeps bleeding."

I resisted the urge to say, *Told you so.*

"Bandage me up again."

"You need stitches."

"Stitch me."

"I'll make a mess, a scar."

I lifted a brow. "A scar? Oh, no. I shiver. I shudder. That would be such a shame."

He ran a hand over his face, leaving a trail of my blood across his cheek.

"Forget it," I said. "It's not going to make a difference in another day anyway."

"That's right." He straightened. "You'll heal."

I wouldn't. But once again, he didn't need to know that.

"Which reminds me, why doesn't Hector's tattoo heal?"

"He has a tattoo? Like Cowboy?"

"Obviously, since they're the same person."

"Which makes no sense."

"You'd be surprised." I didn't have the energy or the time to explain super-duper shape-shifting powers, even if I could.

"But the wolf morphing into the crow made no sense, either," he murmured.

"Getting back to the tattoo?" I reminded him as he used a towel to bind my arm.

"What? Oh. That's easy. You stay the way you were when you were made a wolf. If . . . Was it Hector?" I nodded. "If he had a tattoo when he became a werewolf, he'll have one forever. Any injury *after* that will heal."

Damien pointed to his thigh and I remembered the thin white scar that marred his nearly perfect flesh. "I got that as a kid. It'll never go away."

This was all news to me. Why didn't we *know* this in the *J-S* society? Because we didn't stop to ask questions before we shot them, and maybe that wasn't so bright.

"But what about this?" I lifted my bandaged arm. "Happened before I became a werewolf."

"The wound that infected you with the virus will heal."

"Convenient."

"Can you imagine people walking around with their throats ripped out? It isn't pretty."

I'd wondered when I first became a *Jäger-Sucher* how people with kill wounds could heal. There was a simple, disgusting explanation. People were food. If a werewolf ate you, you died. If he nibbled but didn't snack, you got to be one of them.

"What about diseases?" I pressed.

"They'll heal, because you still have them after you're a werewolf. At least until you shift the first time."

"But not scars?"

"Sorry, Leigh."

He thought I was worried about my back. I hadn't even considered it. Guess I got to keep the scar. Oh, boy.

"Who is Hector?" he asked.

"Cowboy."

"No, who is he to you?"

I lifted my eyes. Sympathy shone in his, caring, understanding, love. How could he love me? Because he didn't know.

"I had sex with him," I blurted. "I saw him, wanted him, took him. Then he sacrificed everyone I loved so he could become like you."

Damien frowned. I waited for the recriminations, the disgust. Instead he murmured, "Interesting."

"Interesting? Is that all you can say?"

"I didn't know someone could become a werewolf without being bitten."

"You'd be surprised what you don't know."

The door to my apartment banged open. Jessie and Will spilled into the room, Jessie shouting my name and cursing.

I was so damn glad to see them alive, I didn't hear what they were saying. I got off the toilet and inched past Damien. As I went by, his palm slid along my good arm in a gentle, reassuring touch. My fingers clung to his for just an instant and it was good.

"I'm here," I said.

They both went silent as if I'd thrown a switch, staring at me as if I were a ghost.

"Thank God," she breathed. "I thought we were too late."

"Too late for what?"

"We talked to Cora. He has to—"

"Make me a werewolf before the full moon."

Jessie shut her mouth, tilted her head. "How did you know that?"

"He told me." I lifted my bandaged arm.

She drew her gun and pointed it at my head. I smiled. "I knew you were the best friend I ever had."

Damien barreled out of the bathroom and shoved me behind him. My hero.

"What the hell?" he asked.

"Get lost," Jessie snapped.

"I don't think I will. This is murder, Sheriff."

"It's none of your business, Fitzgerald. Get out of my way."

"Jess." Will spoke for the first time. "Maybe you should call in before you make any rash decisions."

Indecision flickered over her face.

"You can always shoot her after she grows a tail," Damien murmured.

I kicked him in the leg. He ignored me.

"You told him?" Jessie demanded.

I shrugged and didn't answer.

"Jeez, Leigh, he's a civilian."

"So was Cadotte, once upon a time."

"Got you there," Will said.

"Shut up."

Jessie's answer to everything. She still pointed her gun at Damien. I didn't like it. She had silver in that gun. I tried to slide around him, but he shoved me right back.

"Without her, he can't become the supreme alpha," Jessie argued. "Wolves mate for life."

"What does that have to do with anything?" Damien asked.

"Thought you knew it all."

"I know werewolves exist. I haven't gotten the details on what you're up against."

Will filled him in as I fought a sudden craving for raw steak.

"It seems to me," Damien murmured, "that you have Hector at a disadvantage."

"How so?" Jessie asked.

"Leigh can get close to him. He'll trust her."

Jessie and Will both turned to me. "He's right."

Jessie holstered her gun. "I guess I can always shoot you later."

"Yeah, look at the bright side." I pushed past Damien and moved farther into the room. "Hector plans to use Damien for his sacrifice."

Damien frowned, blinked, then shrugged. "Let him try."

"You need to protect him, Jessie."

"I don't need anyone to protect me," Damien protested. "I can take care of myself."

Jessie ignored him. "We could always shoot him before they kill him."

"Would you *quit* with the shooting?" I said. "Sacrifice is sacrifice. He doesn't necessarily need Damien. He just wants him."

"Because?"

"He touched me."

Jessie glanced at Damien.

"She's worth it," he said.

Her gaze went shrewd, and she turned her attention to me with a lift of her brow.

I shook my head. I wasn't going to discuss my feelings for Damien. Not now. Probably not ever.

"Hector told me you and Will wouldn't make it back from Cora's."

"We almost didn't," Will muttered.

"What happened?"

"My car is kind of like yours now."

"They attacked."

"When we were halfway between Cora's and home. Thankfully Jessie brought a lot of guns and even more ammo."

She patted her Magnum. "Pays to be prepared."

"A regular Boy Scout," I agreed.

"We left quite a few dead ones behind."

"You didn't burn them?"

"We didn't want to get out of the car. There were more waiting."

I nodded. "Did you happen to see a crow?"

Will frowned. "It settled on the kills. Started pecking. Scavenger."

"That was Hector."

Jessie and Will exchanged glances.

"You'd better tell us everything," he urged.

When I was through, Will murmured, "Not good." He spread his hands. "But hey, if this job were easy, everyone would do it."

That startled a laugh out of me.

"Mandenauer?"

My head whipped around. Jessie held the cell phone to her ear.

"You'd better get to Crow Valley. Leigh's been bitten."

She listened for an instant, then hung up.

"Dammit, Jessie, you'll only upset him. What can he do?"

"I guess we're gonna find out. Because he's on his way, and he's bringing Dr. Hanover."

36

I wanted to ask what Edward had said. I hoped he wasn't coming to shoot me. If I had to go, I wanted Jessie to do it, not Edward. He seemed so frail lately. My dying would not help. My dying by his hand would certainly hurt.

I wanted to ask, but I never got the chance. As we sat down to formulate some kind of plan, the room suddenly went dark and cool. I heard the trees rustle, even though the windows and the doors were shut. I smelled leaves, evergreens.

I was hungry. Starving. My belly growled, or maybe the sound came from my mouth. I wasn't sure. I had to eat or the hunger would consume me. The madness flickered at the edge of my brain. Food. Blood. Meat.

Dimly I felt myself slide from the couch to the floor. Damien was there, lifting me, carrying me to the bed. I turned my mouth toward his neck, but he smelled like wolf, not man. I scented fresh meat nearby. My gaze went to Jessie.

She narrowed her eyes. "Don't even think about it."

But I did. The hunger was a living, breathing, aching thing in my stomach. I half-expected it to burst out and devour everyone near me. I placed my hands over my middle and moaned. But the sound that came out of my mouth was something else entirely.

I understood how the hunger caused sane men to go mad. I was a little crazed myself. Then the fever ripped through my body; like a fire it blazed. My skin burned, my scalp tingled, and darkness cloaked my mind.

I awoke in the woods—naked, alone, covered in blood. My hunger was gone, my belly distended. The sun was rising in the east. I had no idea where I was. I remembered nothing of what I had done.

And I didn't care.

That was the strange part. I'd in all likelihood killed, then eaten, my friends, maybe even my lover—though I doubted Damien would have stood still and let me devour him. Literally, anyway.

But now that the hunger was appeased, all I cared about was making sure that the next time it came I had plenty of people to hunt.

I ran through the forest, felt the breeze on my skin, through my hair. I reveled in the dirt beneath my feet. I jumped into a river and washed the blood away, then lay in the sun and let the water drip from my body into the earth. The remnants dried in the heat, and I drifted to sleep.

When I awoke again, someone was pressed spoonlike against my back. I turned and found Hector, naked like me and aroused. He kissed me and as he did, we both changed.

I sat bolt upright in bed. Or at least I tried. Someone had tied me down. Again.

I was sweating, shaking, crying, but I wasn't in the woods. Obviously I never had been.

"What happened?"

I fell back on the pillow, turned my head. Jessie sat in a chair.

"Kill me," I rasped. "Promise."

"I already did."

I closed my eyes. "It's awful, Jessie. I don't want to be like that."

"I know."

We sat together, silent. I kept my eyes closed until I stopped seeing myself in the woods, with Hector, stopped tasting . . . horrible things, stopped hearing screams that had never truly happened. At least not yet.

"Where are the boys?" I asked.

"Gone."

"What?" I tried to sit up again. The bonds scraped along my already-raw wrists and ankles. "You didn't let them go after Hector. He'll eat—"

I stopped. "Eat them alive" had once been an expression; now it was reality.

"They aren't hunting. They went to pick up Elise and Mandenauer."

"But they shouldn't be alone."

"Someone had to go, and I thought it was best if I stay."

She left unspoken the reason why. Damien wouldn't kill me. Will probably couldn't.

I wanted to stay awake, but the virus made me weak. The fever made me toss and turn. The changes made me ache. My back burned, which wasn't new. However, my bones were doing something weird. Snapping, popping, shifting. My eyes hurt. My nose tickled. My teeth seemed too big for my mouth.

I fell back into the void where Hector waited. My

dreams, fantasies, or whatever the hell they were remained pretty much the same. Blood, death. A little bit of doggie-style sex.

I awoke to a silver sheen drifting through the windows and across my bed. The moon was cool. It soothed the fever, calmed my racing heart, called me to come and dance in its light, naked and alive.

Murmurs on the porch. My ears tuned in. I could hear everything they said.

"This could kill her." I recognized the voice of Dr. Elise Hanover. "We haven't tested the serum yet."

I'd never seen the woman, only spoken to her on the phone. I couldn't see her now, except for a slim shadow among all the other shadows clumping together on the porch.

"We will test it now."

That was Edward, always calm, in control, regardless of the situation.

"I won't let you kill her on the off chance you might save her," Damien insisted.

"You have nothing to say about it."

"I do!" I called.

The group went silent and still, then filed into the room.

"The gang's all here," I murmured.

Jessie, Will, Edward, Elise, and Damien hovered near the door, as if afraid to come near me. I didn't want to know why.

Elise was the first to move. She clipped across the wood floor wearing heels the shade of fine porcelain. Her stockings were sheer. Her suit a pure sea green.

She could have been a model—tall, bone thin, with platinum hair that would be long if she ever released the tight coil cemented to the back of her head.

Her skin matched her shoes; her eyes were dark blue,

nearly violet. There wasn't a flaw on her face. And she had a Ph.D., too. Life was hardly fair.

"I've invented a serum," she said.

Her voice was as lovely as she was—low, husky, far too sexy for a scientist. Every man in the room, except for Edward, stared at her with his mouth open.

"However, I don't know if it works."

"So I heard."

They all exchanged glances. If I'd been able to hear them whispering on the porch, the change had already begun.

Behind Elise's back, Jessie made a face and rolled her eyes. Dr. Hanover was too perfect for words. We had to hate her. It was a matter of pride.

"The choice is up to you, Leigh."

I turned my gaze to Edward. He appeared older, sadder, quite tired. I wondered what he'd been doing while he'd been away, but I didn't have time to ask.

My body bowed. My spine seemed to be cracking in two. I opened my mouth to cry out, and a howl escaped instead. When the pain went away and the echo of the howl faded, I glanced at everyone, only to find them studying the ceiling. Except for Damien. He shook his head.

I held his eyes as I said, "Do it, Doctor."

"Wait!" he blurted.

"No."

"Let me talk to her before—"

"Damien," I interrupted. "I know what you want to say."

He loved me. I loved him, too. But I wasn't going to tell him. He'd only agonize longer if I died. I wasn't going to tell anyone what he was, either, even if it went against every vow I'd ever made, every oath I'd ever taken. I couldn't sentence him to death, even if he wanted me to.

"I don't think you do know," he continued. "Everyone get out."

"Just one minute, young man—" Edward began.

"Get out!" Damien shouted.

Edward's eyes narrowed, but Jessie took his arm and Will took Elise's.

"One minute," Jessie said. "No more."

The door closed, and Damien was at my side; his fingers tugged on the knots of the rope.

"What are you doing?"

"Let's get out of here."

"What? No. Are you crazy?"

He let go of the knots, cupped my face in both his hands, and kissed me. I barely had a taste of him before he lifted his mouth and stared into my eyes. "Run away with me. Be *my* mate. In my mind you already are."

"We can't hide from them forever."

"I've been hiding from them for fifty years."

True, but I couldn't spend my life running. Not even for him.

"Damien—"

"We'll be together." His voice held a desperate edge. "You'll be like me."

"But I won't be like you. I'll be evil."

"I don't care."

"Yes, you do. And so do I."

Damien let me go, ran his fingers through his already-tousled hair. "I remember how intense the hunger is at first, but it gets better."

"Only because I'll forget what it was like to be human."

He didn't answer, because I was right.

Edward came in. His eyes went to the ropes, narrowed;

then he crossed the room and tightened the bonds. He ignored Damien as if he weren't even there, sitting in the chair beside me and patting my head like a pet. Damien inched away to hover near the kitchenette.

"Liebchen," Edward murmured. "I am sorry."

"Don't be. My fault."

"I got you into this."

"I wanted to be into this."

"I know." His eyes slid toward Damien, and he lowered his voice to a whisper. "You asked me if he was a rogue agent. Why?"

I didn't want to explain . . . anything now. "Later, Edward."

It was an indication of how much he cared for me that he didn't press the issue. "If I'd realized you were involved with him I'd have checked him out more thoroughly."

"Jessie ran him through her system."

"I have a much better system."

He did. I glanced at Damien. He could hear everything we said, but Edward didn't know that. Damien would have to disappear when this was over. Once Edward ran his name through the system, he'd learn more than was healthy for both of them.

"I never thought to see you with a companion," Edward murmured. "Why this one?"

Why Damien? I had no idea.

Maybe it was the sadness in him that called to the sadness in me. Maybe it was a secret fascination with the monster. Frankenstein complex? Dracula delusions? Werewolf syndrome? At least Damien wouldn't die as easily as everyone else I'd ever loved.

Hell, maybe it was just the incredible sex. But, in truth, I felt so much more for Damien than lust.

"Take care of him," I whispered. "If I can't."

Edward's eyes widened.

"Promise," I insisted.

"Whatever you wish." He squeezed my bound hand. "Leigh, you should have told me your nightmare was back. I would have killed him for you, gladly."

"I know."

The others came into the room. Elise crossed to the kitchen table, where an old-fashioned medical bag rested. She rustled around inside.

"Is this why you had to stay at headquarters?"

Edward hesitated an instant, then nodded. "It is the first breakthrough we've had."

"You said she hadn't found anything."

"I was wrong. Or I hope that I was. Elise wanted to test the serum further, but we have no time."

"Let Elise do her thing."

Edward nodded, then patted me again and moved away. He had never been very good with emotion, even worse with affection. Sometimes I wondered what he'd been like before the war.

Elise swabbed my arm. I resisted the urge to sneer. An infection couldn't hurt me now.

The others crept up behind her, as if they couldn't make themselves stay away.

"You understand I haven't tried the serum on anyone yet?"

"I got that. What's the recipe?"

"Little bit of this, little bit of that." She walked back to her bag. "I need the blood of a live werewolf, in human form."

I frowned. "But how—?"

Damien's arm shot out. "Use mine."

37

Edward's gun was pressed to Damien's head the next instant.

"No!" I shouted, tugging at the ropes. "Edward, you promised me you'd take care of him."

Edward frowned, confused. "I am taking care of him."

"You know I didn't mean for you to kill him."

"I do?"

The room was suddenly pandemonium, everyone talking at once.

In the midst of everything, Damien's eyes met mine. I saw no one but him. He'd revealed himself for me. Knowing Edward, he would die for it.

"Silence," Elise snapped.

Amazingly, everyone complied.

"I don't need the blood of a live werewolf in human form right now." She lifted her hand out of the bag. Her fingers held a full syringe. "I already have it."

"Oops," Damien murmured.

"Yes." Edward shoved the gun into Damien's ear. "Oops."

"Take it outside," Elise ordered.

"No." I struggled, again to no avail. "Don't hurt him. He's not what you think."

"Not the fanged and furry?" Jessie asked. "What exactly does *werewolf* mean, Leigh?"

"He's different."

"That is what they all say," Edward murmured.

"Why don't you tell us what you're talking about?" This was Will, a voice of reason always. Despite his Forrest Gump manner, he was starting to grow on me.

"The brown wolf," I blurted. "The one that was killing the others but not eating them."

"You?" Jessie asked Damien.

He tried to nod, but it was a little hard with a gun in his ear.

"Him," I confirmed. "He's been helping us."

"No, he's been helping Hector." Jessie drew her weapon.

"He didn't know about the legend."

Jessie rolled her eyes. "Are you that naive?"

My body stiffened as if I'd been hit with a cattle prod. Every muscle, every joint, tightened in agony. My eyes bugged.

I saw the moon, felt its sheen on my skin like a caress. Then it was gone, and I lay there panting, aching, bleeding, but there was no blood.

"I'd like to inject this before the first change," Elise said. "Upsetting her is only making that happen more quickly. Perhaps we could let him live until I'm done here?"

"Fine, whatever." Jessie put up her gun.

"Edward?" Elise murmured.

Edward's gaze flicked toward her, then away. "I will not shoot him. Unless he makes me. But I will not put away my weapon."

He removed the gun from Damien's ear—barely. With Edward, that was the best I could hope for.

The fit, or whatever it had been, passed. I was covered with sweat. My skin seemed too small, the hair on my arms too big. My scalp tingled, as did the base of my spine. Hell, I was probably sprouting a tail.

"Get on with it," I ordered.

Elise stuck me. Frowning, she depressed the syringe and shot every last drop into my vein.

She pulled the needle out, pressed a cotton pad to the prick, lifted it, scowled. "No blood," she murmured. "The wound healed already."

"Is that good or bad?"

"I have no idea."

Oh, yeah, I was the guinea pig.

I waited for . . . something. What I got was nothing at all.

Everyone stared at me. I stared back. We waited for what seemed like forever but was probably only an hour.

"How do you feel, Leigh?" Elise asked for the fifth time.

"Fine," I repeated.

"Any strange visions, odd pains?"

"Not anymore."

"I'll stay with her," she said.

"No," Edward stated, gun still pointed at Damien.

"If she hasn't changed by morning, the serum works. There's no reason for all of us to stay here. Don't you have something to do?"

Edward glanced at Damien. "Why, yes, I do."

"No!" I said. "If the serum works, we can use it on him."

Damien blinked. His eyes met mine; something flickered in the gray-green depths. I think it was hope.

"She's right," Elise murmured.

Edward scowled, but he lowered his gun. "Do not make me come after you. You will not like what happens then."

"I'm not leaving Leigh. Ever."

"If the serum does not work, I will kill you."

"If the serum doesn't work, I'll let you."

The world receded, but at least I didn't smell the forest, hear the trees, feel the wind. I didn't taste blood; I didn't even want to. I had to sleep. But before I did, just in case I never woke up, I wanted one last kiss.

"Damien," I whispered.

He knelt by the bed. His fingertips brushed my hand. I turned my face, and his mouth was there. How had he known what I wanted without my saying a word?

The kiss was gentle, sweet, everything I could ask for in a final embrace. His tongue tasted of mint—fresh and clean, new. He nibbled my lower lip, rubbed his thumb along my cheekbone.

"Reverse Sleeping Beauty complex," Jessie muttered. "His kiss puts her to sleep."

I fell into the satin darkness with a smile on my face as his breath mingled with mine.

There was a tunnel or maybe a cave. Dark, not a flicker of light to stay away from—or perhaps run to. But the darkness was peaceful. There was no one there but me. No Jimmy, no family, but the best part . . . no Hector. I went down that tunnel gladly and fell off the edge of the world.

The next instant, or so it seemed, I jerked awake. I was alone, and the gray light of dawn shivered on the horizon. I looked down. I was still me. No fangs, no fur. It was a good day.

A soft footfall drew my attention to the door. Damien
stood in the entryway, barefoot, tousled, his chin shad-
owed, skin pale. For an instant I wondered what had happened to the good doctor; then I realized I didn't care.
Damien was here. He was the only one I wanted to see
right now.

"Did you sleep?" I asked.

"Of course not."

"Wanna come to bed?"

His eyes widened. His mouth opened, then shut. He
shrugged.

"Untie me."

"Leigh—" he began.

"Do it, Damien. I won't bite." I let a slow smile spread
across my face. "Unless you want me to."

He crossed the room, stood over the bed, staring down
at me. Suddenly I was embarrassed. Wanting him at a
time like this—what was the matter with me?

"You don't have to untie me," I muttered. "Maybe you
shouldn't."

"We can't—"

"We can. I think we've proved that quite a few times."

"But we've never . . ."

He was having a helluva time articulating this morning.

"Are you trying to say that we've never been together
when I knew what you were and I knew that you knew
what I was?"

He gave a half-laugh. "Something like that."

"Why do you think I want us to be together now?"

He lifted his eyes. There was that hope again.

"Why?" he whispered.

I'd awoken this morning a human being. No tail, no
snout, no savage bloodlust. Maybe, one day, Damien

would, too. And if he could, then we might have a future.
All I had to do was kill the demon who wanted to mate
with me beneath the full moon.

My life—what can I say?—it wasn't for sissies.

"Why?" I repeated. "Because I love you."

I hadn't planned to say that. What if I had to shoot
him? But what if he died—what if I did—before I told
him the truth? At least Jimmy had known how I felt and
he'd died without discovering how I'd betrayed him.

I pushed away the thought. I needed to let the past go
and focus on the future. I'd been close to death and worse
last night. Every day from now on was a gift.

Dwelling on what I'd done, punishing myself with it,
was getting me nowhere. I needed to live or get out of the
game. With Damien in my life, I knew which one I would
choose.

He knelt by the bed. His clever fingers released the
knots. My hands went around his neck and pulled him
close.

"Tell me again," he demanded.

"I love you."

Our lips met and I forgot everything but him. There
was no one, nothing, else. No werewolves, no demons,
no power eaters. Just Damien and me—until Edward
walked in.

I had my tongue down Damien's throat; he had his hand
up my shirt. A gasp from the doorway made us freeze. I
glanced past Damien's shoulder and met the shocked eyes
of the man who'd saved, then given me back, my life.

"You have lost your mind."

Damien yanked his hand out of my shirt and tried to
pull away. I held on, kissed his cheek, smoothed his hair,
then let him go.

"Maybe." Standing, I crossed the room and stopped right in front of Edward. "But it's *my* mind."

"I see now why you didn't want him dead." He shook his head. "I thought better of you, Leigh."

I frowned. "What's that supposed to mean?"

"Werewolves are . . ." He seemed to struggle for the words. "Accomplished at the physical."

"Is that your way of saying they're great in the sack?"

He winced. "If you must. They are carnal creatures. Their senses are heightened. They have lived long enough to learn many things."

I glanced at Damien. He shrugged. What could he say? He knew how to make me scream. Let's shoot him.

"I should have warned you of their allure. But I thought after Hector you would understand."

"Leave Hector out of this. They're nothing alike."

"No? Did they not both seduce you while in human form? Hector killed everyone you ever loved in order to have you. How do you know this animal will not do the same?"

"Because he won't."

The excuse sounded lame, even to my own ears. Edward actually laughed in my face. "If you needed a boyfriend, why not pick one with the same interests as you?"

"I did. He's been killing werewolves for months."

"So he says."

"So I've seen. Tell him, Damien. Tell him what you told me about the magic woman in Arkansas."

Edward stopped laughing. His faded blue eyes sharpened. "What is this?"

Quickly Damien told him his story. I give Edward credit: he listened. He no longer laughed, so I pressed the advantage.

"He was with you last night. Did he kill anyone?"

The two of them exchanged glances.

"What?" I demanded.

Edward cleared his throat. "You've been asleep longer than one night."

"How long?"

"The hunter's moon is tonight," Damien told me.

I let that sink in. Well, at least I wouldn't have to wait around to find out if my life was over or just begun.

I scowled at Edward. "That just makes my point stronger. What true werewolf could hold back from killing this close to a full moon?"

"That is true," Edward murmured. "I'd hoped he would lose his patience so I could—" He broke off.

"No wonder you were so agreeable. You thought he'd be unable to resist all that tender meat. Then you could kill him."

Edward shrugged, unrepentant.

"But he didn't."

"No, he did not." Edward stared at Damien as if he were a bug under a microscope. "Maybe what has happened to him could be of help to Elise."

"Maybe. If you don't shoot him."

"Fine. He lives. For now. But please refrain from sucking face around me. It makes me ill."

"Sucking face?" Damien asked.

"He hears things on television." I shrugged. "He's still lost in the forties."

"Me, too."

It hit me then that Edward and Damien were compatriots. They would be of an age if Damien hadn't become a werewolf. Still, I doubted they'd embrace and become best friends—even if Elise's serum was a success.

"When will Elise test the cure on Damien?" I asked.

"When she returns from the lab with more."

I frowned. "She's gone?"

"As soon as she knew you were all right, she left for Montana to make more serum and . . ." He hesitated. "There are some other issues she must deal with at headquarters. She will return after the hunter's moon."

Footsteps pounded outside. Jessie and Will spilled into the room. "We figured out how to get Hector," Jessie said.

Will's glasses were crooked, his hair all mussed. It appeared that he and Jessie had been sucking face, too. "He doesn't know about the serum."

The light dawned. "He thinks I'll change. He'll be coming after me."

"No, Leigh," Damien said. "He's dangerous."

My eyes met his. "He'll be coming after you, too. You're the sacrifice."

Our eyes met. We had to do this together if we wanted any kind of future.

Damien took my hand. He'd be right next to me tonight. Suddenly I felt as if I could accomplish anything. I doubted the feeling would last.

You'd think we'd have all sorts of preparations to make, but since we were basically going to let Hector get away with it, our business was to wait. Not my strong suit.

"You cannot go out and about today, Leigh," Edward warned. "Hector could be anywhere. He could be anyone."

"I thought we *wanted* him to snatch me."

"We do not want him to know you have been cured. What would you do if you had been bitten, then changed?"

"Kill myself."

"Besides that?" Jessie asked.

"How should I know?"

Everyone glanced toward Damien, who shrugged. "You wouldn't kill yourself, Leigh. Not once you'd changed. Then you'd be different. You'd no longer be like you; you'd be like him."

Swell. "What did you do? That first time?"

"Went mad in the woods. Munched on Nazis. A few Allies, too. It was a werewolf buffet over there."

"The good old days," Jessie muttered.

I shot her a warning glare. Damien was trying to help us. She needed to let him.

"He was in the war?" Edward glanced in my direction. Why he couldn't just ask Damien the question I have no idea. Except he wasn't used to conversing with werewolves—only killing them.

"He was bitten after the invasion," I explained. "He was a soldier."

"Bitten by one of Mengele's wolves."

"Looks that way."

Edward sighed. He still felt guilty that he'd been unable to prevent the release of the monsters in the Black Forest. He'd dedicated his life to righting what he considered his greatest wrong.

I returned my attention to Damien. "What did you do in the days after you'd shifted the first time?"

"Slept. The physical changes take some getting used to."

"Sleeping sounds good."

Even though I'd slept most of the night, I was exhausted.

"Then you will sleep," Edward ordered. "The rest of us will watch."

"Like hell."

"I didn't mean watch you sleep. I meant watch this place."

"You don't think Hector will be watching us, too? Or one of his wolf boys?"

"I know how to watch a residence, Leigh. I am not completely senile. Yet."

I had a thought—one I should have had before, but I'd been a little busy.

"Did Cora have any fascinating ideas on how to kill Hector?"

Jessie and Will shook their heads. "Nothing more than what she told us the first time."

"Terrific."

"I have an idea," Will said.

"I'm glad someone does."

"Often doing the opposite of a ritual will reverse the outcome."

"English, Slick."

He blinked and adjusted his glasses. "I thought that was."

"Do you have any idea what he was talking about?" Jessie asked.

I shrugged.

"If the ritual is . . ."

Was he blushing? I kind of thought so.

"The ritual is doing me under the hunter's moon in front of all the other wolves."

"Right. So not *doing* you will keep him from becoming all-powerful."

"That works well for me. But how do we kill the son of a bitch?"

"He became a Weendigo by killing, then eating the flesh of his enemy. Reverse it."

I thought about what he'd said. "His enemy kills, then eats him?"

"Can't hurt."

Yes, it could. Because Hector's enemy was me.

38

"Can you do it, Leigh?" Will's voice, his face, was concerned.

"Of course she can." Jessie smacked me on the back. "If it means getting rid of Hector, you can handle anything, right? He murdered your family."

"I remember."

The room went silent, as if in respect for those who had died. I thought of them—went over their names again in my mind.

Jessie was right. I could do anything if it meant sending Hector to hell.

"Let's make a plan," I said.

Edward ran a hand over my head. "There's my girl."

Warmth spread through me at his praise. However, when he saw I was still holding Damien's hand he frowned and stepped away. I hoped I wouldn't have to choose between the two of them. But that was a worry for another time. If I lived past tonight.

We sat around the kitchen table. Will made coffee. Since I had no cinnamon, the secret ingredient, it wasn't as good as the last time. But it was certainly better than any coffee I'd ever made.

The planning didn't take long. "Shoot him with silver," Edward advised. "It is all you can do."

"Cora said silver will kill a Weendigo. But a power eater, she wasn't sure."

"Silver wasn't supposed to kill the wolf god," Jessie murmured.

"But it did?"

"Only because *I* shot her." Will took Jessie's hand, and she squeezed his fingers with a sad, wistful smile. "I loved her."

"The wolf god ritual was about love," Will explained. "Zee needed the blood of the one who loved her to complete the ritual. Therefore, only the hand of the one who loved her could end her life. This ritual is about hate, enemies, lust, and not love."

"Nice," I muttered.

Will continued as if I hadn't spoken. "So it follows that if the power eater is shot by the one who hates him, his enemy, he should be wounded, disabled at the least. Then, to end his existence forever . . ."

Will looked at me.

"Conquering of the enemy, by eating of the flesh."

"Precisely."

I could hardly wait.

The meeting broke up. The others dispersed to take their hiding places and wait for Hector. Damien and I, the bait, waited, too.

I wanted to finish what Edward had interrupted. Sex with love—for the first time.

Damien touched me and I felt reborn. If we could get through tonight alive we could share love, life, a future.

The door burst open and in strode Hector. My back flared with agony, and I fell to the floor, writhing, helpless. Hector grabbed Damien by the neck and tossed him across the room as if he were a doll. Damien cracked against the wall and slid into a heap.

A man would be dead. A werewolf should be fine. Damien lay still. He appeared broken.

I crawled toward him. My back was on fire, but I had other things to worry about.

I placed my palm against his chest. He was breathing, but a tiny trickle of blood ran out of his ear. I had to remember that Hector was stronger than the average werewolf. I reached for Damien's face, and suddenly Hector yanked me to my feet.

"I'll kill him later. Under the full moon." He prodded Damien with his toe. "I will enjoy it. No one touches my mate."

Hector turned his back on Damien as if he were nothing. He stared down at me, then grasped the neck of my T-shirt and tore it off with a single jerk. Shocked, I could only stand there as he made short work of my jeans and underwear.

"Trust me, *querida*. You won't need them."

I nearly gagged at the thought of what he had planned. I soothed myself with the knowledge that his plan would not go as he wanted it to. I had to soothe myself with something. Damien was unconscious; I had no clothes, no weapon, and the blood moon glistened heavy on the horizon.

With one hand Hector tossed me over his shoulder, and he carried me down the steps. We passed others on the way. Black, white, red, I recalled many of their faces from the tavern. I guess race relations were tip-top among the ranks of the fanged and furry.

Perhaps that was one of the reasons Hector had made

himself a werewolf. With them it was all about strength, power, who could kill whom—not the color of your skin, the amount of money you made, or who your parents had been.

Understanding werewolves—what next?

"I'm going to throw up if you don't put me down," I managed.

"Werewolves do not throw up."

It was on the tip of my tongue to say something smart about the best-laid plans, but I contained myself. I needed to wait until I had him where I wanted him before he learned the truth. But where exactly would that be?

I managed to glance back at my apartment right before Hector hauled me into the woods. The others, still in human form, carted Damien down the steps. Hands had their uses, it seemed.

The cool, damp air of the forest closed around us. Darkness descended, nearly complete, the time between sunset and moonrise a still, peaceful, eager place. I waited for that first sliver of silver to spill through the leaves. What would happen then?

Where was Jessie? Will? Edward? I knew they wouldn't leave me. They had to be following as closely as they dared.

"How did you like your first change?"

I wasn't sure what to say, since I hadn't had one. I didn't want to make a mistake, tip Hector off.

He laughed; his exquisite voice lowered to a rumbling growl, rippling through my belly, setting panic to my brain. "Don't worry; the first change is always the worst. You will love the second. Especially what comes after."

Somehow I doubted that.

He turned his head, nuzzled my thigh. His palm stroked my scar, then lower. "I remember how we were together. You were hot, wet. I've never come so hard." His teeth grazed my hip. He licked me, took a fold of my skin between his lips, and suckled. "I can't wait to be inside you again. It'll be even better this time. I promise."

My mind raced, trying to find a way out of this pickle. My brain felt like a hamster on a wheel, running, running, getting nowhere. I had to kill Hector, but how?

We came to a clearing I'd never seen before. How would Jessie and the others find me?

My heart beat as fast as my mind twirled. I was long past scared and halfway to terrified. Killing Hector and becoming free of him forever had sounded good, but doing it was another matter.

I didn't want to be alone with this man, this beast. The very thought paralyzed me. If I was paralyzed, how could I stop him? Even if I knew what to do.

Hector dumped me onto the ground. I looked up. Blinked. Sighed.

Jessie, Will, and Edward sat in a row, each tied to a pole and gagged for good measure.

Well, at least I wouldn't be alone.

39

"You thought you could catch me?" Hector stared at Jessie and the others, then shook his head. "I received not only the strength of a hundred wolves but also their senses. I can hear better, see farther, smell for miles. I can become anything or anyone. *Jäger-Suchers* are no longer any match for me. Soon they will be no match for us, my darling Leigh."

I guess I didn't have to ask if he'd chowed down on his werewolf quota. I *really* needed to kill this guy. If I didn't, he'd decimate not only the *J-S* ranks but the human population as well. Armageddon, thy name is Hector.

He stared at me strangely. Though the thought of what he had planned made a cold sweat break out on my body, I needed to pretend I was just like him. If I wasn't careful, he'd bite me again, and then I'd be in serious shit. Elise was gone, and no one here would be able to call her back.

I stood, crossed my arms over my breasts, then realized I had nothing left to cover my crotch and my back was on full display. Decisions, decisions.

"I don't suppose you have a towel?" I asked.

Hector frowned. Oops, wrong question.

Werewolves no doubt could care less if they were naked in the night. Smiling, I tried to remember what it had felt like to be attracted to him. He was a very handsome package, before the fur came out.

"I'm cold," I said. "Once I change, I'll be fine."

His eyes drifted over me. He licked his lips.

That phrase about skin crawling? It's not so much a phrase as a fact.

"I've dreamed of you," he murmured. "I've spent every night reliving our one night. It was never like that for me again. No matter who I screwed, who I killed, nothing, no one, made me feel like you did."

Gee, just what every girl longs to hear.

"I will take you as the change does. I will make you scream for more. You will forget the other one. He is nothing compared to me."

Hector took off his shirt and tossed it across the space between us. Though the garment smelled like him, the very scent making me light-headed, I slipped it over my shoulders and buttoned it to my chin. Being naked and thinking straight were two mutually exclusive conditions in my world.

Hector continued to disrobe, slipping off his pants and his shoes, too. His body was amazing—long, strong, supple skin over glistening muscles. I could see why I'd been tempted.

But hadn't my mother always told me pretty is as pretty does? I should have listened more carefully.

The moon shivered at the tops of the trees. Soon it would spill over and into the clearing. Once the light touched him, he would change. Once it touched me, I wouldn't. Then what would I do?

The brush rustled as the minion werewolves carried

Damien into the clearing. He was still unconscious. That couldn't be good. I expected them to tie him up anyway. Instead, a man and a woman stood on either side as guards; the rest moved away.

"Come. It is time."

The clearing filled with people. Each one stared at us as if expecting a show. Oh, right. They were.

My heart thundered. My skin tingled. I had a hard time focusing whenever Hector touched me, because my scar would flare like I'd been stuck with a red-hot poker. I didn't want to think about what I would feel if he accomplished what he had planned.

But he couldn't. I wasn't going to turn into a werewolf when they did, and pretty soon everyone would know it.

Hector stood next to Damien and beckoned. I had no choice but to go. When I reached Hector's side, his hand slid over my hip, dipped beneath the shirt, skidded over my ass. I fought not to flinch or gag. I was supposed to be a werewolf. I needed him to believe that, to trust me, or all of us would die. We'd probably die anyway, but at least I had to try.

Hector urged me to face him. His hands were everywhere beneath the material. Palm at my belly, then cupping my breast. His arousal pressed against me. He lowered his head and his mouth took mine. I forced myself to respond, open my lips, meet his tongue. I'd done this before—eagerly. It was fit punishment I should do so again before I died.

My back was in agony. My stomach roiled. My mind was frantic, searching for a way to kill him before he killed us all.

God, help me.

Hector yanked his mouth away, though his hands

stayed right where they were. He leaned his forehead against mine. He was breathing heavily—the change or just plain lust. Maybe both.

"I am sorry, *querida*. You make me forget what we have come here to do."

"I thought we'd come here to do this?"

My throat tight with revulsion, my voice came out breathless and sexy, as if I wanted to do him right here on the ground. He smiled and touched my hair.

"Soon. But first . . ." He pointed to Damien.

Oh, hell. The sacrifice.

He turned away. I glanced at Jessie and the others. They would be no help. I stared down at Damien. Big mistake. One look at him and I wanted to fall on the ground, cover his body with mine, protect him from whatever Hector had planned. But I couldn't.

"Here."

I turned. Hector held a gun in each hand. He offered one to me. Was he stupid?

I took it. He put the barrel of the other to my head. Nope, not stupid.

"What—?" I began.

"The sacrifice. It is for you to make."

"Me?"

"Of course. Only by killing him can you truly put the past behind you. I made a mistake with Jimmy Renquist. You pined for him because you did not understand why he had to go. But this time you will kill your lover, and then you can forget him."

Was he insane?

Yes.

"Why the extra pistol?" I asked.

"I do not plan to leave anything to chance this time, *querida*. You will be mine. We will rule them all. Tonight.

But if you have managed to thwart my plan somehow, I will kill you. I may love you, but I love me more."

Wasn't that romantic?

I stared at Hector and weighed my options. I only had one. Kill him before he killed me. Snatch the other gun and blow away some of his pals. If I was going to die, I was going to take as many of them with me as I could.

Hector's pentagram tattoo gleamed slick and black as a tiny ray of moonlight trickled through the leaves. It reminded me of something . . . something important. I lost the train of thought as he urged me to my knees with the gun at my temple.

Damien's eyes opened. He saw the gun, frowned, glanced up at Hector, and blinked. "Bull's-eye," he murmured.

And I remembered what Hector's tattoo reminded me of.

"Do it," Hector urged.

I spun and fired into the center of the pentagram, ducking as I did. I surprised him so completely he dropped the gun instead of blowing my brains out.

Not a single flame erupted from the wound. Hell, that wasn't right.

The moon skimmed over the tops of the trees. Hector howled, as did every other werewolf in the clearing. They began to change. Damien did, too.

I could shoot close to a dozen, but I decided to save my bullets. There were at least thirty in the clearing. No telling what they'd do or who would need to be shot first.

Hector remained a man. Maybe the silver bullet in his chest prevented the change. It wasn't preventing anything else—like his breathing. I aimed the pistol at his head and Hector laughed.

"You think you can kill me with the usual weapons? I am far too powerful for that. I will heal anything."

As if he'd willed it, the bullet hole slid shut. Blood still glistened on his skin, black beneath the hunter's moon. Memories assaulted me. Another place, other bodies, different blood. Dizziness threatened, but I bit my lip, focusing on the pain until my vision cleared. For the ones who had gone before, for the future I could still have, I needed to be strong.

There had to be a way to kill him. What had Will told me to do?

Shoot Hector with silver. That wasn't working very well.

No, wait. Will's exact instructions had been to shoot Hector with silver, then eat his flesh. I stared at the shiny black blood, the smooth brown skin. My stomach heaved. Strong was one thing; this was another. I didn't think I could do it.

Hector glanced at the moon, then at me, his eyes narrowed. "The *Jäger-Sucher* society appears a bit more advanced than I realized. Ah well, a quick nip or two near something vital and you should change yet tonight. No harm, no foul, as they say."

A chorus of howls rose into the sky. The others had finished their change. Hector reached for me. There was a snarl of warning, and Damien in wolf form knocked him away. Before he hit the ground, Hector had become a great white wolf.

The two of them rolled, end over end, struggling for dominance. Hector was bigger, stronger. It didn't take long before Damien was pinned. I had to do something. No matter how much my hands shook, my heart thundered, my back burned, I had to get close enough to kill him. I took one step in their direction and five wolves blocked my path.

I shot the closest one. The silver worked damn good on him. He burst into flames and the others retreated, prancing and whimpering.

Hector prepared to tear out Damien's throat, and I shot him behind the ear. He slumped to the ground. Damien scampered out from beneath him.

"Heal *that*," I muttered.

Sadly, he began to.

There'd been no flame when I shot him, just as there'd been none the first time. As I watched, mesmerized, horrified, his head began to knit together with a slick, sucking sound.

Helplessly I glanced toward Jessie, Will, and Edward. Will nodded. Jessie tried to talk around her gag. I didn't need to hear her to understand what she was saying.

Eat his flesh. Now. Before he healed completely.

I turned, fell to my knees, retched. Where was the heap big werewolf hunter now? When the going got tough, looked like I threw up.

Suddenly Damien shoved me away. Before I could stop him, he tore a hunk from Hector's flank and swallowed.

The body burst into a fireball. I shielded my eyes, sat back on the ground. Hector's minions howled, but the sound was far away, not worth worrying about.

When the heat diminished, I lowered my arm. Hector was gone. The only thing left was a pile of ashes where his body had been.

I sat there for several moments, dazed, uncertain. My back no longer ached and burned. I wondered if the scar had disappeared along with Hector.

The clearing was empty except for me, Jessie, Will, and Edward. Damien and all the other wolves were gone.

I crawled across the space separating us, yanked the gags loose.

"What the hell was that?" Jessie demanded as I picked at the knots on her wrists. "I thought his enemy had to eat him."

I winced but kept tugging on her bonds.

"Jess," Will murmured.

"What?"

Her arms came free and she dealt with her own ankles. I moved to Edward.

"*Liebchen*," he murmured, and I lifted my eyes to his. Concern deepened the rheumy blue. "Are you all right?"

"He's dead. I'm damn near ecstatic."

"Hmm," was all he said.

I *should* be ecstatic. I should be dancing in the freaking streets. If there were any streets around here. Instead I felt let down. The world wasn't suddenly brighter. Jimmy wasn't alive and neither was my family. My back didn't burn anymore, but I'd kind of gotten used to the pain. And where the hell was Damien? Was he ever coming back? What if he did?

My shoulders sagged. I was tired. All I wanted to do was go to bed and stay there for an eternity.

"Why the hell didn't you do what you were supposed to do?" Jessie was suddenly in my face. "Squeamish?"

She shoved me. Fury erupted. Warmth drove out the cold; the need for action replaced the lethargy. I shoved her back. "How did you manage to get captured, supergirl?"

"It wasn't easy. I was too busy watching your back to watch my own. Or theirs."

"I do not need anyone watching my back," Edward grumbled. "Or at least I never used to."

Jessie and I had been circling each other, searching for a weakness, an opportunity to step in and kick a little ass. We'd both feel better. But at Edward's quietly voiced comment we straightened and turned toward him.

"Ah, hell," Will muttered. "No tearing clothes. No naked wrestling. Again?"

We ignored him.

"You're fine," Jessie and I said at the same time, then scowled at each other.

"No, I am not," Edward said. "I am old. I am no longer an asset in the field. That is why I stayed with Elise. That and . . ."

He broke off.

"What?" I demanded.

He shrugged. "I guess it does not matter now."

He glanced at the pile of ashes that had been Hector, then kicked them apart. Little particles flew all over the place.

"The mission is finished. We have all survived."

"I don't understand," Jessie said.

"The odds of surviving your first mission are twenty to one," he murmured. "I did not want to be here if you succumbed."

I frowned. That wasn't like Edward. How many agents had he lost? How many times had he found another one, then moved on?

He saw my expression and patted my hand. "I never considered I might come this close to losing you. I could not have endured that, Leigh. I have lost far too many people in my life whom I loved."

My eyes were hot, full. I looked away. "I'm alive."

"Thanks to wolf boy," Jessie interjected. "Where'd he go?"

"He went after the others," Will said.

My head came up and my eyes scanned the forest. I wanted to follow and help.

"Do you think . . . ?" Jessie let her voice trail off.

"Think what?" I asked, gaze still focused on the trees.

"He ate Hector. Does that transfer the power? Is Damien the supreme alpha now?"

I frowned and glanced at Will. "No. There's more to

the ritual than that. Hector is ashes now, and so is his power."

I hoped Will was right.

"He will be fine." Edward squeezed my hand once and released me. "He is a hunter, like us."

That was probably the nicest thing he'd ever said about Damien and probably ever would.

"Why did Hector burst into flames when Damien ate him?" Jessie asked.

"Because he was my enemy, too."

Damien's voice made us all turn toward him. He was naked, dirty, bloody. Not his most attractive.

"That would work," Will murmured.

"What happened to the others?" Edward demanded.

Damien ignored everyone but me, crossing the distance between us, stopping an arm's length away. "He hurt you. He had to die."

I didn't know what to say. Damien had saved me, saved us all. He had done my job for me. I should be embarrassed. But I was just glad it was over. I wanted to move on, and I wanted to do it with him. I reached across the space between us and linked our fingers together.

"Hector's pals got away," he said. "I could have kept chasing them, but . . . I wanted to get back."

"How do you feel?" Jessie asked. "Supreme in any way?"

He glanced at her, then back at me. "I feel the same way I always have."

Only I knew what that meant. Damien wasn't a happy man.

"I love you," I blurted, right there before Edward and everyone.

The shadows in his eyes remained. Maybe they always would. Who was I to complain? I had my ghosts, too.

I expected him to draw me into his arms and kiss me, maybe tell me he loved me. Instead, he pulled his hand from mine and moved away.

I frowned, took a single step after him, but he shook his head. "We need to call Elise."

"That doesn't matter—"

"Yes," he interrupted. "It does. Call her."

So I did.

40

The hunter's moon had set. The sun had risen. Elise had returned with the moon and more serum.

"Just because the cure worked on Leigh before she changed doesn't mean it will work on Damien," she cautioned. "It could very well kill him."

"That's a chance I'm willing to take," Damien said. "Just do it."

"No," I said.

Everyone looked at me.

"Leigh." Edward patted my back, still scared, thank you very much. No magic cure for me. "Let Elise do her job. She has researched every cure ever written, every method even whispered. None work. This is the only way."

"I don't want him dead."

"You'd rather he was furry?" Jessie asked.

"Damn straight. I seem to recall your saying you wouldn't have cared if Cadotte was a werewolf."

Will glanced at Jessie. "You say the sweetest things," he murmured.

"Shut up, Slick. I was out of my head at the time." She

turned to me. "Think about what you're saying, Leigh. That's no kind of life."

I moved closer to Damien, took his hand, held on when he would have pulled away. "It's no kind of life without him." I tightened my fingers. "Don't leave me. I need you."

He sighed and closed his eyes. "Leigh, I have to try."

I guess I had to let him.

Elise, her hands covered with protective, plastic gloves—I guess I couldn't blame her for being cautious—stuck the needle into Damien's arm, then released the serum into his veins.

"What's supposed to happen?" he asked.

"I have no idea. Why don't you step outside and see how you feel."

Elise had insisted on waiting until the moon was high in the sky before attempting the cure. That way we'd know immediately if it had worked or not.

I followed Damien out of my apartment and down the steps to the ground. The tavern was deserted, all of Hector's werewolves fled to parts unknown. Crow Valley was awful deserted, too. It was amazing how many residents had been secretly fanged and furry.

Damien kissed my forehead, touched my cheek. "I love you, too, you know."

"I know," I whispered.

He turned his face up to the moon and he changed.

Hours later I waited alone. Elise had returned to Montana with Edward. She had a lot of work to do, since it appeared her cure only worked before the initial change of the just bitten. She seemed more upset about that than I would have thought.

Everyone had given me their advice. Elise wanted

Damien to be her guinea pig. Edward had offered him a job. Having a werewolf as a werewolf hunter wasn't a bad idea. Jessie and Will agreed. They thought we should be a tag team *J-S* unit.

I'd pretended to listen to them all while my eyes scanned the trees searching for Damien. Nothing mattered unless he came back.

The door opened. I could smell him—woods, wind, water—the man I loved.

"I don't care what you are," I said. "All I care about is who we can be together."

"We can never be parents, Leigh."

"Never is a long time. Give Elise a chance."

"What if she can't find a cure? What if I'm always a werewolf?"

"Wolves and werewolves do one thing right. They mate for life. We can, too."

"Having a family, a home, that white picket fence—it was your dream."

"Now you are."

I looked at him then, opened my palm, showed him the ring he'd worn, the one I'd taken and never given to anyone else.

"Marry me?" I asked. "Be mine forever."

He stared at the ring, then lifted his eyes to mine. "Forever means something different to me. Like this I'll never die, Leigh. And you will."

I'd thought of that, and I didn't care. In fact, I was glad. He'd be damn hard to kill—unlike everyone else I'd ever loved.

Besides, I'd learned something at last.

"We need to live for now, because tomorrow everything, hell, everyone, could change. If I have a day, a month, a century, I want to spend it with you."

He reached for the shiny circlet, lifted it to the waning silver night. I held my breath, half-afraid he'd take the ring and leave me behind.

"The werewolf and the werewolf hunter," he murmured, "we're going to have quite an adventure."

"I thought we already did."

Damien slipped his mother's ring onto my finger. "This is only the beginning."

Read on for an excerpt from
Lori Handeland's next book

Dark Moon

Now available from St. Martin's Paperbacks

I have always loved the dark of the moon, when the night is still and serene, when all that can be seen are the stars.

There are those who term the dark moon a new moon, but there is nothing new about the moon. It has been here from time forgotten and will be here long after we are dead.

I spend my days, and most of my nights, inside a stone fortress in the wilds of Montana. I'm a doctor by trade, though not the kind who give out lollipops after dispensing vaccines and pills. Instead I mix a little of this and a little of that, over and over again.

My degree reads virologist. In English, that means I have a Ph.D. in the study of viruses. Don't worry, I won't let the excitement kill me. The boredom might, though, if the loneliness doesn't do it first.

Of course, I'm not *completely* alone. There's a guard at the door and my test subjects, but none of them are great conversationalists. Lately I've started to feel watched, which is pretty funny considering I'm the one in charge of the surveillance cameras.

Paranoia is one of the first signs of dementia, except I

don't *feel* crazy. Does anyone? I've come to the conclusion I need to get out more. But where would I go?

Most days I don't mind being locked safe inside the safest place in the west. The world is pretty scary. Scarier than most people realize.

You think the monsters aren't real? That they're merely the figment of childish imaginations or delusional psychosis? You're wrong.

There are things walking the earth worse than any Grimm's fairy tale. *Unsolved Mysteries* would have a stroke if they got a look at my X-files. But since lycanthropy is a virus, werewolves are my specialty. I've devoted my life to finding a cure.

I have a personal interest. You see, I'm one of them.

The powers that be say a life is formed by changes—decisions made, roads not taken, people we've left behind. I'm inclined to agree.

On the day my whole world changed—again—a single decision, that fork in the road, and the one I left behind walked into my office without warning.

I was at my desk updating files, when the scuff of a shoe against concrete made me glance up. The man in the doorway made my heart go *ba-boom*. He always had.

"Nic," I murmured, and in my voice I heard more than I wanted to.

The strong nose, full lips, wide forehead were as I remembered. But the lines around his mouth and eyes, the darker shade of his skin hinted at a life in the elements. The flicker of silver in his short hair was as shocking as him being here in first place.

He didn't smile, didn't return my greeting. I couldn't blame him. I'd professed love, then disappeared. I hadn't spoken to him since.

Seven years. How had he found me? And why?

Concern replaced curiosity, and my hand inched toward the drawer where I kept my gun. The guard hadn't called to clear a visitor, so I should shoot first, ask questions later. In my world, an enemy could lurk behind every face. But I'd always had a tough time shooting people. One of the many reasons the boss kept me isolated in the forest.

I'd learned long ago how to gauge a suit for a shoulder holster. Nic had one. A disturbing change in a man who'd once been both studious and dreamy, in love with the law and me, not necessarily in that order. Why was he carrying a gun?

Since he hadn't drawn his, I drew mine, then pointed the weapon at Nic's chest. Loaded with silver, I was ready for anything. Except the punch of his deep blue eyes and the familiar timbre of his voice. "Hey, sweetheart."

In college that endearment had made me all warm and stupid. I'd promised things I had no right to promise. Now the same word, uttered with cool sarcasm, annoyed me.

I'd left for his own good. However *he* didn't know that.

I got to my feet, stepped around the desk, came a little too close. "What are you doing here?"

"I didn't think you'd be thrilled to see me, but this isn't exactly the welcome I expected."

His gaze lowered to the gun, and I was distracted by the scent of him. Fresh snow, mountain air, my past.

He grabbed the weapon, twisted it away, then tucked me against his body with an elbow across my throat. I was no good with firearms. Never had been.

I choked, and Nic released the stranglehold on my windpipe, though he didn't release me. Out of the corner of my eye I caught a glimpse of metal on the desk. He'd put my gun aside. One less thing to worry about.

"What do you want?" I managed.

Instead of answering, he nuzzled my hair and his breath brushed my ear. My knees quivered; my eyes burned. Having Nic so close was making me remember things I'd spent years trying to forget. And the memories hurt. Hell, I still loved him.

An uncommon rush of emotion caused my muscles to clench, my stomach to roil. I wasn't used to feeling anything. I prided myself on being cool, patrician, in charge—Dr. Elise Hanover, ice queen. When I let my anger loose, bad things happened.

But no one had ever affected me like Nic. No one had ever made me as happy or as sad. No one could make me more furious.

I slammed my spike heel onto his shiny black shoe and ground down with all my weight. Nic flinched, and I jabbed my elbow into his stomach. I forgot to pull my punch, and he flew into the wall. Spinning around, I watched him slide to the floor, eyes closed.

Oops.

I resisted the urge to run to him, touch his face, kiss his brow. For both our sakes, we couldn't go back to the way things had been.

Nic's eyelids fluttered, and he mumbled something foul. I let out the breath I'd been holding. He'd be all right.

I doubted he was often on the losing end of a fight. Since I'd seen him last he'd bulked up—the combination of age and a few thousand hours with a weight machine.

What else had he been doing in the years we'd been apart? He'd planned to become a lawyer, except he didn't resemble any lawyer I'd ever seen. The suit, yes, but beneath the crisp charcoal material he was something more than a paper-pushing fast talker. Perhaps a soldier decked out in his Sunday best.

My gaze wandered over him, catching on the dark sunglasses hooked into his pocket.

Suit. Muscles. *Men in Black* glasses.

"FBI," I muttered.

Now I was really ticked off.

Nic's eyes snapped open, crossing once before focusing on my face. "You always were smarter than you looked."

I'd been the victim of enough dumb blonde jokes to last me several lifetimes. The moronic jabs and riddles had bothered me, until I realized I could use the speaker's attitude to my advantage. If people thought I was stupid, they weren't expecting anything else.

So I didn't rise to Nic's bait. He'd been sent here by the big boys, without warning, and that meant trouble.

"I suppose you want me to hand over my gun?" he grumbled.

I shrugged. "Keep it."

A weapon filled with lead was the least of my worries.

He struggled to his feet, and I experienced an instant of concern when he wobbled. I'd hit him way too hard.

"Let me give you some advice," he said. "I've always found that the people we least expect to shoot us, usually do."

Funny, I'd found that, too.

"What are you doing here?" I demanded.

His brows lifted. "No hugs, no kisses? You aren't glad to see me? If I remember correctly, I should be the one who's angry."

He sat on a chair without being invited.

"Oh, wait." His eyes met mine. "I am."

Nic had every reason to be furious. I'd snuck out in the night as if I had something to hide.

Oh, wait. I did.

Nevertheless, being near him hurt. I couldn't tell Nic why I'd left. I couldn't apologize because I wasn't really sorry. I couldn't touch him the way I wanted to. I couldn't ever touch anyone that way.

"You didn't come here to talk about our past," I snapped. "What does the FBI want with the *Jäger-Suchers*?"

I wasn't the only one fighting monsters. I was merely the geeky member of a select group—hunter-searchers for those a little rusty on their German.

Though financed by the government, the *Jäger-Suchers* were a secret from all but those who needed to know. If it got out that there were monsters running all over the place, people would panic.

Not only that, but heads would roll. Unlimited cash for a special forces monster-hunting unit? Someone would definitely lose their job, and we'd lose our funding. So we pretended to be things we weren't.

For instance, I was a research scientist investigating a new form of rabies in the animal population. Most of our field agents carried documentation identifying them as wardens for various natural resource departments.

Until today, the precautions had worked. No one had ever come snooping before.

The question was: Why now?

And why him?